Pete Lilling

S0-AWD-621

A CHILD OF THE JAGO

Of all the dark corners of London in the 1890s, the old Nichol, lying off Bethnal Green Road, was the murkiest. In 1895, Arthur Morrison, a successful journalist and writer of short stories, was invited to visit it by the Rector of Shoreditch, who had read and admired Morrison's stories about the East End, but felt that they reflected only part of East End life. Even Morrison, born in the East End and familiar with its ways, was horrified by what he saw. Within a year he had shaped his experiences into his first full-length novel, lightly disguising the Nichol as 'the Jago'. *A Child of the Jago* is the story of Dicky Perrott, born and bred in this area; but it is also a brilliant portrait of a community where crime and violence are the only way of life, and from which there is no escape for the inhabitants. Only the characters themselves are fictional: Morrison's descriptions of the fearful physical conditions are based directly on what he saw. He conjures up an extraordinarily vivid picture of a world which, even as he wrote, was about to vanish in one of the first of the slum clearance schemes. Although Morrison, as an excellent teller of tales, disliked the label 'realist', this is indeed one of the great realist novels in English literature, the equivalent in fiction of Hogarth's fierce artistic observation of the London slums.

Arthur Morrison was born in the East End in 1863; little is known of his early life, but he became a journalist in 1890, after working for the idealistic 'People's Palace' in the East End. He wrote short stories and detective fiction as a side-line, *Tales of Mean Streets* (1894) being his first success. After *A Child of the Jago* he wrote two historical novels, *Cunning Murrell* and *The Hole in the Wall*, the latter being his best-known book. He became an expert on oriental art (partly through buying Japanese prints in the East End), and after 1913 made his career in this field. He died in 1945.

A CHILD OF THE JAGO

Arthur Morrison

THE BOYDELL PRESS

© 1969, 1982
National Society for the Prevention of Cruelty to Children
and Westminster Hospital

Biographical Study © 1969
MacGibbon and Kee Ltd

First published in the BOOKMARKS series 1982
by The Boydell Press
an imprint of Boydell and Brewer Ltd
PO Box 9, Woodbridge, Suffolk, IP12 3DF

British Library Cataloguing in Publication Data

Morrison, Arthur
A child of the Jago
I. Title
823'.8[F]   PR6025.0/

ISBN 0 85115 203 1

Printed in Great Britain by
Nene Litho, Wellingborough, Northants

To
ARTHUR OSBORNE JAY
Vicar of Holy Trinity, Shoreditch

CONTENTS

FOREWORD

THE BIOGRAPHICAL study of Arthur Morrison that introduces this edition of A Child of the Jago is a piece of literary detective work based on a number of small items of information drawn from a wide variety of sources, both published and unpublished. I would like to thank the many people who replied to my queries even when, as was unfortunately often the case, they were unable to give me any definite answers. I am especially grateful to Mrs Lavinia Thurley and the late Lady Ethel Parlett, both of whom kindly told me what they remembered of Morrison; and to Professor Asa Briggs, Mr B. Harding-Edgar, Mr A. L. Hellicar, Dr K. G. T. McDonnell and Mr Oscar Tapper, who helped me in various ways. The details of Morrison's connection with the People's Palace were first published as an article in *East London Papers* and I would like to thank the editors for their permission to reprint them here; also the Librarian of Queen Mary College for allowing me to examine certain papers in the People's Palace archives: and the Librarian of the Central Library, London Borough of Tower Hamlets, for allowing me to consult the original manuscript of A Child of the Jago.

The only full-length study of Morrison I know is Dr D. I. Nwoga's unpublished London University M.A. thesis, 'The Novels and Tales of Arthur Morrison' (1962) which I read when my own researches were well under way. Owing to the civil war in Nigeria I have been unable to contact Dr Nwoga and would therefore like to acknowledge here that I am indebted to him for several biographical details.

Because of the conjectural nature of my biographical study of Morrison, footnotes have been kept to a minimum. Further details can be found in the Bibliographical Note which lists the printed sources I have used. This Note is obviously selective and is not intended as a definitive bibliography of writings by or about Morrison.

After consulting the original manuscript I have made several small corrections; otherwise the present text is that of the first edition.

P.J.K.

ARTHUR MORRISON

So LITTLE is known of Arthur Morrison's early life that any biographical study of him must rely more on conjecture than established fact. His birth certificate shows that he was born at 14 John Street, Poplar, on the 1st November 1863; that his father, George Richard Morrison, was an engine fitter; and that his mother's maiden name was Jane Cooper. Nothing further is definitely known until, at the age of twenty-three, his signature appears on a cash receipt in respect of one month's salary (September 1886) as Clerk to the Beaumont Trustees, a charitable institution that administered the People's Palace in the East End of London. By the middle years of the 1890s he was firmly established as a successful writer and when questioned about his early life provided the details which are still erroneously reproduced in standard works of reference. According to Morrison's own account he was born in Kent, the son of a 'professional man' and was educated at private schools. Two of these three statements flatly contradict the evidence of his birth certificate and the third is sufficiently vague as to raise doubts about its reliability.

His employment before he became a full-time journalist in 1890 he described variously as 'the secretary of an old Charity Trust' or as a 'civil servant', both of which terms are half-truths calculated to add social respectability to the post he actually held. This particular connection with the East End was doubtless too well known by his friends for him to disclaim it completely even had he wished to do so; and indeed, there was a good reason why, in this respect at least, he should have been eager to embellish rather than suppress the truth. For when Morrison began writing short stories and novels about the East End he was able to assure those critics who praised or doubted his intimate knowledge of working-class life that he was speaking from first-hand experience, without this being taken to mean that he himself came from a working-class home. When called upon to defend his 'realism' he would sometimes refer directly to the years spent at the People's Palace, but more often he would avoid this and write

11

in a vague equivocal manner: 'For a good few years I have lived in the East End of London, and have been, not an occasional visitor, but a familiar and equal friend in the house of the East-Ender'; or, replying angrily to criticisms of his portrayal of East End life 'which . . . I *do* happen to know at first hand, and without the help of a note-book.' Thus by openly acknowledging his public connection with the East End he was able to conceal his more personal relationship with it.

Throughout a long life Morrison neither elaborated nor supplemented these few misleading statements. He appears to have been a shy, retiring man who refused to develop any kind of public persona, and this in spite of the fact that several of his books attained widespread critical approval and the status of best-sellers. What is even more surprising is the almost total absence of his name from late Victorian and Edwardian literary memoirs. The few friendships he formed with literary personalities of the nineties (those with W. E. Henley, W. W. Jacobs and Rudyard Kipling being the most notable) were private, and he was as shadowy a figure to his contemporaries as he is to us today. When discussing Morrison's life it is as well to keep this fact in mind, for if he was a 'snob' (as my opening paragraphs must be taken to imply) his snobbery was clearly of an unobjectionable nature. In the early nineties he was extremely ambitious for literary fame but when this was achieved he made no attempt to capitalise on it. Instead he devoted himself to the study of art and retreated into a still more private world.

The period of Morrison's life that is of special relevance here stretches from his birth in 1863 to the end of the century. In the history of the English novel the working classes play a small though fascinating part, and Morrison's contribution to the genre remains one of the most valuable. What distinguishes his best working-class fiction from that of most other English novelists is the feeling it creates (despite the violence and occasional melodrama) of presenting working-class life from the inside. In the nineties, critics explained this away by reference to Morrison's great skill as a reporter, but once we realise that he himself came from a working-class family then this explanation, by itself, has little validity. Thus for the literary historian an examination of the relationship between Morrison's life and work offers new insights into the very nature of working-class fiction, and to probe deeper than he himself might have wished is no matter of idle curiosity. That Morrison tried to conceal all details of his early life merely increases its interest, for as Vincent Brome has pointed out: 'It was almost as if the man who so vividly evokes the horror, the poverty, the seaminess of late nineteenth-century London, wanted to forget or run away from his roots.' The present study aims to cast some light on this relationship.

EARLY LIFE

In 1863 there were two John Streets in Poplar, very near each other, just off of the East India Dock Road to the north of the Isle of Dogs, and there is no way of knowing which one contained Morrison's birthplace. John Street (north) was amalgamated with Grundy Street in 1865 and ten years later John Street (south) was renamed Rigden Street. The original houses were demolished in the Festival of Britain slum clearances but in this neighbourhood there still remain rows of houses, built according to a standard early Victorian working-class accommodation pattern, to show us exactly what the two John Streets looked like. In 1863 these houses were still quite new and the area was by no means a slum; its predominant characteristic being not poverty but a stultifying monotony as described by Morrison in the introduction to *Tales of Mean Streets*:

> Of this street there are about one hundred and fifty yards—on the same pattern all. It is not pretty to look at. A dingy little brick house twenty feet high, with three square holes to carry the windows, and an oblong hole to carry the door, is not a pleasing object; and each side of the street is formed by two or three score of such houses in a row, with one front wall in common.

It is unlikely that the Morrison family lived for very long in John Street. Their name is not included in the Rate Books for Poplar (which at this time listed only the names of owners) nor in the Post Office Directory (which only partially listed John Street North). One must draw the conclusion that either the period of residence was extremely short or that they were lodgers and would not therefore be mentioned in official lists. It is possible that they moved away from the East End; to, perhaps, Kent

13

where Morrison claimed to have been born, or to Essex, the county which Morrison throughout his life loved more than any other. Essex is the more likely of the two as at this time East London was rapidly expanding and working-class suburbs mushroomed on the Essex boundaries. Certainly there are good reasons for arguing that at least some, if not all, of Morrison's childhood was spent in or near the East End. In his early work, before the autobiographical references became so guarded, Morrison occasionally introduced reminiscences of his childhood. In 1889 he wrote: 'There is much less of old Bromley and other old-fashioned East End spots than I recollect ten or fifteen years ago'; and in an article written in 1892 he talks of the fascination Leadenhall Market held for him 'fifteen years ago'. These recollections refer to when Morrison was aged between ten and fifteen and would therefore place him in the East End during the mid-seventies.

When acting upon such slight evidence one must, of course, beware of making fanciful interpretations of intrinsically harmless statements, and this is especially true of attempting to establish not merely that Morrison was living in the East End during the seventies but what kind of life he led. But there is one further reference made by him to his childhood that it is impossible to resist. In *Zig-Zags at the Zoo* (1894), a collection of facetious animal sketches, Morrison breaks away from the objective narrative to make one personal aside:

> I quite believe I skipped the crocodiles; at any rate, I find little hereditary affinity between us. When a crocodile objects to its surroundings it refuses its food; as a boy at school I objected very much to my surroundings but without any effect of that sort.

Coming in such an innocuous setting these sentences are quite striking. The reference to 'school' is obviously a subconscious safeguard or the comparison makes no sense at all (crocodiles not going to school) and should be taken to mean general childhood environment. Of all the images used by Victorian novelists and sociologists to describe slum life, that of the jungle is the most common, and in a zoo one would expect to be constantly reminded of it. But it is only brought home to Morrison by the odd snippet of information he has about the crocodile, and this, as the tone of the quotation indicates, forces the 'hereditary affinity'

14

upon him. Within the context of the sketch there is no reason why Morrison should suddenly speak of his childhood 'objection' to his environment, nor why this should lead to an implied hint that he did not get sufficient food as a child, unless he was constantly aware of the uneasy relationship between the working-class background, which he wished to reject, and the new life as a journalist and writer in which he was beginning to feel his way.

Bearing this in mind it is worth glancing briefly at certain recurrent features of Morrison's three full-length working-class novels: A Child of the Jago (1896), To London Town (1899) and The Hole in the Wall (1902). In each of these novels the central character is a child who is faced with the problem of how to escape from the lower strata of working-class life. This has been a dominant theme of working-class fiction for the last century and a half, but in Morrison's case it takes an especially significant form. A Child of the Jago tells the story, in Morrison's own words, of a 'boy, who, but for his environment, would have become a good citizen.' The working classes in this novel are indistinguishable from criminals and Dicky Perrott dies because the author could not bear to think of the form his adult life would inevitably take. Dicky's mother descends from a respectable working-class woman into a slattern and his father is hanged. In To London Town Johnny May is born in Essex (thus escaping the hereditary taint of the East End) but comes to live in East London while still young. The working classes in this novel are much more respectable and Johnny rises within the community by attending night school and serving an apprenticeship. When the novel opens Johnny's father is already dead and the family is supported by the grandfather who urges upon his grandson the need to be trained for a skilled job, and whose murder necessitates the sudden move to London. While in London Johnny's mother marries a worthless drunkard from whom she is released by the discovery that he is a bigamist, but not before Johnny has beaten him up. In The Hole in the Wall Stephen Kemp is born in the East End but his mother has just died when the novel opens and his father is later murdered without ever appearing in the book. Stephen is looked after by his grandfather who is obsessed (and not merely because of his own criminal activities) with the need to send Stephen away to school. This novel ends with the burning down of the grandfather's pub (and thus symbolically his shady past)

15

and the separation of Stephen and Grandfather Kemp: 'For Captain Nat Kemp turned to enlarging and improving his wharf, and he bought lighters and Wapping saw him no more. As for me, I went to school at last.'

There are several features of this, the last of Morrison's working-class novels, that distinguishes it from the other two. It is, for instance, the only one which is historical in setting (and could not therefore be explained away by reference to observed experience at the People's Palace) and the period chosen is the late sixties/ early seventies. Also, the structure of the novel is curious and has puzzled many critics. The story is told from two alternating points of view. One, in the first person, traces Stephen's impressions of the East End from the moment when, at the age of eight, his mother dies in childbirth, to the moment when he 'goes to school at last'; the other, in the third person, pursues the melodramatic aspect of the novel. What truly impresses about *The Hole in the Wall* is the unforced, but effective, grasp of child psychology that Morrison displays; a sense of realness about Stephen Kemp (in spite of the basically romantic nature of the story) that is lacking in the portraiture of Dicky Perrott and Johnny May.

Whether or not Stephen's tale has any direct relation to Morrison's own it is impossible to say. But the little we do know about Morrison's attitude to his childhood is fully complemented by the obsessive themes barely hidden in his working-class novels; of which, the wholesale slaughter of parents or parent figures, the need to escape from and yet remain in the East End, and the power of education to effect a total break with the past, are the most striking.

Wherever Morrison did go to school it is reasonably clear that his formal education was not extensive and was later supplemented by his own exertions. As nothing is known of his father except his occupation (which, by itself, tells us little) it is idle to speculate upon the kind of education he might have been able to afford for his son. If, however, we assume only that Morrison's family background was steady, that he conscientiously attended a local Board or Charity School, later became a clerk (perhaps with the Beaumont Trust) and during this time nurtured literary ambitions, then this would provide quite enough education for his future career. Indeed, it can be regarded as an archetypal example of a late nineteenth- early twentieth-century working-class writer's educational development. We do not have to look far for parallel cases. H. M. Tomlinson was born in the East End in 1873 and the only formal education he received was at a Board School which he left at the age of twelve on the death of his father. He worked as a clerk in a shipping office for nineteen years studying and writing in his spare-time before becoming a journalist and later a novelist.[1]

Morrison himself provides some support for this interpretation of his early life. In one of his rare interviews he claimed that his 'literary career began with the acceptance of some cycling verses contributed by him as a lad to a cycling magazine', and that while working for the charity trust he published many articles on sport and other subjects. His principal interests at this time were literature, boxing and cycling; the very interests that a robust, intelligent working-class boy would have little difficulty in developing. His love of painting is an exception but, as we shall see, in this respect he was self-educated.

When the People's Palace was officially opened by Queen Victoria in May 1887, Morrison had already been employed in its administration for several months. It is possible that he was initially appointed to the post because of his wide-ranging interest in art, literature and sport, as in its early days, when still reeling under the influence of Walter Besant's misguided idealism, the People's Palace placed almost total stress on the power of vocational education to transform working-class life into something full and valuable. What is even more possible is that Morrison gained from the People's Palace as much as he contributed. One of the most frequent charges made against such institutions (and by no one so bitterly as Morrison, as his treatment of the East End Elevation Mission and Pansophical Institute in *A Child of the Jago* shows)[2] was that by their very nature they catered more for the pretentious young clerks of the East End than the manual workers. Morrison's criticism of the clerks was not that they used

[1] A. E. Coppard, a more important writer than either Morrison or Tomlinson, can stand as another example. Born in 1878 he attended a Brighton Board School until the age of nine. He then spent two years as a tailor's apprentice in the East End, after which he returned to Brighton where he took a job as a clerk. He did not become a full-time writer until 1919.

[2] The East End Elevation Mission, however, is based on Toynbee Hall, not the People's Palace.

the Institute but that they misused it. For someone like himself, with little formal education but a sincere interest in art and literature, the People's Palace could bring about a widening perspective, a whole range of experiences not readily available elsewhere. The large number of societies, clubs, musical evenings, art exhibitions, visiting lecturers and public debates would have been ignored by the majority, patronised by the pretentious and attended avidly by the few; and Morrison as an administrator enjoyed advantages above the enrolled members.

Certainly while working at the People's Palace he was conscious of serving an apprenticeship for an entirely different kind of work. During this period, as we have seen, he was a practising part-time journalist and also seems to have sought and received advice on the writing of fiction from Walter Besant. In 1888, perhaps beginning to feel the limitations of the local libraries, he obtained a reader's ticket to the British Museum. The People's Palace thus provided Morrison with the perfect opportunity to pursue his personal interests and furthermore brought him into contact with a number of people sympathetic to his ideas and ambitions. Walter Besant has already been mentioned but it was also while working at the People's Palace that Morrison met his future wife, Elizabeth Thatcher, and one of his closest friends, Harold Parlett who was then working for the Church Commissioners and who was later to play an important part in Morrison's study of Japanese painting.

In March 1889 he was offered the sub-editorship of the *Palace Journal* and leapt at the practical opportunity it offered him. By this time the People's Palace was running into serious financial trouble and Morrison's appointment was part of an attempt to streamline the early, over-ambitious plans for the *Journal*. In spite of this he tackled the job with enthusiasm; recommending books for the members to read and paintings for them to look at, urging upon them the need to develop proper standards of critical discrimination and announcing that henceforth the connection between the *Journal* and the Literary Society would be much closer.[3]

[3] Besant always expected to find a vast untapped source of working-class literary talent in the East End. He was appalled when a literary competition held by the People's Palace in February 1888 received only one entry.

What is of special interest about Morrison's connection with the *Palace Journal* is that it provides examples of his journalistic writing earlier than anything known of before. The weekly sub-editorial followed the conventional lines laid down by his predecessor, consisting of general information about the Palace and snippets of knowledge about local or world affairs. Apart from this Morrison also probably wrote many of the leading articles (Besant at this time being an overseer rather than active editor) and some of the unsigned articles. Of much more significance are the three descriptive studies he published, under the general heading 'Cockney Corners', in which he can be observed groping his way towards his later more individual style of writing about the East End.

On 29th July 1890 the Beaumont Trustees accepted Morrison's resignation from his post as clerk, to take effect from 30th September, and offered him their thanks 'for the services he has rendered since the commencement of the institution'; it being likely that he had given up his post on the *Journal* some months earlier. Although there is no indication given as to why he resigned, the reasons are not difficult to guess.

In the early months of 1890 the financial crisis that had long threatened the People's Palace came to a head, amid worsening relations between Sir Edmund Hay Currie (the chairman of the Palace and the man who more than any other had almost turned a crazy dream into reality), the Beaumont Trustees, and the Drapers' Company (which had generously provided large sums of money and was now demanding a greater say in the running of the Palace). The history of the People's Palace still remains to be written and it is by no means clear exactly what happened. It was, however, sufficiently unsavoury for the *Palace Journal*, which had always represented Currie as the universal much-loved father figure but which was no longer under Besant's or Morrison's complete control, virtually to ignore his resignation. The *Journal* itself suffered a severe shake-up and pressure was continually put on Besant to change the nature of the *Journal* or to discontinue it altogether.

The rapidly deteriorating atmosphere at the People's Palace forced Morrison into making the complete break with his past he had long contemplated, and in October 1890 he moved from East to West London where he joined the editorial staff of an evening newspaper. He was immediately disillusioned with the work he had to do, feeling that his present post was little different from that which he had held on the *Palace Journal*. As it was later reported: 'He became convinced that he could not long continue the daily round of hurried scribbling at ordinary journalism without permanently destroying any ability for better work that he might possess.' He therefore rejected permanent employment and took his chance as a free-lance writer. Although he continued to contribute unsigned articles to various magazines, he also began to write short stories and sketches; producing a great variety of work, feeling his way.

In 1891 he published his first book *The Shadows Around Us*, a collection of stories presented as authentic, verifiable evidence of supernatural powers. The most interesting aspect of the book today is the perfect seriousness of the author, but apart from this it has little value and in later life Morrison longed to disown it. As a compensation for this failure he achieved his first literary success in October of the same year with the appearance in *Macmillan's Magazine* of an article called 'A Street'. The difference in quality between this article and the supernatural stories written at the same time is quite startling: and not the least puzzling thing about Morrison is why, even after he must have known where his true talent lay, he should have continued to produce, side-by-side with excellent studies of working-class life, feeble imitations of popular literature of the day. It is not enough to speak of his desire for wealth and literary fame, as these came to him from his working-class fiction. It is rather as if the man who had so painstakingly learnt how to write refused to deal only, or even mainly, with the subject most suited to his gifts and needed to prove that he could turn his hand to other more purely imaginative fields.

In 'A Street' Morrison attempted to capture the very essence of East End life, the 'deadly monotony and respectability of the mean streets', which he saw as more characteristic of the East End as a whole than the poverty and brutal violence with which the reading public was usually regaled. The tone of the article is detached, melancholy and quietly despairing, expressed in a simple, terse style that made it unlike any previous piece of writing on the working classes:

The East-end is a vast city, as famous in its way as any city men have built. But who knows the East-end? It is down through Cornhill and out beyond Leadenhall Street and Aldgate pump, one will say; a shocking place, where he once went with a curate. An evil growth of slums which hide human creeping things; where foul men and women live on penn'orths of gin, where collars and clean shirts are not yet invented, where every citizen wears a black eye, and no man combs his hair. Our street is not a place like this.

One sentence is of special biographical interest: 'A Palace of Delight was once set in the midst of this street, but Commissioners brandished their pens over it and it became a Polytechnic Institution'; which implies that Morrison still supported the original aims of the People's Palace and was disillusioned only with the changes wrought by the Drapers' Company.[4]

This article attracted the attention of W. E. Henley who arranged to meet the young author. When he learnt that Morrison planned to write a series of short stories centred on the original article Henley urged him to go ahead with the idea, promising to publish them in the magazine he edited. The stories appeared in the *National Observer* throughout 1893 and in the following year were collected together, with a slightly re-written version of the original article acting as an introduction, and published as *Tales of Mean Streets.*[5]

From their first meeting Henley and Morrison became close friends. Henley was renowned for the brilliant group of young writers he had gathered around him (sometimes referred to admiringly as 'Henley's young men'; sometimes sarcastically as 'Henley's Regatta') and Morrison immediately felt at home in this company. The two men shared a common interest in art, sport and literature, and the older man enthused over Morrison's passion for Japanese prints which were only just becoming known in England. Kennedy Williamson has recorded how at this time Morrison was scouring the East End docks for prints and how: 'When he had found a new choice specimen in some dingy

[4] This sentence was omitted from the revised edition of 'A Street' when it became the introduction to *Tales of Mean Streets* three years later.
[5] Two of the stories had originally appeared in the *Pall Mall Budget* and one of them was new.

marine-store in Wapping or Limehouse, he would return so agog with his discovery that the Henley Household would be roused from their slumbers to rejoice with him, even though it was past midnight.'

It would be difficult to overestimate Henley's influence on Morrison. Not merely did he publish Morrison's work and introduce him to literary London, but read his short stories and, like Besant before him, gave Morrison advice on how to improve his style; advice which was willingly accepted. Morrison, in his turn, offered Henley companionship during the dark final years of his life. After Henley's death Morrison described the intense devotion he had inspired in his young friends: 'The like of it I never saw elsewhere and never expect to see again. It moved not only his nearer friends, not a man of whom but would give his last breath in Henley's service and memory today: but every honest man who came near it.'

Apart from the *Mean Street* stories Morrison was also trying his hand at other kinds of fiction in the early nineties. In February 1892 he formed a partnership with a book illustrator, J. A. Shepherd, and published an article in the *Strand* called 'My Neighbours' Dogs'. Initially begun as a typographical experiment in which illustration and text were interlocked, it was followed by a great number of similar sketches, most of which were published in book form as *Zig-Zags at the Zoo* (1894). Not satisfied with producing such diverse work as the *Zig-Zag* sketches and *Mean Streets* tales, he began to plan a completely different series of short stories. In December 1893 Arthur Conan Doyle had stunned the British reading public and horrified the editors of the *Strand* by allowing Sherlock Holmes and Moriarty to plunge over the Reichenbach Falls. Morrison undertook to create a successor to Sherlock Holmes and the first Martin Hewitt story 'The Lenton Croft Robberies' appeared in the *Strand* in March 1894. Today only the most dedicated historian of detective fiction can find much to praise in the Martin Hewitt stories but they were popular in the nineties and for many years Morrison continued to write them; publishing the later series in the *Windsor Magazine* and all of them in book form.

In the four years since becoming a freelance writer Morrison had gone some way to establishing himself in the public mind. His material position had improved and his prospects looked good, and in August 1892 he married Elizabeth Thatcher. Immediately after the marriage they lived at Chingford and a little later moved to a house in Loughton, Essex, where their only child, Guy, was born the following year.

The turning point of Morrison's early life was the publication of *Tales of Mean Streets* late in 1894. The book was an immediate success, running into several editions and provoking widespread critical discussion from which Morrison emerged as a leading figure of English realism. There was only one aspect of the reviews that upset him and which has plagued discussion of his work ever since. The reviewers concentrated almost entirely on 'Lizerunt' the one really violent story in the collection of fourteen; so much so that Morrison wrote a letter to the *Spectator* complaining of this unnecessary bias and denying that he had 'generalised half London as a race of Yahoos'. It must be admitted that 'Lizerunt' was the best as well as the most violent story in *Mean Streets* but there was much else that deserved serious consideration. No doubt in answer to his critics he immediately began to write *To London Town*, a much gentler study of working-class life, but then suddenly put this aside and wrote instead *A Child of the Jago* in which working-class violence was presented with a detailed frankness unlike anything the English novel had seen before.

THE JAGO

Early in 1895 the Reverend A. Osborne Jay, Vicar of Holy Trinity, Shoreditch, read *Tales of Mean Streets* and wrote a letter of appreciation to Morrison. While praising the general truthfulness of his East End portrait, Jay pointed out that there were certain isolated areas of East London that did not conform with the *Mean Streets* image, and as an example instanced part of his own parish, the Old Nichol, which he invited Morrison to visit. Morrison had long planned to write a novel about the corrupting effect of heredity and environment on a slum child but could not decide what form the novel should take nor its precise East End setting. His meeting with Jay immediately settled these problems. The impact of his visit to the Old Nichol and how it persuaded him to write a novel with a direct social message was later described by Morrison: 'I resolved therefore to write the "Child of the Jago", in which I should tell the story of a boy who, but for his environment, would have become a good citizen; also the story of the horrible Nichol; and, lastly, I wished to show that Father Jay's method is the only one that it is possible to employ in such a district.'

Jay's parish was situated on the boundary of Bethnal Green and Shoreditch; a small, densely-populated area which, according to Charles Booth, possessed the highest poverty level in East London. The Old Nichol consisted of only some half-dozen streets but it lay at the heart of the parish and largely dictated the tone and quality of life in the entire district, and it was here that Jay decided to settle when he first accepted the living in December 1886. From the beginning he was convinced that only by adopting drastic methods appropriate to the environment could a priest hope to make any lasting impact on such a community. As at this time there was no church in the parish (services being held in the loft of an old stable), Jay moved freely about the Old Nichol, steadfastly studying this alien way of life and gradually improvising an idiosyncratic technique for dealing with his unruly parishioners. Supported by a regular grant from Magdalen College, Oxford, he seized every opportunity to publicise his work and in the space of ten years raised a sum of £25,000 with which he built, in the centre of Old Nichol Street, a church, social club, gymnasium and lodging house. His greatest achievement, however, was in persuading the newly-formed L.C.C. to give high priority on its slum clearance schedules to the Old Nichol, or the Boundary Street Improvement Scheme as it was officially called. When Morrison accepted Jay's invitation to visit his parish the first houses were just being pulled down. These details of Jay's life are familiar to readers of A Child of the Jago as Morrison faithfully reproduced them in his portrait of Father Sturt. Jay also has told his own story, and that of the Old Nichol, in three lively books: Life in Darkest London (1891), The Social Problem and Its Solution (1893) and A Story of Shoreditch (1896).

Morrison, as we have seen, already possessed considerable personal knowledge of both the East End and slum workers but in spite of this he was horrified by the Old Nichol and deeply impressed by Jay. For a period of eighteen months he made frequent trips to Shoreditch where, under Jay's guidance, he met all of the characters later to appear in his book; talking with them (his knowledge of boxing once again standing him in good stead), drinking with them in local pubs, visiting their homes and even learning how to make matchboxes. Occasionally he would invite some of the Old Nichol inhabitants back to his house at Loughton where he carefully recorded their conversation. Jay later testified to the intensity of Morrison's research: 'Mr Morrison's laborious and persistent care amazed me. He would take nothing for granted; he examined, cross-examined and examined again as to the minutest particulars, until I began to fear his book would never be begun. Till then I never realised what conscientious labour art involved. And this remember, was the man who had already proved his intimate knowledge of the poor classes by his "Tales of Mean Streets".'

But the kind of knowledge of the London working classes possessed by Morrison was of little use in writing about the Jago, as he now renamed the Old Nichol. It was a special case: 'A plague spot in the East End which for the greater part is respectable to the gloomiest point of monotony.' And in the opening chapter of the novel Morrison was careful to emphasise that he was dealing with the semi-criminal rather than the working classes: 'What was too vile for Kate Street, Seven Dials, and Ratcliff Highway in its worst day, what was too useless, incapable and corrupt—all that teemed in the Jago.' Determined that nothing in the novel should be invented Morrison needed to depend almost entirely on his notebook (though there is a biographical point here that must be explored later) and even went so far as to set 'traps' for his future reviewers, many of whom fell into them.

As so much criticism of the book concerned the veracity of the Old Nichol portrait, it is worthwhile setting out some of the sober statistics gathered by the L.C.C. for the Boundary Street Improvement Scheme. The area covered is slightly larger than Morrison's Jago and the following statistics therefore give a relatively favourable picture:

The streets were 20 in number and the average population per room was about 2¼, 107 rooms having five or more inhabitants each.

The streets and courts were very narrow, the widest being only 28 feet across. In very many cases there was a great difference between the level of the street and that of the ground floor of the houses, the latter in some cases being 18 inches below the former. A large number of the houses had no back yards and many of the small courts were of a very bad class.

There were 730 houses, of which 652 were occupied, wholly or partly, by persons of the labouring classes; the remaining 78 houses consisted of 12 public-houses and beer shops, 21 shops and factories, 2 registered lodging-houses (153 beds); and 43 empty houses. The population, exclusive of those in lodging-houses, was 5,566—viz., 3,370 adults and 2,196 children, who occupied 2,545 rooms.

The L.C.C. report goes on to point out that 'a large proportion of the inhabitants of the area belonged to the criminal classes. Living in one street only there were at one time no less than 64 persons who had served varying terms of penal servitude.' We also learn that the death rate in the Boundary Street area was twice as high as in other parts of Bethnal Green and four times that of London as a whole; and that one child in every four born in the area died before his first birthday. These statistics had been gathered four years before Morrison came in contact with the Old Nichol and no doubt, through Jay, he was fully aware of them. His task, however, was to write not about statistics but people: not about relative levels of poverty but a way of life. Even so it is a mark of the accuracy of his portrait that it should be so totally vindicated by the L.C.C. report.

The first thirteen chapters of *A Child of the Jago*, constituting 'an episode which is, in a sense, complete', were serialised by Henley in the *New Review* before the book appeared in November 1896. Its publication was a great personal triumph for Morrison. Although *Mean Streets* had brought him critical approval he was extremely sensitive to the charge sometimes made against him, that his reputation rested entirely on his ability to satisfy the voracious demand for short stories that existed in the nineties. The only satisfactory way to refute the charge was to produce a successful novel and this he achieved with *A Child of the Jago*. H. G. Wells' opinion can be taken as representing that of the literary world as a whole:

We have admired Mr Morrison already for his 'Lizerunt'; we have disliked him for his despicable detective stories; and we will frankly confess we did not think him capable of anything nearly so good as this admirably conceived and excellently written story.

All the reviewers followed Wells in acknowledging the artistic power of the novel, but sharply divided over the crucial question of realism. On the one hand there were those critics who praised the book while doubting its veracity; and on the other, those who personally vouched for its truth and claimed that if Morrison erred at all it was in making the Jago less vile than it actually was. In the main, the former attitude was that of professional critics and the latter that of clergymen and philanthropists, many of whom reviewed the book and, to a man, supported Morrison. The critical debate that followed was unmarred by the moral denunciation that only a few years earlier had plagued the reception of Zola's novels in England, and centred on a discussion of the word 'realism'.

In December 1896 the *St James's Gazette* published a long review of *A Child of the Jago* called 'How Realistic Fiction is Written' which amounted to a charge against Morrison of having plagiarised Jay's first book *Life in Darkest London*. Parallel passages were carefully chosen and analysed showing how in some cases Morrison had brought the original brilliantly to life, and how in others he had crudely exaggerated. The reviewer claimed that *A Child of the Jago* provided a rare opportunity for observing 'how fiction is worked up out of a nucleus of fact' and concluded that the reader was impressed by such realistic fiction only because of 'his own ignorance of the subject'. Six days later, in a letter apologising for his delay in writing, Jay furiously rejected the parallel passages and completely exonerated Morrison from the charge of plagiarism.[6] He claimed that two men studying the same small district would inevitably 'agree as to certain main features' and, in the passage quoted earlier, testified to Morrison's lengthy and patient researches in the Old Nichol. In a brief footnote the editor closed the correspondence by praising Morrison's

[6] Charges of plagiarism (in effect a refusal to believe the widespread nature of the life described) were often made against slum novelists and workers of the nineties. Several years earlier Jay had been accused by George Gissing of having plagiarised parts of *The Nether World* (1889); and later Somerset Maugham's *Liza of Lambeth* (1897) was described as a plagiarism of Morrison's *Jago*.

'very artistic story' and assuring Jay that he was 'exciting himself needlessly'.

Morrison had remained aloof from this discussion but in January 1897 the *Fortnightly Review* published an article by H. D. Traill called 'The New Realism' which represented a more serious challenge.[7] Traill was one of the most respected late Victorian critics and his pronouncements on such a topical subject as realism carried great weight with the reading public. His principal argument was that while Morrison was clearly a 'trained craftsman' and a 'writer of promise' the kind of realism he practised produced an impression of 'extraordinary unreality'. After a minute examination of detail Traill decided that the inhabitants of the Jago could no more be regarded as true to life than the Houyhnhnms, and rashly said he was not surprised that 'many who know the East-End of London well have protested against this picture'. Jay, rising to the bait, refused to believe that anyone knew the Old Nichol better than he did and challenged Traill to name his authorities. This time, however, Morrison chose to defend himself and published a refutation of Traill's article, which appeared first in the *New Review* and later as a preface to the third edition of *A Child of the Jago*.

The title of Morrison's article, 'What is a Realist?' leads one to expect a critical manifesto, and perhaps he had intended it to be so, but although his defence was low pitched and dignified, it hardly raised the level of the debate above that of Jay and the *St James's Gazette*. Describing himself as 'a simple writer of tales, who takes whatever means lie to his hand to present life as he sees it', Morrison denied any allegiance to a school of realism, showed how loosely the term could be applied by referring to Japanese art (thus skilfully avoiding Traill's superiority in the field of literature) and reaffirmed the social purpose of his novel:

> If I had been a rich man I might have attempted to discharge my peculiar responsibility in one way; if I had been a statesman I might have tried another. Being neither of these things, but a simple writer of fiction, I endeavoured to do my duty by writing a tale wherein I hoped to bring the condition of this place within the comprehension of others.

[7] Morrison did, however, provide the necessary information for a friend of his to refute the *St. James's Gazette* article. See C.R. 'The Methods of Mr. Morrison', *The Academy*, 12 Dec. 1896.

He proceeded to outline the now familiar argument that *A Child of the Jago* was an exact transcript of life in the Old Nichol, that many notable authorities had already publicly testified as to its reality, and finally that if Traill wished to substantiate his criticisms he should 'trot out his experts'.[8]

When considered in relation to the wider debate on realism then taking place in England, Europe and America, the contributions of Morrison, Jay, Traill and the *St James's Gazette* must be regarded as of little significance. In the present context, however, there is both biographical and historical interest in the kind of defence so stubbornly adhered to by Morrison. For while the total weight of sociological evidence is in Morrison's favour, this does not help to explain at all the continuing interest for today's reader of *A Child of the Jago*: the field of working-class fiction is scattered with lifeless novels written with strict sociological exactness. Nor does it explain why the techniques which were so successful in this novel are barely observable in Morrison's other work; in, for instance, the detective stories where the narrative skill exhibited in *Jago* is sadly lacking.

It seems reasonable to assume that Morrison's horror at discovering this criminal ghetto among the mean streets he already knew so well, awakened in him some kind of deep personal association (of what nature exactly can never be determined, but possibly realisation of what he himself in slightly different circumstances might have come to) that served to raise the quality of this novel far above the level of his normal work; just as a similar sense of involvement had inspired the best sketches in *Mean Streets* and was later to inform those parts of *The Hole in the Wall* narrated by Stephen. Before writing about the Old Nichol Morrison did need to study the district and he did rely heavily on Jay's memoirs, or at least on Jay's special point of view: a comparison of *A Child of the Jago* and Jay's books brings out too many points of similarity (and not merely in the portrait of Father Sturt) for the charge of plagiarism to be completely discounted. What he did not need to study was the subtle relationship that existed, and the existence of which, as we have seen, he consistently denied, between ordinary working-class life and the semi-criminals of the

---

[8] Traill took up the challenge when his article was reprinted as *The New Fiction and other Essays* (1897), but by this time both parties seem to have tired of this rather futile exchange.

Old Nichol. And it is this ability to describe life in the Jago as though it represented a universally accepted norm that gives the novel its distinctive quality.

As Morrison so doggedly stressed the didactic aims of *A Child of the Jago* it is surprising that they rarely obtrude upon the reader. Dicky Perrott's death scene now seems mawkish rather than genuinely pathetic, as late Victorian readers found it: and there are moments when the hero-worship of Father Sturt is a little too obvious, but for the most part the reader is compelled by the fast-flowing narrative into a state of total acceptance of events, a mood induced by almost no other English working-class novel. One serious weakness is the undigested influence of Dickens, especially *Oliver Twist*, which is most apparent in the portrait of Mr Weech, Josh Perrott's flight from the police and in the trial scene; even though the total pattern of the novel suggests that Morrison was deliberately reacting against the prevalent image in Victorian fiction of the slum child as upper-class changeling.

Where the novel really succeeds is in its portrayal of violence as a way of life. Initially violence had been an immediate reaction against the deadening grind of unemployment and poverty (the characters in the book are, it is important to note, *working-class* criminals) but the Jago has long since taken control of its inhabitants, moulding their speech, establishing their values, creating their culture; until violence and brutality have become ends in themselves, truly exciting and valuable. There are, for instance, various kinds of violence presented in the novel, not all of which are indulged in for material gain. 'Cosh-carrying' certainly is but this is directed against any outsider foolish enough to stray close to the Jago and is also 'near to being the major industry of the Jago'. The gang-fights, on the other hand, take place within the community and only incidentally involve innocent bystanders. The atmosphere of infectious excitement they create is neatly shown by the effect they have upon old Beveridge who neglects his cadging business and strides 'wildly about the streets, lank and rusty, stabbing the air with a carving knife, and incoherently defying "all the lot" to come near him'. The boxing match in Jago Court is more highly organised and conducted according to sporting rules, but for the inhabitants of the Jago it possesses much the same importance as the faction feuds, in that it establishes, publicly and irrefutably, Kingship within the district. This is not, of course, to argue that Morrison approved of such conduct, merely that in tracing the 'degraded' Jago behaviour, he frequently conveyed, perhaps against his will, elements of genuine communal excitement: a sense of kinship that serves to bind people together as well as isolate them from the outside world.

The only people to escape moral corruption by the Jago are the Ropers, who run away pursued by a hooting crowd of 'Jago rats', and Kiddo Cook, the working-class hero of the novel, who prospers by running a successful barrow and thus remains both in and out of the Jago. The Perrott family represent the reverse of this process. They were once typical inhabitants of *Mean Streets* who allowed their respectability to slip from them. At first, memories of the past serve as a goad to their conscience, but the moment they begin to find Jago life attractive then the 'ghost of respectability' is exorcised and they are trapped.

Just as few Jago inhabitants ever move to the outside world unless it is to 'do a click' or spend a 'holiday in the country', so the outside world has hitherto made little impact on the Jago. Until the arrival of Father Sturt, the only regular contact with the rest of London has been through the High Mobsmen, the aristocrats of the Jago. There have been other intruders or intrusive forces (the Elementary Education Act, the East End Elevation Mission, and the 'Panjandrum of philanthropy, a mummer of the market-place' i.e. General William Booth of the Salvation Army)[9] but these have had so slight an influence that they might never have been. Father Sturt changes all this. He himself is an outsider who by studying the Jago ways easily becomes 'wider' than the widest Jago rat, and thus beats them at their own game. Because he is the victor, the fate of the Jago lies in his hands (just as ordinarily it belongs to the victors of the permanent faction feud) and from him it is passed to the L.C.C. Morrison makes it clear that the physical destruction of the Jago is not a total answer to the problem. Many of the Jago inhabitants refuse to accept the new flats, which would destroy the clan basis of their lives, and move on to other areas.

Thus the novel really ends with a question mark, for if the

[9] Morrison's harsh treatment of Booth in Chap. XIV was probably influenced by Jay whose first book *Life in Darkest London* was in part a bitter attack on the methods of the Salvation Army.

Jago rats can survive the moral influence of Jay and the physical power of the L.C.C., then what can society do about them? That Morrison believed they could not be reformed is clear from *A Child of the Jago* and he later publicly endorsed Jay's proposal for the establishment of Penal Settlements which would solve the problem of heredity by wiping out the entire strain. At first it seems incredible that so humane a man as Jay could advocate building Penal Settlements in isolated parts of the country where the inmates would be well treated but 'actually sentenced to remain there for life, and will not under any conceivable circumstances be allowed to propagate their species and so perpetuate their type'. But the seemingly contradictory mixture of profound humanity and unbelievable inhumanity or stupidity, was a common characteristic of many late-Victorian slum workers; an ambivalence created by their fear of failing at the vast work of character transformation they had eagerly undertaken.

For Morrison Jay's plan was attractive because it confirmed what he wished to believe—that the London working-class comprised two distinct races; the one, debased, hooligan and semi-criminal; the other, eminently respectable. Two articles Morrison later wrote show how he tried to keep these different races apart. In 'A Workman's Budget' he wrote sympathetically of the problems that a working-class housewife faced in trying to balance the weekly accounts. He objected to the term 'working man' being applied only to 'men whose work is of the manual sort' and based his generalisations on the assumption that: 'The workman is merely a human being, and generalisation may safely go as far with him as with his race, and no farther.' But in the second article, 'Hooliganism', written in the same year, he defined the hooligan as a 'mere unlicked cub of a peculiarly vicious type, and he flourishes more openly of late by reason of his long immunity from licking'; and once again took up the cause of penal settlements. He seems never to have been aware that in his own novels he had convincingly shown that the line separating the respectable from the violent working man was almost entirely a matter of environment and had little to do with heredity.[10]

[10] H. G. Wells, in his review of *Jago* for the *Saturday Review*, had taken up one aspect of this. Seizing upon the slum surgeon's comments in Chap. XIV Wells argued that 'the Jago people are racially indistinguishable from the people who send their children to Oxford' and that

By the time *A Child of the Jago* was published the Old Nichol had all but ceased to exist. In its place was rising the new style L.C.C. housing estate (consisting of huge blocks of flats centred on a circular park) that still stands on the spot. Morrison's novel had played no part in the clearance of the Old Nichol, but it had brought the district vividly to the public mind; so much so that when the Prince of Wales officially opened the estate in March 1900 he naturally gave precedence to the slum novelist above the slum priest: 'Few, indeed, will forget this site who have read Mr Morrison's pathetic tale of "A Child of the Jago", and all of us are familiar with the labours of that most excellent philanthropist, Mr Jay, in this neighbourhood.'

LATER LIFE

The remainder of Morrison's fiction need only be mentioned briefly. In the same year as *A Child of the Jago* he published a further collection of Martin Hewitt stories and followed this with *The Dorrington Deed-Box* (1897), a more unusual if hardly successful work of detective fiction. He did not return to a working-class theme until *To London Town* (1899) which was intended to complete the trilogy begun with *Mean Streets*. The reviewers were kind to it but it is by far the weakest of the three working-class studies, lacking the sharp observation of *Mean Streets* and the spontaneity of *A Child of the Jago*. Deserving of much more attention are the two historical novels he then wrote, *Cunning Murrell* (1900) and *The Hole in the Wall* (1902). The latter, as has already been sufficiently stressed, ranks with the very best of Morrison's work, and the former, a study of witchcraft in mid-nineteenth-century Essex, is a regional novel of considerable distinction. During the Edwardian period he published four further collections of short stories: *The Red Triangle* (1903), *The Green Eye of Goona* (1904), *Divers Vanities* (1905) and *Green Ginger* (1909). The best of these stories are those which deal with working life. Although they cannot be said to constitute any significant development they do testify to a mellowing of

---

Morrison had undermined his own case by allowing Mrs Perrott to be assimilated to the Jago way of life and Kiddo Cook to become a useful citizen.

personal attitudes. There is a new lightness of touch about them and an attempt at balancing the sardonic aspects of working-class speech (so exactly captured in the early work) with a gentler, more domesticated Cockney humour.

It is disappointing that Morrison did not develop as a novelist. The working-class novels and *Cunning Murrell* testify to the possibility of artistic growth, especially in dealing with those areas of life he knew well, Essex and the East End; but it is doubtful whether Morrison felt this himself. He had always regarded the writing of fiction as a part-time occupation and until his retirement in 1913 continued to work as a journalist. It is possible, as Jocelyn Bell has suggested, that 'his best writing went into newspaper articles which were often unsigned or written under an assumed name'. For a while he was also attracted to the stage and with professional advice from various collaborators successfully turned some of his short stories into one-act plays. But from the mid-nineties onwards these various activities were subordinated to his study of Japanese painting. In this Morrison found a subject that profoundly absorbed his interest and which brought in its wake financial reward and social respect, without the emotional disturbance created by working-class fiction.

The East End in the late eighties and nineties was a perfect hunting ground for Japanese prints which at this time were in the main regarded more as novelties than works of art. The cosmopolitan nature of the East End, enhanced by the steady influx of foreign immigrants and sailors returning home with mementoes of their voyages, provided him with the opportunity of buying valuable prints cheaply. Furthermore, he was able to benefit from the expert advice of his friend, Harold Parlett, who went to Japan in 1890 as a student interpreter and later held a number of consular posts, becoming the Consul at Dairen in 1910. Morrison later publicly thanked Parlett for his 'unselfish aid, extending over many years of his long residence in Japan, in the acquisition of many of my best pictures.' At the same time Morrison began to supplement the rudimentary knowledge of Japanese art he had gradually picked up, by systematic courses of study under Japanese scholars and painters in London; and in 1902 published a series of articles on the subject in the *Monthly Review*. The culminating point of his studies was the publication in 1911 of a two-volume work, largely illustrated from his own collection, *The*

Painters of Japan. Two years later Sir Watkin Gwynne Evans purchased Morrison's Chinese and Japanese prints and presented them to the British Museum where, in 1914, they were placed on public exhibition.[11]

According to William Pett Ridge, Morrison received £4,000 for his collection and used the money to buy a motor-car: but this was obviously only one of the less important reasons why he sold the paintings he had so lovingly collected. In 1913, at the early age of fifty, he retired from regular employment as a journalist and settled into a house at High Beech, Essex, on the borders of Epping Forest, where he continued to devote much of his time to the study, purchase, and presumably speculative sale, of works of art. During the first world war his son Guy served in the army and Morrison in the Essex Special Constabulary, attaining the peculiar distinction of telephoning news of the first Zeppelin raid on London. After the war the Morrison family moved to Cavendish Square, London, where Guy, who was suffering from malaria contracted during his army service, died in 1921.

Almost as little is known of Morrison's later as his early life. In 1930 he moved to 'High Barn', Chalfont St Peter, Buckinghamshire, where he lived until his death fifteen years later. During this period he published one further book, a volume of short stories *Fiddle o' Dreams* (1933) and lived quietly, adding to his art collections (which now contained many outstanding English watercolours as well as a great number of Oriental *objets d'art*) and working conscientiously for the Royal Society of Literature, to which he had been elected a member in 1924 and a member of the Council in 1935. He was also a freemason and an honorary member of the Japanese Art Association.

When Morrison died in December 1945 he was a wealthy but little known figure. The books with which he had made his name were fifty years old and long out of print; the critical and social debates they had occasioned were not yet of historical interest. Before he died he might well have read V. S. Pritchett's enthusiastic article 'An East End Novelist' in the *New Statesman* which

---

[11] Apart from this Morrison had sold a collection of Japanese woodcuts to the B.M. in 1906, and in his will presented a further 140 Japanese paintings and woodcuts and a small collection of Japanese tea ceremony porcelain to the B.M. His wife added a collection of Chinese lacquer to these when she died in 1956.

inspired a minor revival of interest in his work, but it is impossible to say how he would have received it. Although proud of his working-class fiction he had early vowed to keep his public and private lives apart, and this vow he always kept. After his death, Elizabeth Morrison, acting according to her husband's wishes, sold his library, dispersed his art collections and burnt his personal notebooks and papers. Only the original manuscript of *A Child of the Jago*, which he had presented to Bethnal Green Library in 1936, escaped the flames.

P. J. KEATING

PREFACE

I AM glad to take this, the first available opportunity, to acknowledge the kindness with which *A Child of the Jago* has been received: both by the reading public, from which I have received many gratifying assurances that what I have tried to say has not altogether failed of its effect, and by the reviewers, the most of whom have written in very indulgent terms.

I think, indeed, that I am the more gratified by the fact that this reception has not been unanimous; because an outcry and an opposition, even from an unimportant minority, are proofs that I have succeeded in saying, however imperfectly, something that was worth being said. Under the conditions of life as we know it there is no truth worth telling that will not interfere with some hearer's comfort. Various objections have been made to *A Child of the Jago*, and many of them had already been made to *Tales of Mean Streets*. And it has been the way of the objectors, as well as the way of many among the kindest of my critics, to call me a 'realist'. The word has been used sometimes, it would seem, in praise; sometimes in mere indifference as one uses a phrase of convenient description; sometimes by way of an irremediable reproach. It is natural, then, not merely that I should wish to examine certain among the objections made to my work, but that I should feel some interest in the definition and description of a realist. A matter never made clear to me.

Now it is a fact that I have never called myself a 'realist', and I have never put forth any work as 'realism'. I decline the labels of the schoolmen and the sophisters: being a simple writer of tales, who takes whatever means lie to his hand to present life as he sees it; who insists on no process; and who refuses to be bound by any formula or prescription prepared by the cataloguers and the pigeon-holers of literature.

So it happens that when those who use the word 'realist' use it with no unanimity of intent and with a loose, inapprehensive application, it is not easy for me, who repudiate it altogether, to make a guess at its meaning. Nevertheless, it seems to me that the man who is called a 'realist' is one who, seeing things with his own eyes, discards the conventions of the schools, and presents his matter in individual terms of art. For a while the schoolmen abuse him as a realist; and in twenty years' time, if his work have life in it, he becomes a classic. Constable was called a realist; so was Corot. Who calls these painters realists now? The history of Japanese art affords a continuous illustration. From the day when Iwasa Matahei impudently arose and dared to take his subjects from the daily life of the people, to the day when Hiroshigé, casting away the last rag of propriety, adventurously drew a cast shadow, in flat defiance of all the canons of Tosa and Kano—in all this time, and through all the crowded history of the School of Ukioyé, no artist bringing something of his own to his art but was damned for a realist. Even the classic Harunobu did not escape. Look now at the work of these men, and the label seems grotesque enough. So it goes through the making of all art. A man with the courage of his own vision interprets what he sees in fresh terms, and gives to things a new reality and an immediate presence. The schoolmen peer with dulled eyes from amid the heap of precedents and prescriptions about them, and, distracted by seeing a thing sanctioned neither by precedent nor by prescription, dub the man realist, and rail against him for that his work fits none of their pigeon-holes. And from without the schools many cry out and complain: for truth is strong meat, and the weakling stomach turns against it, except in minim doses smothered in treacle. Thus we hear the feeble plea that the function of imagination is the distortion of fact; the piteous demand that the artist should be shut up in a flower-garden, and forbidden to peep through the hedge into the world. And they who know nothing of beauty, who are innately incapable of comprehending it, mistake it for mere prettiness, and call aloud for comfits; and among them that cannot understand, such definitions of the aims of art are bandied, as mean, if they mean anything, that art finds its most perfect expression in pink lollipops and gilt boxes. But in the end the truth prevails, if it be well set forth; and the schoolmen, groaning in their infinite labour, wearily write another prescription, admit another precedent, and make another pigeon-hole.

I have been asked, in print, if I think that there is no phase of life which the artist may not touch. Most certainly I think this. More, I know it. It is the artist's privilege to seek his material where he pleases, and it is no man's privilege to say him nay. If the community have left horrible places and horrible lives before his eyes, then the fault is the community's; and to picture these places and these lives becomes not merely his privilege, but his duty. It was my fate to encounter a place in Shoreditch, where children were born and reared in circumstances which gave them no reasonable chance of living decent lives: where they were born fore-damned to a criminal or semi-criminal career. It was my experience to learn the ways of this place, to know its inhabitants, to talk with them, eat, drink, and work with them. For the existence of this place, and for the evils it engendered, the community was, and is, responsible; so that every member of the community was, and is, responsible in his degree. If I had been a rich man I might have attempted to discharge my peculiar responsibility in one way; if I had been a statesman I might have tried another. Being neither of these things, but a mere writer of fiction, I sought to do my duty by writing a tale wherein I hoped to bring the conditions of this place within the apprehension of others. There are those who say that I should have turned away my eyes and passed by on the other side: on the very respectable precedent of the priest and the Levite in the parable.

Now, when the tale was written and published it was found, as I have said, to cause discomfort to some persons. It is needless to say more of the schoolmen. Needless, too, to say much of the merely genteel: who were shocked to read of low creatures, as Kiddo Cook and Pigeony Poll, and to find my pages nowhere illuminated by a marquis. Of such are they who delight to read of two men in velvet and feathers perforating each other's stomachs with swords; while Josh Perrott and Billy Leary, punching each other's heads, present a scene too sickening and brutal to consider without disgust. And it was in defiance of the maunderings of such as these that Charles Lamb wrote much of his essay *On the Genius and Character of Hogarth*. But chiefly this book of mine disturbed those who had done nothing, and preferred to do nothing, by way of discharging their responsibility toward the Jago and the people in it. The consciousness of duty neglected is discomforting, and personal comfort is the god of their kind. They firmly believe it to be the sole function of art to minister to their personal comfort—as upholstery does. They find it comfortable to shirk consideration of the fate of the Jago

39

children, to shut their eyes to it, to say that all is well and the whole world virtuous and happy. And this mental attitude they nickname optimism, and vaunt it—exult in it as a quality. So that they cry out at the suggestion that it is no more than a selfish vice; and finding truth where they had looked for the materials of another debauch of self-delusion, they moan aloud: they protest, and they demand as their sacred right that the bitter cup be taken from before them. They have moaned and protested at *A Child of the Jago*, and, craven and bewildered, any protest seemed good enough to them. And herein they have not wanted for allies among them that sit in committee-rooms, and tinker. For your professed philanthropist, following his own spirit, and seeing nothing, honestly resents the demonstration that his tinkering profits little. There is a story current in the East End of London, of a distracted lady who, being assailed with a request for the loan of a saucepan, defended herself in these words: 'Tell yer mother I can't lend 'er the saucepan, consekince o' 'avin' lent it to Mrs Brown, besides which I'm a-usin' of it meself, an' moreover it's gone to be mended, an' what's more I ain't got one.' In a like spirit of lavish objection it has been proclaimed in a breath that I transgress: because (1) I should not have written of the Jago in all the nakedness of truth; (2) my description is not in the least like; (3) moreover, it is exaggerated; (4) though it may be true, it is quite unnecessary because the Jago was already quite familiar, and everybody knew all about it; (5) the Jago houses have been pulled down; and (6) there never was any such place as the Jago at all.

To objections thus handsomely variegated it is not easy to reply with the tripping brevity wherewith they may be stated; and truly it is little reply that they call for, except, perhaps, in so far as they may be taken to impugn the sincerity of my work and the accuracy of my picture. A few of the objectors have caught up enough of their wits to strive after a war in my own country. They take hold of my technical method, and accuse me of lack of 'sympathy'; they claim that if I write of the Jago I should do so 'even weeping'. Now, my technical method is my own, and is deliberately designed to achieve a certain result, as is the method of every man—painter, poet, sculptor, or novelist—who is not the slave and the plaything of his material. My tale is the tale of my characters, and I have learned better than to thrust myself and my emotions between them and my reader. The cant of the charge stares all too plainly from the face of it. It is not that these good people wish me to write 'even weeping': for how do they know whether I weep or not? No: their wish is, not that I shall weep, but that I shall weep obscenely in the public gaze. In other words, that I shall do their weeping for them, as a sort of emotional bedesman: that I shall make public parade of sympathy in their behalf, so that they may keep their own sympathy for themselves, and win comfort from the belief that they are eased of their just responsibility by vicarious snivelling.

But the protest, that my picture of the Jago is untrue, is another thing. For the most part it has found very vague expression, but there are instances of rash excursion into definiteness. Certain passages have been denoted as exaggerations—as impossibilities. Now, I must confess that, foreseeing such adventurous indiscretions, I had, for my own diversion, set *A Child of the Jago* with traps. For certain years I have lived in the East End of London, and have been, not an occasional visitor, but a familiar and equal friend in the house of the East-Ender in all his degrees; for, though the steps between be smaller, there are more social degrees in the East End than ever in the West. In this experience I have seen and I have heard things that persons sitting in committee-rooms would call diabolical fable; nevertheless, I have seen them, and heard them. But it was none of my design to write of extreme instances: typical facts were all I wanted; these, I knew, would be met—or shirked—with incredulity; so that, whenever I saw reason to anticipate a charge of exaggeration—as for instance, in the matter of faction fighting—I made my typical incident the cold transcript of a simple fact, an ordinary, easy-going fact, a fact notorious in the neighbourhood, and capable of any amount of reasonable proof. If I touched my fact at all, it was to subdue it; that and no more. The traps worked well. Not one definite charge of exaggeration has been flung but it has been aimed at one of the normal facts I had provided as a target: not one. Sometimes the effect has had a humour of its own; as when a critic in a literary journal, beginning by selecting two of my norms as instances of 'palpable exaggeration', went on to assure me that there was no need to describe such life as the life in the Jago, because it was already perfectly familiar to everybody.

41

Luckily I need not vindicate my accuracy. That has been done for me publicly by independent and altogether indisputable authority. In particular, the devoted vicar of the parish, which I have called the Jago, has testified quite unreservedly to the truth of my presentation. Others also, with special knowledge, have done the same; and though I refer to them, and am grateful for their support, it is with no prejudice to the validity of my own authority. For not only have I lived in the East End of London (which one may do, and yet never see it) but observation is my trade.

I have remarked in more than one place the expression of a foolish fancy that because the houses of the Old Jago have been pulled down, the Jago difficulty has been cleared out of the way. That is far from being the case. The Jago, as mere bricks and mortar, is gone. But the Jago in flesh and blood still lives, and is crowding into neighbourhoods already densely over-populated.

In conclusion: the plan and the intention of my story made it requisite that, in telling it, I should largely adhere to fact; and I did so. If I write other tales different in scope and design, I shall adhere to fact or neglect it as may seem good to me: regardless of anybody's classification as a realist, or as anything else. For though I have made a suggestion, right or wrong, as to what a realist may be, whether I am one or not is no concern of mine; but the concern (if it be anybody's) of the tabulators and the watersifters.

February 1897   A.M.

. . . Woe unto the foolish prophets, that follow their own spirit, and have seen nothing! . . .

Because, even because they have seduced my people, saying, Peace; and there was no peace; and one built up a wall, and lo, others daubed it with untempered mortar:

Say unto them which daub it with untempered mortar, that it shall fall; there shall be an overflowing shower; and ye, O great hailstones, shall fall; and a stormy wind shall rend it.

Lo, when the wall is fallen, shall it not be said unto you, Where is the daubing wherewith ye have daubed it?

EZEKIEL xiii, 3, 10–12

Sketch Plan of

THE OLD JAGO

1

IT WAS past the mid of a summer night in the Old Jago. The
narrow street was all the blacker for the lurid sky; for there was
a fire in a farther part of Shoreditch, and the welkin was an in-
fernal coppery glare. Below, the hot, heavy air lay a rank oppression on the contorted forms of those who made for sleep on the
pavement: and in it, and through it all, there rose from the foul
earth and the grimed walls a close, mingled stink—the odour of
the Jago.

From where, off Shoreditch High Street, a narrow passage, set
across with posts, gave menacing entrance on one end of Old
Jago Street, to where the other end lost itself in the black beyond
Jago Row; from where Jago Row began south at Meakin Street,
to where it ended north at Honey Lane—there the Jago, for one
hundred years the blackest pit in London, lay and festered; and
half way along Old Jago Street a narrow archway gave upon Jago
Court, the blackest hole in all that pit.

A square of two hundred and fifty yards or less—that was all
there was of the Jago. But in that square the human population
swarmed in thousands. Old Jago Street, New Jago Street, Half
Jago Street lay parallel, east and west: Jago Row at one end and
Edge Lane at the other lay parallel also, stretching north and
south: foul ways all. What was too vile for Kate Street, Seven
Dials, and Ratcliff Highway in its worst day, what was too useless, incapable and corrupt—all that teemed in the Old Jago.

Old Jago Street lay black and close under the quivering red
sky; and slinking forms, as of great rats, followed one another
quickly between the posts in the gut by the High Street, and
scattered over the Jago. For the crowd about the fire was now
small, the police was there in force, and every safe pocket had
been tried. Soon the incursion ceased, and the sky, flickering and
brightening no longer, settled to a sullen flush. On the pavement
some writhed wearily, longing for sleep; others, despairing of it,
sat and lolled, and a few talked. They were not there for lack of
shelter, but because in this weather repose was less unlikely in
the street than within doors; and the lodgings of the few who

45

nevertheless abode at home were marked here and there by the lights visible from the windows. For in this place none ever slept without a light, because of three kinds of vermin that light in some sort keeps at bay: vermin which added to existence here a terror not to be guessed by the unafflicted: who object to being told of it. For on them that lay writhen and gasping on the pavement; on them that sat among them; on them that rolled and blasphemed in the lighted rooms; on every moving creature in this, the Old Jago, day and night, sleeping and waking, the third plague of Egypt, and more, lay unceasing.

The stifling air took a further oppression from the red sky. By the dark entrance to Jago Court a man rose, flinging out an oath, and sat with his head bowed in his hands.

'Ah—h—h—h,' he said, 'I wish I was dead: an' kep' a cawfy shop.' He looked aside from his hands at his neighbours; but Kiddo Cook's ideal of heaven was no new thing, and the sole answer was a snort from a dozing man a yard away.

Kiddo Cook felt in his pocket, and produced a pipe and a screw of paper. 'This is a bleed'n' unsocial sort o' evenin' party, this is,' he said. 'An' 'ere's the on'y real toff in the mob with 'ardly 'arf a pipeful left, an' no lights. D' y' 'ear, me lord'—leaning toward the dozing neighbour—'got a match?'

'Go t' 'ell!'

'O wot 'orrid langwidge! It's shocking, blimey. Arter that y' ought to find me a match. Come on.'

'Go t' 'ell!'

A lank, elderly man, who sat with his back to the wall, pushed up a battered tall hat from his eyes, and, producing a box of matches, exclaimed 'Hell? And how far's that? You're in it!' He flung abroad a bony hand, and glanced upward. Over his forehead a greasy black curl dangled and shook as he shuddered back against the wall. 'My God, there can be no hell after this!'

'Ah,' Kiddo Cook remarked, as he lit his pipe in the hollow of his hands, 'that's a comfort, Mr Beveridge, any'ow.' He returned the matches, and the old man, tilting his hat forward, was silent.

A woman, gripping a shawl about her shoulders, came furtively along from the posts, with a man walking in her tracks—a little unsteadily. He was not of the Jago, but a decent young workman, by his dress. The sight took Kiddo Cook's idle eye, and when the couple had passed, he said meditatively: 'There's Billy Leary in luck ag'in: 'is missis do pick 'em up, s'elp me. I'd carry the cosh meself if I'd a woman like 'er.'

Cosh-carrying was near to being the major industry of the Jago. The cosh was a foot length of iron rod, with a knob at one end, and a hook (or a ring) at the other. The craftsman, carrying it in his coat sleeve, waited about dark staircase corners till his wife (married or not) brought in a well-drunken stranger: when, with a sudden blow behind the head, the stranger was happily coshed, and whatever was found on him as he lay insensible was the profit on the transaction. In the hands of capable practitioners this industry yielded a comfortable subsistence for no great exertion. Most, of course, depended on the woman: whose duty it was to keep the other artist going in subjects. There were legends of surprising ingatherings achieved by wives of especial diligence: one of a woman who had brought to the cosh some six-and-twenty on a night of public rejoicing. This was, however, a story years old, and may have been no more than an exemplary fiction, designed, like a Sunday School book, to convey a counsel of perfection to the dutiful matrons of the Old Jago.

The man and woman vanished in a doorway near the Jago Row end, where, for some reason, dossers were fewer than about the portal of Jago Court. There conversation flagged, and a broken snore was heard. It was a quiet night, as quietness was counted in the Jago; for it was too hot for most to fight in that stifling air— too hot to do more than turn on the stones and swear. Still the last hoarse yelps of a combat of women came intermittently from Half Jago Street in the farther confines.

In a little while something large and dark was pushed forth from the door-opening near Jago Row which Billy Leary's spouse had entered. The thing rolled over, and lay tumbled on the pavement, for a time unnoted. It might have been yet another would-be sleeper, but for its stillness. Just such a thing it seemed, belike, to two that lifted their heads and peered from a few yards off, till they rose on hands and knees and crept to where it lay: Jago rats both. A man it was; with a thick smear across his face, and about his head the source of the dark trickle that sought the gutter deviously over the broken flags. The drab stuff of his pockets peeped out here and there in a crumpled bunch, and his waistcoat gaped where the watch-guard had been. Clearly, here was an uncommonly remunerative cosh—a cosh so good that the boots had been neglected, and remained on the man's feet. These the kneeling two unlaced deftly, and, rising, prize in hand, vanished in the deeper shadow of Jago Row.

A small boy, whom they met full tilt at the corner, staggered out to the gutter and flung a veteran curse after them. He was a slight child, by whose size you might have judged his age at five. But his face was of serious and troubled age. One who knew the children of the Jago, and could tell, might have held him eight, or from that to nine.

He replaced his hands in his trousers pockets, and trudged up the street. As he brushed by the coshed man he glanced again toward Jago Row, and, jerking his thumb that way, 'Done 'im for 'is boots,' he piped. But nobody marked him till he reached Jago Court, when old Beveridge, pushing back his hat once more, called sweetly and silkily, 'Dicky Perrott!' and beckoned with his finger.

The boy approached, and as he did so the man's skeleton hand suddenly shot out and gripped him by the collar. 'It—never—does—to—see—too—much!' Beveridge said, in a series of shouts close to the boy's ear. 'Now go home,' he added in a more ordinary tone, with a push to make his meaning plain: and straightway relapsed against the wall.

The boy scowled and backed off the pavement. His ragged jacket was coarsely made from one much larger, and he hitched the collar over his shoulder as he shrank toward a doorway some few yards on. Front doors were used merely as firewood in the Old Jago, and most had been burnt there many years ago. If perchance one could have been found still on its hinges, it stood ever open and probably would not shut. Thus at night the Jago doorways were a row of black holes, foul and forbidding.

Dicky Perrott entered his hole with caution, for anywhere, in the passage and on the stairs, somebody might be lying drunk, against whom it would be unsafe to stumble. He found nobody, however, and climbed and reckoned his way up the first stair-flight with the necessary regard for the treads that one might step through and the rails that had gone from the side. Then he pushed open the door of the first-floor back and was at home.

A little heap of guttering grease, not long ago a candle end, stood and spread on the mantelpiece, and gave irregular light from its drooping wick. A thin-railed iron bedstead, bent and staggering, stood against a wall, and on its murky coverings a half-dressed woman sat and neglected a baby that lay by her, grieving and wheezing. The woman had a long dolorous face, empty of expression and weak of mouth.

'Where 'a' you bin, Dicky?' she asked, rather complaining than asking. 'It's sich low hours for a boy.'

Dicky glanced about the room. 'Got anythink to eat?' he asked.

'I dunno,' she answered listlessly. 'P'raps there's a bit o' bread in the cupboard. I don't want nothin', it's so 'ot. An' father ain't bin 'ome since tea-time.'

The boy rummaged and found a crust. Gnawing at this, he crossed to where the baby lay. ''Ullo, Looey,' he said, bending and patting the muddy cheek. ''Ullo!'

The baby turned feebly on its back, and set up a thin wail. Its eyes were large and bright, its tiny face was piteously flea-bitten and strangely old. 'Wy, she's 'ungry, mother,' said Dicky Perrott, and took the little thing up.

He sat on a small box, and rocked the baby on his knees, feeding it with morsels of chewed bread. The mother, dolefully inert, looked on and said: 'She's that backward I'm quite wore out; more 'n ten months old, an' don't even crawl yut. It's a never-endin' trouble, is children.'

She sighed, and presently stretched herself on the bed. The boy rose, and carrying his little sister with care, for she was dozing, essayed to look through the grimy window. The dull flush still spread overhead, but Jago Court lay darkling below, with scarce a sign of the ruinous back yards that edged it on this and the opposite sides, and nothing but blackness between.

The boy returned to his box, and sat. Then he said: 'I don't s'pose father's 'avin' a sleep outside, eh?'

The woman sat up with some show of energy. 'Wot?' she said sharply. 'Sleep out in the street like them low Ranns an' Learys? I should 'ope not. It's bad enough livin' 'ere at all, an' me being used to different things once, an' all. You ain't seen 'im outside, 'ave ye?'

'No, I ain't seen 'im: I jist looked in the court.' Then, after a pause: 'I 'ope 'e's done a click,' the boy said.

His mother winced. 'I dunno wot you mean, Dicky,' she said, but falteringly. 'You—you're gittin' that low an' an'—'

'Wy, copped somethink, o' course. Nicked somethink. You know.'

'If you say sich things as that I'll tell 'im wot you say, an' 'e'll pay you. We ain't that sort o' people, Dicky, you ought to know I was alwis kep' respectable an' straight all my life, I'm sure, an'—'

'I know. You said so before, to father—I 'eard: w'en 'e brought 'ome that there yuller prop—the necktie pin. Wy, where did 'e git that? 'E ain't 'ad a job for munse and munse: where's the yannups come from wot's bin for to pay the rent, an' git the toke, an' milk for Looey? Think I dunno? I ain't a kid. I know.'

'Dicky, Dicky! you mustn't say sich things!' was all the mother could find to say, with tears in her slack eyes. 'It's wicked an'— an' low. An' you must alwis be respectable an' straight, Dicky, an' you'll—you'll git on then.'

'Straight people's fools, I reckon. Kiddo Cook says that, an' 'e's as wide as Broad Street. W'en I grow up I'm goin' to git toffs' clo'es an' be in the 'igh mob. They does big clicks.'

'They git put in a dark prison for years an' years, Dicky—an'— an' if you're sich a wicked low boy, father 'll give you the strap— 'ard,' the mother returned, with what earnestness she might. 'Gimme the baby, an' you go to bed, go on; 'fore father comes.'

Dicky handed over the baby, whose wizened face was now re-laxed in sleep, and slowly disencumbered himself of the ungainly jacket, staring at the wall in a brown study. 'It's the mugs wot git took,' he said, absently. 'An' quoddin' ain't so bad.' Then, after a pause, he turned and added suddenly: 'S'pose father 'll be smugged some day, eh, mother?'

His mother made no reply, but bent languidly over the baby, with an indefinite pretence of settling it in a place on the bed. Soon Dicky himself, in the short and ragged shirt he had worn under the jacket, burrowed head first among the dingy coverings at the foot, and protruding his head at the farther side, took his accustomed place crosswise at the extreme end.

The filthy ceiling lit and darkened by fits as the candle-wick fell and guttered to its end. He heard his mother rise and find another fragment of candle to light by its expiring flame, but he lay still wakeful. After a time he asked: 'Mother, why don't you come to bed?'

'Waitin' for father. Go to sleep.'

He was silent for a little. But brain and eyes were wide awake, and soon he spoke again. 'Them noo 'uns in the front room,' he said. 'Ain't the man give 'is wife a 'idin' yut?'

'No.'

'Nor yut the boy—'umpty-backed 'un?'

'No.'

'Seems they're mighty pertickler. Fancy theirselves too good for their neighbours; I 'eard Pigeony Poll say that; on'y Poll said—'

'You mustn't never listen to Pigeony Poll, Dicky. Ain't you 'eard me say so? Go to sleep. 'Ere comes father.' There was, indeed, a step on the stairs, but it passed the landing, and went on to the top floor. Dicky lay awake, but silent, gazing upward and back through the dirty window just over his head. It was very hot, and he fidgeted uncomfortably, fearing to turn or toss lest the baby should wake and cry. There came a change in the hue of the sky, and he watched the patch within his view, until the red seemed to gather in spots, and fade a spot at a time. Then at last there was a tread on the stairs, that stayed at the door; and father had come home. Dicky lay still, and listened.

'Lor, Josh, where ye bin?' Dicky heard his mother say. 'I'm almost wore out a-waitin'.'

'Awright, awright'—this in a hoarse grunt, little above a whisper. 'Got any water up 'ere? Wash this 'ere stick.'

There was a pause, wherein Dicky knew his mother looked about her in vacant doubt as to whether or not water was in the room. Then a quick, undertoned scream, and the stick rattled heavily on the floor. 'It's sticky!' his mother said. 'O my Gawd, Josh, look at that—an' bits o' 'air, too!' The great shadow of an open hand shot up across the ceiling and fell again. 'O Josh! O my Gawd! You ain't, 'ave ye? Not—not—not that?'

'Not wot? Gawblimey, not what? Shutcher mouth. If a man fights, you've got to fight back, aincher? Any one 'ud think it was a murder, to look at ye. I ain't sich a damn fool as that. 'Ere— pull up that board.'

Dicky knew the loose floor-board that was lifted with a slight groaning jar. It was to the right of the hearth, and he had shammed sleep when it had been lifted once before. His mother whimpered and cried quietly. 'You'll git in trouble, Josh,' she said. 'I wish you'd git a reg'lar job, Josh, like what you used—I do—I do.'

The board was shut down again. Dicky Perrott through one opened eye saw the sky a pale grey above, and hoped the click had been a good one: hoped also that it might bring bullock's liver for dinner.

Out in the Jago the pale dawn brought a cooler air and the chance of sleep. From the paving of Old Jago Street sad grey faces, open-mouthed, looked upward as from the Valley of Dry Bones. Down by Jago Row the coshed subject, with the blood dry on his face, felt the colder air, and moved a leg.

2

THREE-QUARTERS of a mile east of the Jago's outermost limit was the East End Elevation Mission and Pansophical Institute: such was the amazing success whereof, that a new wing had been built, and was now to be declared open by a Bishop of great eminence and industry.

The triumphs of the East End Elevation Mission and Pansophical Institute were known and appreciated far from East London, by people who knew less of that part than of Asia Minor. Indeed, they were chiefly appreciated by these. There were kept, perpetually on tap for the aspiring East Ender, the Higher Life, the Greater Thought, and the Wider Humanity: with other radiant abstractions, mostly in the comparative degree, specifics all for the manufacture of the Superior Person. There were many Lectures given on still more subjects. Pictures were borrowed and shown, with revelations to the Uninformed of the morals ingeniously concealed by the painters. The Uninformed were also encouraged to debate and to produce papers on literary and political matters, while still unencumbered with the smallest knowledge thereof: for the Enlargement of the Understanding and the Embellishment of the Intellect. And there were classes, and clubs, and newspapers, and games of draughts, and musical evenings, and a brass band, whereby the life of the Hopeless Poor might be coloured, and the Misery of the Submerged alleviated. The wretches who crowded to these benefits were tradesmen's sons, small shopkeepers and their families, and neat clerks, with here and there a smart young artisan of one of the especially respectable trades. They freely patronised the clubs, the musical evenings, the brass band, and the bagatelle board; and those who took themselves seriously debated and Mutually-Improved with pomp. Others, subject to savage fits of wanting-to-know, made short rushes at random evening classes, with intervals of disgusted apathy. Altogether, a number of decently-dressed and mannerly young men passed many evenings at the Pansophical Institute in harmless pleasures, and often with an agreeable illusion of intellectual advance.

Other young men, more fortunately circumstanced, with the educational varnish fresh and raw upon them, came from afar, equipped with a foreign mode of thought and a proper ignorance of the world and the proportions of things, as Missionaries. Not without some anxiety to their parents, they plunged into the perilous depths of the East End, to struggle—for a fortnight—with its suffering and its brutishness. So they went among the tradesmen's sons and the shopmen, who endured them as they endured the nominal subscription; and they came away with a certain relief, and with some misgiving as to what impression they had made, and what they had done to make it. But it was with knowledge and authority that they went back among those who had doubted their personal safety in the dark region. The East End, they reported, was nothing like what it was said to be. You could see much worse places up West. The people were quite a decent sort, in their way: shocking Bounders, of course; but quite clean and quiet, and very comfortably dressed, with ties and collars and watches.

But the Missionaries were few, and the subscribers to the Elevation Mission were many. Most had been convinced, by what they had been told, by what they had read in charity appeals, and perhaps by what they had seen in the police-court and inquest reports, that the whole East End was a wilderness of slums: slums packed with starving human organisms without minds and without morals, preying on each other alive. These subscribers visited the Institute by twos and threes, on occasions of particular festivity among the neat clerks, and were astonished at the wonderful effects of Pansophic Elevation on the degraded classes, their aspect and their habits. Perhaps it was a concert where nobody was drunk: perhaps a little dance where nobody howled a chorus, nor wore his hat, nor punched his partner in the eye. It was a great marvel, whereunto the observers testified: so that more subscriptions came, and the new wing was built.

The afternoon was bright, and all was promising. A small crowd of idlers hung about the main door of the Institute, and stared at a string of flags. Away to the left stood the new wing, a face of fair, clean brick; the ornamentation of approved earnestness, in terra-cotta squares at regular intervals. Within sat many friends and relations of the shopmen and superior mechanics, and waited for the Bishop; the Eminences of the Elevation Mission

54

sitting apart on the platform. Without, among the idlers, waited
Dicky Perrott. His notions of what was going on were indistinct,
but he had a belief, imbibed through rumour and tradition, that
all celebrations at such large buildings were accompanied by the
consumption, in the innermost recesses, of cake and tea. Even to
be near cake was something. In Shoreditch High Street was a
shop where cake stood in the window in great slabs, one slab
over another, to an incalculable value. At this window—against
it, as near as possible, his face flattened white—Dicky would
stand till the shopkeeper drove him off: till he had but to shut
his eyes to see once more, in the shifting black, the rich yellow
sections with their myriad raisins. Once a careless errand-boy,
who had bought a slice, took so clumsy a bite as he emerged that
near a third of the whole piece broke and fell; and this Dicky had
snatched from the paving and bolted with, ere the owner quite
saw his loss. This was a superior sort of cake, at a penny. But
once he had managed to buy himself a slice of an inferior sort
for a halfpenny, in Meakin Street.

Dicky Perrott, these blessed memories in his brain, stood un-
obtrusively near the door, with the big jacket buttoned over as
decently as might be, full of a desperate design: which was to get
inside by whatsoever manner of trick or opportunity he might,
and so, if it were humanly possible, to the cake.

The tickets were being taken at the door by an ardent young
Elevator—one of the missionaries. Him, and all such washed and
well-dressed people, Dicky had learnt to hold in serene contempt
when the business in hand was dodging. There was no hurry: the
Elevator might waste his vigilance on the ticket-holders for some
time yet. And Dicky knew better than to betray the smallest sign
of a desire for entrance while his enemy's attention was awake.

Carriages drew up, and yielded more Eminences: toward the
end the Bishop himself, whom Dicky observed but as a pleasant-
looking old gentleman in uncommon clothes; and on whom he
bestowed no more thought than a passing wonder at what might
be the accident to his hat which had necessitated its repair with
string.

But at the spikes of the Bishop's carriage came another; and
out of that there got three ladies, friends of the ticket-receiver,
on whom they closed, greeting and shaking hands; and in a flash
Dicky Perrott was beyond the lobby and moving obscurely along

the walls of the inner hall, behind pillars and in shadow, seeking cake.

The Choral Society sang their lustiest, and there were speeches. Eminences expressed their surprise and delight at finding the people of the East End, gathered in the Institute building, so respectable and clean, thanks to persistent, indefatigable, unselfish Elevation.

The good Bishop, amid clapping of hands and fluttering of handkerchiefs, piped cherubically of everything. He rejoiced to see that day, whereon the helping hand of the West was so unmistakably made apparent in the East. He rejoiced also to find himself in the midst of so admirably typical an assemblage—so representative, if he might say so, of that great East End of London, thirsting and crying out for—for Elevation: for that—ah —Elevation which the fortunately circumstanced denizens of—of other places, had so munificently—laid on. The people of the East End had been sadly misrepresented—in popular periodicals and in—in other ways. The East End, he was convinced, was not so black as it was painted. (Applause.) He had but to look about him. *Etcetera, etcetera.* He questioned whether so well-conducted, morally-given, and respectable a gathering could be brought together in any West End parish with which he was acquainted. It was his most pleasant duty on this occasion—and so on and so forth.

Dicky Perrott had found the cake. It was in a much smaller room at the back of the hall, wherein it was expected that the Bishop and certain Eminences of the platform would refresh themselves with tea after the ceremony. There were heavy, drooping curtains at the door of this room, and deep from the largest folds the ratling from the Jago watched. The table was guarded by a sour-faced man—just such a man as drove him from the window of the cake shop in Shoreditch High Street. Nobody else was there yet, and plainly the sour-faced man must be absent or busy ere the cake could be got at.

There was a burst of applause in the hall: the new wing had been declared open. Then there was more singing, and after that much shuffling and tramping, for everybody was free to survey the new rooms on the way out; and the Importances from the platform came to find the tea.

Filling the room and standing about in little groups; chatting, munching, and sipping, while the sour-faced man distractedly floundered amid crockery: not a soul of them all perceived an inconsiderable small boy, ducking and dodging vaguely among legs and round skirts, making, from time to time, a silent snatch at a plate on the table: and presently he vanished altogether. Then the amiable Bishop, beaming over the tea-cup six inches from his chin, at two courtiers of the clergy, bethought him of a dinner engagement, and passed his hand downward over the rotundity of his waistcoat.

'Dear, dear,' said the Bishop, glancing down suddenly, 'why—what's become of my watch?'

There hung three inches of black ribbon, with a cut end. The Bishop looked blankly at the Elevators about him.

Three streets off, Dicky Perrott, with his shut fist deep in his breeches pocket, and a gold watch in the fist, ran full drive for the Old Jago.

3

THERE was nobody in chase; but Dicky Perrott, excited by his novel exploit, ran hard: forgetting the lesson first learnt by every child of the Jago, to avoid, as far as may be, suspicious flight in open streets. He burst into the Old Jago from the Jago Row corner, by Meakin Street; and still he ran. A small boy a trifle bigger than himself made a sharp punch at him as he passed, but he took no heed. The hulking group at the corner of Old Jago Street, ever observant of weaklings with plunder, saw him, and one tried to catch his arm, but he had the wit to dodge. Past the Jago Court passage he scudded, in at the familiar doorway, and up the stairs. A pale hunchbacked child, clean and wistful, descended, and him Dicky flung aside and half downstairs with 'Git out, 'ump!'

Josh Perrott sat on the bed, eating fried fish from an oily paper; for it was tea-time. He was a man of thirty-two, of middle height and stoutly built, with a hard, leathery face as of one much older. The hair about his mouth seemed always three days old—never much less nor much more. He was a plasterer—had, at least, so described himself at police-courts. But it was long since he had plastered, though he still walked abroad splashed and speckled, as though from an eruption of inherent plaster. In moments of pride he declared himself the only member of his family who had ever learned a trade, and worked at it. It was a long relinquished habit, but while it lasted he had married a decent boiler-maker's daughter, who had known nothing of the Jago till these latter days. One other boast Josh Perrott had: that nothing but shot or pointed steel could hurt him. And this, too, was near being a true boast; as he had proved in more than one fight in the local arena —which was Jago Court. Now he sat peaceably on the edge of the bed, and plucked with his fingers at the oily fish, while his wife grubbed hopelessly about the cupboard shelves for the screw of paper which was the sugar-basin.

Dicky entered at a burst. 'Mother—father—look! I done a click! I got a clock—a red 'un!'

Josh Perrott stopped, jaw and hand, with a pinch of fish poised in the air. The woman turned, and her chin fell. 'O Dicky, Dicky,' she cried, in real distress, 'you're a awful low, wicked boy. My Gawd, Josh, 'e—'e'll grow up bad: I said so.'

Josh Perrott bolted the pinch of fish, and sucked his fingers as he sprang to the door. After a quick glance down the stairs he shut it, and turned to Dicky. 'Where d'je get that, ye young devel?' he asked, and snatched the watch.

'Claimed it auf a ol' bloke w'en 'e was drinkin' 'is tea,' Dicky replied, with sparkling eyes. 'Let's 'ave a look at it, father.'

'Did 'e run after ye?'

'No—didn't know nuffin' about it. I cut 'is bit o' ribbon with my knife.' Dicky held up a treasured relic of blade and handle, found in a gutter. 'Aincher goin' to let's 'ave a look at it?'

Josh Perrott looked doubtfully toward his wife: the children were chiefly her concern. Of her sentiments there could be no mistake. He slipped the watch into his own pocket, and caught Dicky by the collar.

'I'll give you somethink, you damn young thief,' he exclaimed, slipping off his belt. 'You'd like to have us all in stir for a year or two, I s'pose; goin' thievin' watches like a growed-up man.' And he plied the belt savagely, while Dicky, amazed, breathless and choking, spun about him with piteous squeals, and the baby woke and puled in feeble sympathy.

There was a rip, and the collar began to leave the old jacket. Feeling this, Josh Perrott released it, and with a quick drive of the fist in the neck sent Dicky staggering across the room. Dicky caught at the bed frame, and limped out to the landing, sobbing grievously in the bend of his sleeve.

It was more than his mother had intended, but she knew better than to attempt interference. Now that he was gone, she said, with some hesitation: ''Adn't you better take it out at once, Josh?'

'Yus, I'm goin',' Josh replied, turning the watch in his hand. 'It's a good 'un—a topper.'

'You—you won't let Weech 'ave it, will ye, Josh? 'E—'e never gives much.'

'No bloomin' fear. I'm goin' up 'Oxton with this 'ere.'

Dicky sobbed his way down the stairs and through the passage to the back. In the yard he looked for Tommy Rann, to sympathise. But Tommy was not there, and Dicky paused in his grief to reflect that perhaps, indeed, in the light of calm reason, he would rather cast the story of the watch in a more heroic mould, for Tommy's benefit, than was compatible with tears and a belted back. So he turned and squeezed through a hole in the broken fence, sobbing again, in search of the friend that shared his inmost sorrows.

The belting was bad—very bad. There was broken skin on his shins where the strap had curled round, and there was a little sticky blood under the shirt half way up his back: to say nothing of bruises. But it was the hopeless injustice of things that shook him to the soul. Wholly unaided, he had done, with neatness and credit, a click that anybody in the Jago would have been proud of. Overjoyed, he had hastened to receive the commendations of his father and mother, and to place the prize in their hands, freely and generously, though perhaps with some hope of hot supper by way of celebration. And his reward was this. Why? He could understand nothing: could but feel the wrong that broke his heart. And so, sobbing, he crawled through two fences to weep on the shaggy neck of Jerry Gullen's canary.

Jerry Gullen's canary was no bird, but a donkey: employed by Jerry Gullen in his occasional intervals of sobriety to drag a cranky shallow, sometimes stored with glass bottles, rags, and hearthstone: sometimes with firewood manufactured from a convenient hoarding, or from the joinery of an empty house: sometimes with empty sacks covering miscellaneous property suddenly acquired and not for general inspection. His vacations, many and long, Jerry Gullen's canary spent, forgotten and unfed, in Jerry Gullen's back yard: gnawing desperately at fences, and harrowing the neighbourhood with his bray. Thus the nickname, facetiously applied by Kiddo Cook in celebration of his piteous song, grew into use; and 'Canary' would call the creature's attention as readily as a mouthful of imprecations.

Jerry Gullen's canary was gnawing, gnawing, with a sound as of a crooked centre-bit. Everywhere about the foul yard, ten or twelve feet square, wood was rounded and splintered and bitten white, and as the donkey turned his heavy head, a drip of blood from his gums made a disc on the stones. A twitch of the ears welcomed Dicky, grief-stricken as he was; for it was commonly thus that he bethought him of solace in Jerry Gullen's back yard. And so Dicky, his arms about the mangy neck, told the tale of his wrongs till consolation came in composition of the heroic narrative designed for Tommy Rann.

'O, Canary, it is a blasted shame!'

4

WHEN Dicky Perrott came running into Jago Row with the Bishop's watch in his pocket, another boy punched a fist at him, and at the time Dicky was at a loss to guess the cause—unless it were a simple caprice—but stayed neither to inquire nor to retaliate. The fact was that the Ranns and the Learys were coming out, fighting was in the air, and the small boy, meeting another a trifle smaller, punched on general principles. The Ranns and the Learys, ever at war or in guarded armistice, were the great rival families—the Montagues and the Capulets—of the Old Jago. The Learys, indeed, scarce pretended to rivalry—rather to factious opposition. For the Ranns gloried in the style and title of the 'Royal Family', and dominated the Jago; but there were mighty fighters, men and women, among the Learys, and when a combat arose it was a hard one and an animated. The two families ramified throughout the Jago; and under the Rann standard, whether by kin or by custom, were the Gullens, the Fishers, the Spicers, and the Walshes; while in the Leary train came Dawsons, Greens, and Harnwells. So that near all the Jago was wont to be on one side or the other, and any of the Jago which was not, was apt to be the worse for it; for the Ranns drubbed all them that were not of their faction in the most thorough and most workmanlike manner, and the Learys held by the same practice; so that neutrality meant double drubbing. But when the Ranns and Learys combined, and the Old Jago issued forth in its entire might against Dove Lane, then the battle was one to go miles to see.

This, however, was but a Rann and Leary fight; and it was but in its early stages when Dicky Perrott, emerging from Jerry Gullen's back yard, made for Shoreditch High Street by way of the 'Posties'—the passage with posts at the end of Old Jago Street. His purpose was to snatch a handful of hay from some passing waggon, or of mixed fodder from some unguarded nosebag, wherewith to reward the sympathy of Jerry Gullen's canary. But by the 'Posties', at the Edge Lane corner, Tommy Rann, capless, and with a purple bump on his forehead, came flying into his arms, breathless, exultant, a babbling braggart. He had fought

Johnny Leary and Joe Dawson, he said, one after the other, and pretty nigh broke Johnny Leary's blasted neck; and Joe Dawson's big brother was after him now with a bleed'n' shovel. So the two children ran on together, and sought the seclusion of their own back yard; where the story of Tommy Rann's prowess, with scowls and the pounding of imaginary foes, and the story of the Bishop's watch, with suppressions and improvements, mingled and contended in the thickening dusk. And Jerry Gullen's canary went forgotten and unrequited.

That night fighting was sporadic and desultory in the Jago. Bob the Bender was reported to have a smashed nose, and Sam Cash had his head bandaged at the hospital. At the Bag of Nails in Edge Lane, Snob Spicer was knocked out of knowledge with a quart pot, and Cocko Harnwell's missis had a piece bitten off of one ear. As the night wore on, taunts and defiances were bandied from window to door, and from door to window, between those who intended to begin fighting to-morrow; and shouts from divers corners gave notice of isolated scuffles. Once a succession of piercing screams seemed to betoken that Sally Green had begun. There was a note in the screams of Sally Green's opposites which the Jago had learned to recognise. Sally Green, though of the weaker faction, was the female champion of the Old Jago: an eminence won and kept by fighting tactics peculiar to herself. For it was her way, reserving teeth and nails, to wrestle closely with her antagonist, throw her by a dexterous twist on her face, and fall on her, instantly seizing the victim's nape in her teeth, gnawing and worrying. The sufferer's screams were audible afar, and beyond their invariable eccentricity of quality—a quality vaguely suggestive of dire surprise—they had mechanical persistence, a pump-like regularity, that distinguished them, in the accustomed ear, from other screams.

Josh Perrott had not been home all the evening: probably the Bishop's watch was in course of transmutation into beer. Dicky, stiff and domestically inclined, nursed Looey and listened to the noises without till he fell asleep, in hopeful anticipation of the morrow. For Tommy Rann had promised him half of a broken iron railing wherewith to fight the Learys.

5

SLEEP in the Jago was at best a thing of intermission, for reasons —reasons of multitude—already denoted; nevertheless Dicky slept well enough to be unconscious of his father's home-coming. In the morning, however, there lay Josh Perrott, snoring thunderously on the floor, piebald with road-dust. This was not a morning whereon father would want breakfast—that was plain: he would wake thirsty and savage. So Dicky made sure of a crust from the cupboard, and betook himself in search of Tommy Rann. As to washing, he was never especially fond of it, and in any case there were fifty excellent excuses for neglect. The only water was from the little tap in the back yard. The little tap was usually out of order, or had been stolen bodily by a tenant; and if it were not, there was no basin there, nor any soap nor towel; and anything savouring of moderate cleanliness was resented in the Jago as an assumption of superiority.

Fighting began early, fast and furious. The Ranns got together soon, and hunted the Learys up and down, and attacked them in their houses: the Learys' chances only coming when straggling Ranns were cut off from the main body. The weapons in use, as was customary, rose in effectiveness by a swiftly ascending scale. The Learys, assailed with sticks, replied with sticks torn from old packing-cases, with protruding nails. The two sides bethought them of coshes simultaneously, and such as had no coshes—very few—had pokers and iron railings. Ginger Stagg, at bay in his passage, laid open Pud Palmer's cheek with a chisel; and, knives thus happily legitimised with the least possible preliminary form, everybody was free to lay hold of whatever came handy.

In Old Jago Street, half way between Jago Court and Edge Lane, stood the Feathers, the grimiest and vilest of the four public-houses in the Jago. Into the Feathers some dozen Learys were driven, and for a while they held the inner bar and the tap-room against the Ranns, who swarmed after them, chairs, bottles, and pewter pots flying thick, while Mother Gapp, the landlady, hung hysterical on the beer-pulls in the bar, supplicating and blubbering aloud. Then a partition came down with a crash, bringing shelves and many glasses with it, and the Ranns rushed over the ruin, beating the Learys down, jumping on them, heaving them through the back windows. Having thus cleared the house of the intruding enemy, the Ranns demanded recompense of liquor, and took it, dragging handles off beer-engines, seizing bottles, breaking into the cellar, and driving in bungs. Nobody better than Mother Gapp could quell an ordinary bar riot—even to knocking a man down with a pot; but she knew better than to attempt interference now. Nothing could have made her swoon, but she sat limp and helpless, weeping and blaspheming.

The Ranns cleared off, every man with a bottle or so, and scattered, and this for a while was their undoing. For the Learys rallied and hunted the Ranns in their turn: a crowd of eighty or a hundred sweeping the Jago from Honey Lane to Meakin Street. Then they swung back through Edge Lane to Old Jago Street, and made for Jerry Gullen's—a house full of Ranns. Jerry Gullen, Bill Rann, and the rest took refuge in the upper floors and barricaded the stairs. Below, the Learys broke windows and ravaged the rooms, smashing whatsoever of furniture was to be found. Above, Pip Walsh, who affected horticulture on his window-sill, hurled down flower-pots. On the stairs, Billy Leary, scaling the barricade, was flung from top to bottom, and had to be carried home. And then Pip Walsh's missis scattered the besiegers on the pavement below with a kettleful of boiling water.

There was a sudden sortie of Ranns from Jago Court, but it profited nothing; for the party was small, and its advent being unexpected, there was a lack of prompt co-operation from the house. The Learys held the field.

Down the middle of Old Jago Street came Sally Green: red-faced, stripped to the waist, dancing, hoarse and triumphant. Nail-scores wide as the finger striped her back, her face, and her throat, and she had a black eye; but in one great hand she dangled a long bunch of clotted hair, as she whooped defiance to the Jago. It was a trophy newly rent from the scalp of Norah Walsh, champion of the Rann womankind, who had crawled away to hide her blighted head, and be restored with gin. None answered Sally's challenge, and, staying but to fling a brickbat at Pip Walsh's window, she carried her dance and her trophy into Edge Lane.

The scrimmage on Jerry Gullen's stairs was thundering anew,

and parties of Learys were making for other houses in the street, when there came a volley of yells from Jago Row, heralding a scudding mob of Ranns. The defeated sortie-party from Jago Court, driven back, had gained New Jago Street by way of the house-passages behind the Court, and set to gathering the scattered faction. Now the Ranns came, drunk, semi-drunk, and otherwise, and the Learys, leaving Jerry Gullen's, rushed to meet them. There was a great shock, hats flew, sticks and heads made a wooden rattle, and instantly the two mobs were broken into an uproarious confusion of tangled groups, howling and grappling. Here a man crawled into a passage to nurse a broken head; there a knot gathered to kick a sprawling foe. So the fight thinned out and spread, resolving into many independent combats, with concerted rushes of less and less frequency, till once again all through the Jago each fought for his own hand. Kiddo Cook, always humorous, ran hilariously through the streets, brandishing a long roll of twisted paper, wherewith he smacked the heads of Learys all and sundry, who realised too late that the paper was twisted round a lodging-house poker.

Now, of the few neutral Jagos, most lay low. Josh Perrott, however, hard as nails and respected for it, feared neither Rann nor Leary, and leaving a little money with his missis, carried his morning mouth in search of beer. Pigeony Poll, harlot and outcast, despised for that she neither fought nor kept a cosh-carrier, like a respectable married woman, slunk and trembled in corners and yards, and wept at the sight of bleeding heads. As for old Beveridge, the affair so grossly excited him that he neglected business (he cadged and wrote begging screeves) and stayed in the Jago, where he strode wildly about the streets, lank and rusty, stabbing the air with a carving knife, and incoherently defying 'all the lot' to come near him. Nobody did.

Dicky Perrott and Tommy Rann found a snug fastness in Jago Row. For there was a fence with a loose board, which, pushed aside, revealed a hole where-through a very small boy might squeeze; and within were stored many barrows and shallows, mostly broken, and of these one, tilted forward and bottom up, made a hut or den, screened about with fence and barrows. Here they hid while the Learys swept the Jago, and hence they issued from time to time to pound such youngsters of the other side as might come in sight. The bits of iron railing made imposing weapons, but were a trifle too big and heavy for rapid use in their puny hands. Still, Dicky managed to double up little Billy Leary with a timely lunge in the stomach, and Tommy Rann made Bobby Harnwell's nose bleed very satisfactorily. On the other hand, the bump on Tommy Rann's forehead was widened by the visitation of a stick, and Dicky Perrott sustained a very hopeful punch in the eye, which he cherished enthusiastically with a view to an honourable blackness. In the snuggery intervals they explained their prowess one to another, and Dicky alluded to his intention, when he was a man, to buy a very long sword wherewith to cut off the Learys' heads: Tommy Rann inclining, however, to a gun, with which one might also shoot birds.

The battle flagged a little toward mid-day, but waxed lively again as the afternoon began. It was then that Dicky Perrott, venturing some way from the retreat, found himself in a scrimmage, and a man snatched away his piece of iron and floored a Leary with it. Gratifying as was the distinction of aiding in the exploit, Dicky mourned the loss of the weapon almost unto tears, and Tommy Rann would not go turn-about with the other, but kept it wholly for himself; so Dicky was fain to hunt sorrowfully for a mere stick. Even a disengaged stick was not easy to find just then. So Dicky, emerging from the Jago, tried Meakin Street, where there were shops, but unsuccessfully, and so came round by Luck Row, a narrow way from Meakin Street by Walker's cook shop, up through the Jago.

Dicky's mother, left with the baby, fastened the door as well as she might, and trembled. Indeed she had reason. The time of Josh Perrott's return was a matter of doubt, but when he did come he would want something to eat; it was for that he had left the money. But Dicky was out, and there was nothing in the cupboard. From the window she saw divers fights in Jago Court; and a man lay for near two hours on the stones with a cut on his temple. As for herself, she was no favourite in the neighbourhood at any time. For one thing, her husband did not carry the cosh. Then she was an alien who had never entirely fallen into Jago ways; she had soon grown sluttish and dirty, but she was never drunk, she never quarrelled, she did not gossip freely. Also her husband beat her but rarely, and then not with a chair nor a poker. Justly irritated by such superiorities as these, the women of the Jago were ill-disposed to brook another: which was, that Hannah Perrott had been married in church. For these reasons she was timid at the most peaceful of times, but now, with Ranns and Learys on the war-path, and herself obnoxious to both, she trembled. She wished Dicky would come and do her errand. But there was no sign of him, and mid-day wore into afternoon. It was late for Josh as it was, and he would be sure to come home irritable: it was his way when a bad head from overnight struggled with morning beer. If he found nothing to eat there would be trouble.

At length she resolved to go herself. There was a lull in the outer din, and what there was seemed to come from the farther parts of Honey Lane and Jago Row. She would slip across by Luck Row to Meakin Street and be back in five minutes. She took up little Looey and went.

As Dicky, stickless, turned into Luck Row, there arose a loud shriek, and then another, and then in a changed voice a succession of long screams with a regular breath-pause. Sally Green again! He ran, turned into Old Jago Street, and saw.

Sprawled on her face in the foul road lay a writhing woman who screamed; while squeezed under her arm was a baby with mud in its eyes and a cut cheek, crying weakly; and spread over all, clutching her prey by hair and wrist, Sally Green hung on the nape like a terrier, jaws clenched, head shaking.

Thus Dicky saw it in a flash, and in an instant he had flung himself on Sally Green, kicking, striking, biting, and crying, for he had seen his mother and Looey. The kicks wasted themselves among the woman's petticoats, and the blows were feeble; but the sharp teeth were meeting in the shoulder-flesh, when help came.

Norah Walsh, vanquished champion, now somewhat recovered, looked from a window, saw her enemy vulnerable, and ran out armed with a bottle. She stopped at the kerb to knock the bottom off the bottle, and then, with an exultant shout, seized Sally Green by the hair and stabbed her about the face with the jagged points. Blinded with blood, Sally released her hold on Mrs Perrott, and rolled on her back, struggling fiercely; but to no end, for Norah Walsh, kneeling on her breast, stabbed and stabbed again, till pieces of the bottle broke away. Sally's yells and plunges ceased, and a man pulled Norah off. On him she turned, and he was fain to run, while certain Learys found a truck which might carry Sally to the hospital.

Hannah Perrott was gone indoors, hysterical and helpless. She had scarce crossed the street on her errand when she had met Sally Green in quest of female Ranns. Mrs Perrott was not a Rann, but she was not a Leary, so it came to the same thing. Moreover, there was her general obnoxiousness. She had tried to run, but that was useless; and now, sobbing and bleeding, she was merely conscious of being gently led, almost carried, indoors and upstairs. She was laid back on the bed, and somebody loosened her hair and wiped her neck, giving her hoarse, comforting words. Then she saw the face—scared though coarse and pitted, and red about the eyes—that bent over her. It was Pigeony Poll's.

Dicky had followed her in, no longer the hero of the Jago Row retreat, but with his face tearful and distorted, carrying the baby in his arms, and wiping the mud from her eyes. Now he sat on the little box and continued his ministrations, with fear in his looks as he glanced at his mother on the bed.

Without, the fight rallied once more. The Learys ran to avenge Sally Green, and the Ranns met them with a will. Down by the Bag of Nails a party of Ranns was driven between the posts and through the gut into Shoreditch High Street, where a stand was made until Fag Dawson dropped, with a shoe-maker's knife sticking under his arm-pit. Then the Ranns left, with most of the Learys after them, and Fag Dawson was carried to a chemist's by the police, never to floor a Rann again. For he was chived in the left lung.

Thus the fight ended. For a faction fight in the Jago with a few broken heads and ribs and an odd knife wound here and there— even with a death in the hospital from kicks or what not—was all very well; but when it came to homicide in the open High Street, the police drew the line, and entered the Jago in force. Ordinarily, a peep now and again from a couple of policemen between the 'Posties' was all the supervision the Jago had, although three policemen had been seen to walk the length of Old Jago Street together, and there were raids in force for special captures. There was a raid in force now, and the turmoil ceased. Nothing would have pleased both Ranns and Learys better than to knock over two or three policemen, for kicking-practice; but there were too many for the sport, and for hours they patrolled the Jago's closest passages. Of course nobody knew who chived Fag Dawson. No inquiring policeman ever found anybody in the Old Jago who knew anything, even to the harm of his bitterest foe. It was the sole commandment that ran there: 'Thou shalt not nark.'

That night it was known that there would be a fight between Josh Perrott and Billy Leary, once the latter grew well. For Josh Perrott came home, saw his wife, and turned Rann on the spot. But for the police in the Jago that night, there would have been many a sore head, if no worse, among the Learys, by visitation of Josh Perrott. Sally Green's husband had fled years ago, and Billy Leary, her brother, was the obvious mark for Josh's vengeance. He was near as eminent a fighter among the men as his sister among the women, and a charming scrap was anticipated. It would come off, of course, in Jago Court one Sunday morning, as all fights of distinction did; and perhaps somebody in the High Mob would put up stakes.

6

In the morning the police still held the Jago. Their presence embarrassed many, but none more than Dicky Perrott, who would always take a turning, or walk the other way, at sight of a policeman. Dicky got out of Old Jago Street early, and betook him to Meakin Street, where there were chandlers' shops with sugar in their windows, and cook-shops with pudding. He designed working through by these to Shoreditch High Street, there to crown his solace by contemplation of the cake-shop. But, as he neared Weech's coffee-shop, scarce half through Meakin Street, there stood Weech himself at the door, grinning and nodding affably, and beckoning him. He was a pleasant man, this Mr Aaron Weech, who sang hymns aloud in the back parlour, and hummed the tunes in the shop: a prosperous, white-aproned, whiskered, half-bald, smirking tradesman, who bent and spoke amiably to boys, looking sharply in their eyes, but talked to a man mostly with his gaze on the man's waistcoat.

Indeed, there seemed to be something about Mr Aaron Weech especially attractive to youth. Nearly all his customers were boys and girls, though not boys and girls who looked likely to pay a great deal in the way of refreshment, much as they took. But he was ever indulgent, and at all times accessible to his young clients. Even on Sunday (though, of course, his shutters were kept rigidly up on the Day of Rest) a particular tap would bring him hot-foot to the door: not to sell coffee, for Mr Weech was no Sabbath-breaker.

Now he stood at his door, and invited Dicky with nods and becks. Dicky, all wondering, and alert to dodge in case the thing were a mere device to bring him within striking distance, went.

'W'y, Dicky Perrott,' quoth Mr Weech in a tone of genial surprise, 'I b'lieve you could drink a cup o' cawfy!'

Dicky, wondering how Mr Weech had learnt his name, believed he could.

'An' eat a slice o' cake too, I'll be bound,' Mr Weech added.

Dicky's glance leapt. Yes, he could eat a slice of cake too.

'Ah, I knew it,' said Mr Weech, triumphantly; 'I can always

tell.' He rubbed Dicky's cap about his head, and drew him into the shop, at this hour bare of customers. At the innermost compartment they stopped, and Mr Weech with a gentle pressure on the shoulders, seated Dicky at the table.

He brought the coffee, and not a single slice of cake, but two. True, it was not cake of Elevation Mission quality, nor was it so good as that shown at the shop in High Street: it was of a browner, dumpier, harder nature, and the currants were gritty and few. But cake it was, and to consider it critically were unworthy. Dicky bolted it with less comfort than he might, for Mr Weech watched him keenly across the table. And, indeed, from some queer cause, he felt an odd impulse to cry. It was the first time that he had ever been given anything, kindly and ungrudgingly.

He swallowed the last crumb, washed it down with the dregs of his cup, and looked sheepishly across at Mr Weech.

'Goes down awright, don't it?' that benefactor remarked. 'Ah, I like to see you enjoyin' of yerself. I'm very fond o' you young 'uns: 'specially clever 'uns like you.'

Dicky had never been called clever before, so far as he could recollect, and he wondered at it now. Mr Weech, leaning back, contemplated him smilingly for some seconds, and then proceeded. 'Yus,' he said, 'you're the sort o' boy as can 'ave cawfy and cake w'enever you want it, you are.'

Dicky wondered more, and his face said as much. 'You know,' Mr Weech pursued, winking amain, grinning and nodding. 'That was a fine watch you found the other day. Y'ought to 'a' brought it to me.'

Dicky was alarmed. How did Mr Weech learn about the watch? Perhaps he was a friend of the funny old man who lost it. Dicky half rose, but his affable patron leaned across and pushed him back on the seat. 'You needn't be frightened,' he said. 'I ain't goin' to say nothink to nobody. But I know all about it, mind, an' I could if I liked. You found the watch, an' it was a red 'un, on a bit o' ribbin. Well, then you went and took it 'ome, like a little fool. Wot does yer father do? W'y 'e ups an' lathers you with 'is belt, an' 'e keeps the watch 'isself. That's all you git for yer pains. See—I know all about it.' And Mr Weech gazed on Dicky Perrott with a fixed grin.

''Oo toldjer?' Dicky managed to ask at last.

'Ah!'—this with a great emphasis and a tapping of the fore-finger beside the nose—'I don't want much tellin': it ain't much as goes on 'ereabout I don't know of. Never mind 'ow. P'raps I got a little bird as w'ispers—p'raps I do it some other way. Any'ow I know. It ain't no good any boy tryin' to do somethink unbeknownst to me, mindjer.'

Mr Weech's head lay aside, his grin widened, his glance was sidelong, his forefinger pointed from his temple over Dicky's head, and altogether he looked so very knowing that Dicky shuffled in his seat. By what mysterious means was this new-found friend so well informed? The doubt troubled him, for Dicky knew nothing of Mr Aaron Weech's conversation, an hour before, with Tommy Rann.

'But it's awright, bless yer,' Mr Weech went on presently. 'Nobody's none the wuss for me knowin' about 'em.... Well, we was a-talkin' about the watch, wasn't we? All you got after sich a lot o' trouble was a woppin' with a belt. That was too bad.' Mr Weech's voice was piteous and sympathetic. 'After you a-findin' sich a nice watch—a red 'un an' all!—you gits nothink for yerself but a beltin'. Never mind, you'll do better next time—I'll take care o' that. I don't like to see a clever boy put upon. You go an' find another, or somethink else—anythink good—an' then you bring it 'ere.'

Mr Weech's friendly sympathy extinguished Dicky's doubt. 'I didn't find it,' he said, shy but proud. 'It was a click—I sneaked it.'

'Eh?' ejaculated Mr Weech, a sudden picture of blank incom-prehension. 'Eh? What? Click? Wot's a click? Sneaked? Wot's that? I dunno nothink about no talk o' that sort, an' I don't want to. It's my belief it means somethink wrong—but I dunno, an' I don't want to. 'Ear that? Eh? Don't let me 'ave no more o' that, or you'd better not come near me again. If you *find* somethink, awright: you come to me an' I'll give ye somethink for it, if it's any good. It ain't no business of anybody's *where* you find it, o' course, an' I don't want to know. But clicks and sneaks—them's Greek to me, an' I don't want to learn 'em. Unnerstand that? Nice talk to respectable people, with yer clicks an' sneaks!'

Dicky blushed a little, and felt very guilty without in the least understanding the offence. But Mr Weech's virtuous indignation subsided as quickly as it had arisen, and he went on as amiably as ever.

'When you *find* anythink,' he said, 'jist like you found that watch, don't tell nobody, an' don't let nobody see it. Bring it 'ere quiet, when there ain't any p'liceman in the street, an' come right through to the back o' the shop, an' say, "I come to clean the knives." Unnerstand? "I come to clean the knives." There ain't no knives to clean—it's on'y a way o' tellin' me you got somethink without other people knowin'. An' then I'll give you somethink for it—money p'raps, or p'raps cake or wot not. Don't forgit. "I come to clean the knives." See?'

Yes, Dicky understood perfectly; and Dicky saw a new world of dazzling delights. Cake—limitless cake, coffee, and the like whenever he might feel moved thereunto; but more than all, money—actual money. Good broad pennies, perhaps whole shillings—perhaps even more still: money to buy bullock's liver for dinner, or tripe, or what you fancied: saveloys, baked potatoes from the can on cold nights, a little cart to wheel Looey in, a boat from a toy-shop with sails!

'There's no end o' things to be found all over the place, an' a sharp boy like you can find 'em every day. If you don't find 'em, someone else will; there's plenty on 'em about on the look-out an' you got jist as much right as them. On'y mind!'—Mr Weech was suddenly stern and serious, and his forefinger was raised impressively—'you know you can't do anythink without I know, an' if you say a word—if you say a word,' his fist came on the table with a bang, 'somethink 'll happen to you. Somethink bad.'

Mr Weech rose, and was pleasant again, though business-like. 'Now, you just go an' find somethink,' he said. 'Look sharp about it, an' don't go an' git in trouble. The cawfy's a penny, an' the cake's a penny—ought prop'ly to be twopence, but say a penny this time. That's twopence you owe me, an' you better bring somethink an' pay it off quick. So go along.'

This was an unforeseen tag to the entertainment. For the first time in his life Dicky was in debt. It was a little disappointing to find the coffee and cake no gift after all: though, indeed, it now seemed foolish to have supposed they were; for in Dicky Perrott's world people did not give things away—that was the act of a fool. Thus Dicky, with his hands in his broken pockets, and thought in his small face, whereon still stood the muddy streaks of yesterday's tears, trudged out of Mr Aaron Weech's shop-door, and along Meakin Street.

Now he was beginning the world seriously, and must face the fact. Truly the world had been serious enough for him hitherto, but that he knew not. Now he was of an age when most boys were thieving for themselves, and he owed money like a man. True it was, as Mr Weech had said, that everybody—the whole Jago—was on the look-out for himself. Plainly he must take his share, lest it fall to others. As to the old gentleman's watch, he had but been beforehand. Through foolish ingenuousness he had lost it, and his father had got it, who could so much more easily steal one for himself; for he was a strong man, and had but to knock over another man at any night-time. Nobody should hear of future clicks but Mr Weech. Each for himself? Come, he must open his eyes.

7

THERE was no chance all along Meakin Street. The chandlers
and the keepers of cook-shops knew their neighbourhood too well
to leave articles unguarded. Soon Dicky reached Shoreditch High
Street. There things were a little more favourable. There were
shops, as he well remembered, where goods were sometimes exhibited at the doors and outside the windows; but to-day there
seemed to be no chance of the sort. As for the people, he was too
short to try pockets, and indeed the High Street rarely gave passage to a more unpromising lot. Moreover, from robbery from
the person he knew he must abstain, except for such uncommon
opportunities as that of the Bishop's watch, for some years yet.

He hung about the doors and windows of shop after shop,
hoping for a temporary absence of the shop-keeper, which might
leave something snatchable. But he hoped in vain. From most
shops he was driven away, for the Shoreditch trader is not slow
to judge the purpose of a loitering boy. So he passed nearly two
hours: when at last he saw his chance. It came in an advantageous
part of High Street, not far from the 'Posties', though on the
opposite side of the way. A nurse-girl had left a perambulator at
a shop door, while she bought inside, and on the perambulator
lay loose a little skin rug, from under which a little fat leg stuck
and waved aloft. Dicky set his back to the shop, and sidled to
within reach of the perambulator. But it chanced that at this
moment the nurse-girl stepped to the door, and she made a snatch
at his arm as he lifted the rug. This he dropped at once, and was
swinging leisurely away (for he despised the chase of any nurse-
girl) when a man took him suddenly by the shoulder. Quick as a
weasel, Dicky ducked under the man's arm, pulled his shoulder
clear, dropped forward and rested an instant on the tips of his
fingers to avoid the catch of the other hand, and shot out into the
road. The man tried to follow, but Dicky ran under the belly of a
standing horse, under the head of another that trotted, across the
fore-platform of a tramcar—behind the driver's back—and so
over to the 'Posties'.

He slouched into the Jago, disappointed. As he crossed Edge

Lane, he was surprised to perceive a stranger—a toff, indeed—who walked slowly along, looking up right and left at the grimy habitations about him. He wore a tall hat, and his clothes were black, and of a pattern that Dicky remembered to have seen at the Elevation Mission. They were, in fact, the clothes of a clergyman. For himself, he was tall and soundly built, with a certain square muscularity of face, and of age about thirty-five. He had ventured into the Jago because the police were in possession, Dicky thought; and wondered in what plight he would leave, had he come at another time. But losing view of the stranger, and making his way along Old Jago Street, Dicky perceived that indeed the police were gone, and that the Jago was free.

He climbed the broken stairs and pushed into the first-floor back, hopeful, though more doubtful, of dinner. There was none. His mother, tied about the neck in rags, lay across the bed nursing the damage of yesterday, and commiserating herself. A yard from her lay Looey, sick and ailing in a new way, but disregarded. Dicky moved to lift her, but at that she cried the more, and he was fain to let her lie. She rolled her head from side to side, and raised her thin little hand vaguely toward it, with feverishly working fingers. Dicky felt her head and she screamed again. There was a lump at the side, a hard, sharp lump; got from the stones of the roadway yesterday. And there was a curious quality, a rather fearful quality, in the little wails: uneasily suggestive of the screams of Sally Green's victims.

Father was out, prowling. There was nothing eatable in the cupboard, and there seemed nothing at home worth staying for. He took another look at Looey, but refrained from touching her, and went out.

The opposite door on the landing was wide open, and he could hear nobody in the room. He had never seen this door open before, and now he ventured on a peep: for the tenants of the front room were strangers, late arrivals, and interlopers. Their name was Roper. Roper was a pale cabinet-maker, fallen on evil times and out of work. He had a pale wife, disliked because of her neatly-kept clothes, her exceeding use of soap and water, her aloofness from gossip. She had a deadly pale baby; also there was a pale hunchbacked boy of near Dicky's age. Collectively the Ropers were disliked as strangers: because they furnished their own room, and in an obnoxiously complete style; because Roper did not drink, nor brawl, nor beat his wife, nor do anything all day but look for work; because all these things were a matter of scandalous arrogance, impudently subversive of Jago custom and precedent. Mrs Perrott was bad enough, but such people as these!...

Dicky had never before seen quite such a room as this. Everything was so clean: the floor, the windows, the bed-clothes. Also there was a strip of old carpet on the floor. There were two perfectly sound chairs; and two pink glass vases on the mantelpiece; and a clock. Nobody was in the room, and Dicky took a step farther. The clock attracted him again. It was a small, cheap, nickel-plated, cylindrical thing, of American make, and it reminded him at once of the Bishop's watch. It was not gold, certainly, but it was a good deal bigger, and it could go—it was going. Dicky stepped back and glanced at the landing. Then he darted into the room, whipped the clock under the breast of the big jacket, and went for the stairs.

Half way down he met the pale hunchback ascending. Left at home alone, he had been standing in the front doorway. He saw Dicky's haste, saw also the suspicious bulge under his jacket, and straightway seized Dicky's arm. 'Where 'a' you bin?' he asked sharply. 'Bin in our room? What you got there?'

'Nothin' o' yours, 'ump. Git out o' that!' Dicky pushed him aside. 'If you don't le' go I'll corpse ye!'

But one arm and hand was occupied with the bulge, and the other was for the moment unequal to the work of driving off the assailant. The two children wrangled and struggled downstairs, through the doorway and into the street: the hunchback weak, but infuriate, buffeting, biting and whimpering; Dicky infuriate too, but alert for a chance to break away and run. So they scrambled together across the street, Dicky dragging away from the house at every step; and just at the corner of Luck Row, getting his fore-arm across the other's face, he back-heeled him, and the little hunchback fell heavily, and lay breathless and sobbing, while Dicky scampered through Luck Row and round the corner into Meakin Street.

Mr Weech was busier now, for there were customers. But Dicky and his bulge he saw ere they were well over the threshold.

'Ah yus, Dicky,' he said, coming to meet him. 'I was expectin' you. Come in—

> *In the swe-e-et by an' by,*
> *We shall meet on that beautiful shaw-er!*

Come in 'ere.' And still humming his hymn, he led Dicky into the shop parlour.

Here Dicky produced the clock, which Mr Weech surveyed with no great approval. 'You'll 'ave to try an' do better than this, you know,' he said. 'But any'ow 'ere it is, sich as it is. It about clears auf wot you owe, I reckon. Want some dinner?'

This was a fact, and Dicky admitted it.

'Awright—

> *In the swe-e-et by an' by,—*

come out an' set down. I'll bring you somethink 'ot.'

This proved to be a very salt bloater, a cup of the usual muddy coffee, tasting of burnt toast, and a bit of bread: afterwards supplemented by a slice of cake. This to Dicky was a banquet. Moreover, there was the adult dignity of taking your dinner in a coffee-shop, which Dicky supported indomitably now that he began to feel at ease in Mr Weech's: leaning back in his seat, swinging his feet, and looking about at the walls with the grocers' almanacks hanging thereto, and the Sunday School Anniversary bills of past date, gathered from afar to signalise the elevated morals of the establishment.

'Done?' queried Mr Weech in his ear. 'Awright, don't 'ang about 'ere then. Bloater's a penny, bread a 'a'peny, cawfy a penny, cake a penny. You'll owe thrippence 'a'peny now.'

8

WHEN Dicky Perrott and the small hunchback were hauling and struggling across the street, Old Fisher came down from the top-floor back, wherein he dwelt with his son Bob, Bob's wife and two sisters, and five children: an apartment in no way so clean as the united efforts of ten people might be expected to have made it. Old Fisher, on whose grimy face the wrinkles were deposits of mud, stopped at the open door on the first floor, and, as Dicky had done, he took a peep. Perplexed at the monstrous absence of dirt, and encouraged by the stillness, Old Fisher also ventured within. Nobody was in charge, and Old Fisher, mentally pricing the pink glass vases at threepence, made for a small chest in the corner of the room, and lifted the lid. Within lay many of Roper's tools, from among which he had that morning taken such as he might want on an emergent call to work, to carry as he tramped Curtain Road. Clearly these were the most valuable things in the place; and, slipping the most valuable articles into his pockets, Old Fisher took a good double handful of the larger, and tramped upstairs with them. Presently he returned with Bob's missis, and together they started with more. As they emerged, however, there on the landing stood the little hunchback, sobbing and smearing his face with his sleeve. At the sight of this new pillage he burst into sharp wails, standing impotent on the landing, his streaming eyes following the man and woman ascending before him. Old Fisher, behind, stumped the stairs with a clumsy affectation of absent-mindedness; the woman, in front, looked down, merely indifferent. Scarce were they vanished above, however, when the little hunchback heard his father and mother on the lower stairs.

9

DICKY came moodily back from his dinner at Mr Weech's, plunged in mystified computation: starting with a debt of two-pence, he had paid Mr Weech an excellent clock—a luxurious article in Dicky's eyes—had eaten a bloater, and had emerged from the transaction owing threepence halfpenny. Of what such a clock cost he had no notion, though he felt it must be some inconceivable sum. As Mr Weech put it, the adjustment of accounts would seem to be quite correct; but the broad fact that all had ended in increasing his debt by three halfpence, remained and perplexed him. He remembered having seen such clocks in a shop in Norton Folgate. To ask the price, in person, were but to be chased out of the shop; but they were probably ticketed, and perhaps he might ask some bystander to read the ticket. This brought the reflection that, after all, reading was a useful accomplishment on occasion: though a matter of too much time and trouble to be worth while. Dicky had never been to school; for the Elementary Education Act ran in the Jago no more than any other Act of Parliament. There was a Board School, truly, away out of the Jago bounds, by the corner of Honey Lane, where children might go free, and where some few Jago children did go now and again, when boots were to be given away, or when tickets were to be had, for tea, or soup, or the like. But most parents were of Josh Perrott's opinion: that school-going was a practice best never begun; for then the child was never heard of, and there was no chance of inquiries or such trouble. Not that any such inquiries were common in the Jago, or led to anything.

Meantime Dicky, minded to know if his adventure had made any stir in the house, carried his way deviously toward home. Working through the parts beyond Jago Row, he fetched round into Honey Lane, so coming at New Jago Street from the farther side. Choosing one of the houses whose backs gave on Jago Court, he slipped through the passage, and so, by the back yard, crawled through the broken fence into the court. Left and right were the fronts of houses, four a side. Before him, to the right of the narrow archway leading to Old Jago Street, was the window of his own home. He gained the back yard quietly, and at the kitchen door met Tommy Rann.

'Come on,' called Tommy. "Ere's a barney! They're a-pitchin' into them noo 'uns—Roperses. Roperses sez Fisherses is sneaked their things. They *are* a-gittin' of it!'

From the stairs, indeed, came shouts and curses, bumps and sobs and cries. The first landing and half the stairs were full of people, men and women, Ranns and Learys together. When Ranns joined Learys it was an ill time for them they marched against; and never were they so ready and so anxious to combine as after a fight between themselves, were but some common object of attack available. Here it was. Here were these pestilent outsiders, the Ropers, assailing the reputation of the neighbourhood by complaining of being robbed. As though their mere presence in the Jago, with their furniture and their superiority, were not obnoxious enough: they must turn about and call their neighbours thieves! They had been tolerated too long already. They should now be given something for themselves, and have some of their exasperating respectability knocked off; and if, in the confusion, their portable articles of furniture and bed-clothing found their way into more deserving hands—why, serve them right.

The requisite volleys of preliminary abuse having been discharged, more active operations began under cover of fresh volleys. Dicky, with Tommy Rann behind him, struggled up the stairs among legs and skirts, and saw that the Ropers, the man flushed, but the woman paler than ever, were striving to shut their door. Within, the hunchback and the baby cried, and without, those on the landing, skidding the door with their feet, pushed inward, and now began to strike and maul. Somebody seized the man's wrist, and Norah Walsh got the woman by the hair and dragged her head down. In a peep through the scuffle Dicky saw her face, ashen and sweat-beaded, in the jamb of the door, and saw Norah Walsh's red fist beat into it twice. Then somebody came striding up the stairs, and Dicky was pushed farther back. Over the shoulders of those about him, Dicky saw a tall hat, and then the head beneath it. It was the stranger he had seen in Edge Lane—the parson: active and resolute. Norah Walsh he took by the shoulder, and flung back among the others, and as he turned on him, the man who held Roper's wrist released it and backed off.

'What is this?' demanded the new-comer, stern and hard of face. 'What is all this?' He bent his frown on one and another about him, and, as he did it, some shrank uneasily, and on the faces of others fell the blank lack of expression that was wont to meet police inquiries in the Jago. Dicky looked to see this man beaten down, kicked and stripped. But a well-dressed stranger was so new a thing in the Jago, this one had dropped among them so suddenly, and he had withal so bold a confidence, that the Jagos stood irresolute. A toff was not a person to be attacked without due consideration. After such a person there were apt to be inquiries, with money to back them, and vengeance sharp and certain: the thing, indeed, was commonly thought too risky. And this man, so unflinchingly confident, must needs have reason for it. He might have the police at instant call—they might be back in the Jago at the moment. And he flung them back, commanded them, cowed them with his hard, intelligent eyes, like a tamer among beasts.

'Understand this, now,' he went on, with a sharp tap of his stick on the floor. 'This is a sort of thing I will *not* tolerate in my parish—in this parish: nor in any other place where I may meet it. Go away, and try to be ashamed of yourselves—go. Go, all of you, I say, to your own homes: I shall come there and talk to you again soon. Go along, Sam Cash—you've a broken head already, I see. Take it away: I shall come and see you too.'

Those on the stairs had melted away like punished school-children. Most of the others, after a moment of averted face and muttered justification one to another, were dragging their feet, each with a hang-dog pretence of sauntering airily off from some sight no longer interesting. Sam Cash, who had already seen the stranger in the street, and was thus perhaps a trifle less startled than the others at his advent, stood, however, with some assumption of virtuous impudence, till amazed by sudden address in his own name: whereat, clean discomfited, he ignominiously turned tail and sneaked downstairs in meaner case than the rest. How should this strange parson know him, and know his name? Plainly he must be connected with the police. He had brought out the name as pat as you please. So argued Sam Cash with his fellows in the outer street: never recalling that Jerry Gullen had called aloud to him by name, when first he observed the parson in the street; had called to him, indeed, to haste to the bashing of the Ropers; and thus had first given the stranger notice of the proceeding. But it was the way of the Jago that its mean cunning saw a mystery and a terror where simple intelligence saw there was none.

As the crowd began to break up, Dicky pushed his own door a little open behind him, and there stood on his own ground, as the others cleared off; and the hunchback ventured a peep from behind his swooning mother. 'There y'are, that's 'im!' he shouted, pointing at Dicky. "E begun it! 'E took the clock!' Dicky instantly dropped behind his door, and shut it fast.

The invaders had all gone—the Fishers had made upstairs in the beginning—before the parson turned and entered the Ropers' room. In five minutes he emerged and strode upstairs: whence he returned, after a still shorter interval, herding before him Old Fisher and Bob Fisher's missis, sulky and reluctant, carrying tools.

And thus it was that the Reverend Henry Sturt first addressed his parishioners. The parish, besides the Jago, comprised Meakin Street and some small way beyond, and it was to this less savage district that his predecessor had confined his attention: preaching every Sunday in a stable, in an alley behind a disused shop, and distributing loaves and sixpences to the old women who attended regularly on that account. For to go into the Jago was for him mere wasted effort. And so, indeed, the matter had been since the parish came into being.

10

WHEN Dicky retreated from the landing and shut the door behind
him, he slipped the bolt, a strong one, put there by Josh Perrott
himself, possibly as an accessory to escape by the window in
some possible desperate pass. For a little he listened, but no
sound hinted of attack from without, and he turned to his
mother.

Josh Perrott had been out since early morning, and Dicky, too,
had done no more than look in for a moment in search of dinner.
Hannah Perrott, grown tired of self-commiseration, felt herself
neglected and aggrieved—slighted in her state of invalid privilege. So she transferred some of her pity from her sore neck to
her desolate condition as misprized wife and mother, and the
better to feel it, proceeded to martyrise herself, with melancholy
pleasure, by a nerveless show of 'setting to rights' in the room—
a domestic novelty, perfunctory as it was. Looey, still restless and
weeping, she left on the bed, for, being neglected herself, it was
not her mood to tend the baby; she would aggravate the relish
of her sorrows in her own way. Besides, Looey had been given
something to eat a long time ago, and had not eaten it yet: with
her there was nothing else to do. So that now, as she dragged a
rag along the grease-strewn mantelpiece, Mrs Perrott greeted
Dicky: 'There y'are, Dicky, comin' 'inderin' 'ere jest when I'm
a-puttin' things to rights.' And she sighed with the weight of
another grievance.

Looey lay on her back, faintly and vainly struggling to turn
her fearful little face from the light. Clutched in her little fist was
the unclean stump of bread she had held for hours. Dicky plucked
a soft piece and essayed to feed her with it, but the dry little
mouth rejected the morsel, and the head turned feverishly from
side to side to the sound of that novel cry. She was hot wherever
Dicky touched her, and presently he said: 'Mother, I b'lieve
Looey's queer. I think she wants some med'cine.'

His mother shook her head peevishly. 'O, you an' Looey's a
noosance,' she said. 'A lot you care about *me* bein' queer, you an'
yer father too, leavin' me all alone like this, an' me feelin' ready to

drop, an' got the room to do an' all. I wish you'd go away an' stop 'inderin' of me like this.'

Dicky took but another look at Looey, and then slouched out. The landing was clear, and the Ropers' door was shut. He wondered what had become of the stranger with the tall hat—whether he was in the Ropers' room or not. The thought hurried him, for he feared to have that stranger asking him questions about the clock.

He got out into the street, thoughtful. He had some compunctions in the matter of that clock, now. Not that he could in any reasonable way blame himself. There the clock had stood at his mercy, and by all Jago custom and ethic it was his if only he could get clear away with it. This he had done, and he had no more concern in the business, strictly speaking. Nevertheless, since he had seen the woman's face in the jamb of the door, he felt a sort of pity for her—that she should have lost her clock. No doubt she had enjoyed its possession, as, indeed, he would have enjoyed it himself, had he not had to take it instantly to Mr Weech. And his fancy wandered off in meditation of what he would do with a clock of his own. To begin with, of course, he would open it, and discover the secret of its works and its ticking: perhaps thereby discovering how to make a clock himself. Also he would frequently wind it up, and he would show the inside to Looey, in confidence. It would stand on the mantelpiece, and raise the social position of the family. People would come respectfully to ask the time, and he would tell them, with an air. Yes, certainly a clock must stand eminent among the things he would buy, when he had plenty of money. He must look out for more clicks: the one way to riches.

As to the Ropers, again. Bad it must be, indeed, to be deprived suddenly of a clock, after long experience of the joys it brought; and Norah Walsh had punched the woman in the face, and clawed her hair, and the woman could not fight. Dicky was sorry for her, and straightway resolved to give her another clock, or, if not a clock, something that would please her as much. He had acquired a clock in the morning; why not another in the afternoon? Failing a clock, he would try for something else, and the Ropers should have it. The resolve gave Dicky a virtuous exaltation of spirit, the reward of the philanthropist.

Again he began to prowl after likely plunder that was to be his daily industry. Meakin Street he did not try. The chandlers' and the cook-shops held nothing that might be counted a consolatory equivalent for a clock. Through the 'Posties' he reached Shoreditch High Street at once, and started.

This time his movement aroused less suspicion. In the morning he had no particular prize in view, and loitered at every shop, waiting his chance at anything portable. Now, with a more definite object, he made his promenade easily, but without stopping or lounging by shop-fronts. The thing, whatsoever it might be, must be small, handsome, and of an interesting character—at least as interesting as the clock was. It must be small, not merely for facility of concealment and removal—though these were main considerations—but because stealthy presentation were then the easier. It would have pleased Dicky to hand over his gift openly, and to bask in the thanks and the consideration it would procure. But he had been accused of stealing the clock, and an open gift would savour of admission and peace-offering, whereas in that matter stark denial was his plain course.

A roll of print stuff would not do; apples would not do; and fish was wide of his purpose. Up one side and down the other side of High Street he walked, his eyes instant for suggestion and opportunity. But all in vain. Nobody exposed clocks out of doors, and of those within not one but an attempt on it were simple madness. And of the things less desperate of access nothing was proper to the occasion: all were too large, too cheap, or too uninteresting. Oddly, Dicky feared failure more than had he been hunting for himself.

He tried farther south, in Norton Folgate. There was a shop of cheap second-hand miscellanies: saddles, razors, straps, dumb-bells, pistols, boxing gloves, trunks, bags, and billiard-balls. Many of the things hung about the door-posts in bunches, and within all was black, as in a cave. At one door-post was a pistol. Nothing could be more interesting than a pistol—indeed it was altogether a better possession than a clock; and it was a small, handy sort of thing. Probably the Ropers would be delighted with a pistol. He stood and regarded it with much interest. There were difficulties. In the first place, it was beyond his reach; and in the second, it hung by the trigger-guard on a stout cord. Just then, glancing within the shop, he perceived a pair of fiery eyes regarding him, panther-like, from the inner gloom; and he hastily resumed his walk, as the Jew shopkeeper reached the door, and watched him safely away.

Now he came to Bishopsgate Street, and here at last he chose the gift. It was a toy-shop: a fine, flaming toy-shop, with carts, dolls and hoops dangling above, and wooden horses standing below, guarding two baskets by the door. One contained a mixed assortment of tops, whips, boats, and woolly dogs; the other was lavishly filled with shining, round metal boxes, nobly decorated with coloured pictures, each box with a little cranked handle. As he looked, a tune, delightfully tinkled on some instrument, was heard from within the shop. Dicky peeped. There was a lady, with a little girl at her side who was looking eagerly at just such a shining, round box in the saleswoman's hands, and it was from that box, as the saleswoman turned the handle, that the tune came. Dicky was enchanted. This—this was the thing, beyond debate: a pretty little box that would play music whenever you turned a handle. This was a thing worth any fifty clocks. Indeed it was almost as good as a regular barrel-organ, the first thing he would buy if he were rich.

There was a shop-boy in charge of the goods outside the window, and his eyes were on Dicky. So Dicky whistled absently, and strolled carelessly along. He swung behind a large waggon, crossed the road, and sought a convenient doorstep; for his mind was made up, and his business was now to sit down before the toy-shop, and wait his opportunity.

A shop had been boarded up after a fire, and from its doorstep one could command a perfect view of the toy-shop across the broad thoroughfare with its crowded traffic—could sit, moreover, safe from interference. Here he took his seat, secure from the notice of the guardian shop-boy, whose attention was given to passengers on his own side. The little girl, gripping the new toy in her hand, came out at her mother's side and trotted off. For a moment Dicky reflected that the box could be easily snatched. But after all the little girl had but one: whereas the shopwoman had many, and at best could play on no more than one at a time.

He resumed his watch of the shop-boy, confident that sooner or later a chance would come. A woman stopped to ask the price of something, and Dicky had half-crossed the road ere the boy had begun to answer. But the answer was short, and the boy's attention was released too soon.

At last the shopwoman called the boy within, and Dicky darted across—not directly, but so as to arrive invisibly at the side next the basket of music boxes. A quick glance behind him, a snatch at the box with the reddest picture, and a dash into the traffic did it.

The dash would not have been called for but for the sudden reappearance of the shop-boy ere the box had vanished amid the intricacies of Dicky's jacket. Dicky was fast, but the boy was little slower, and was, moreover, bigger, and stronger on his legs; and Dicky reached the other pavement and turned the next corner into Widegate Street, the pursuer scarce ten yards behind.

It was now that he first experienced 'hot beef'—which is the Jago idiom denoting the plight of one harried by the cry 'Stop thief'. Down Widegate Street, across Sandys Row and into Raven Row he ran his best, clutching the hem of his jacket and the music box that lay within. Crossing Sandys Row a loafing lad shouldered against the shop-boy, and Dicky was grateful, for he made a gain of several yards.

But others had joined in the hunt, and Dicky for the first time began to fear. This was a bad day—twice already he had been chased; and now—it was bad. He thought little more, for a stunning fear fell upon him: the fear of the hunted, that calculates nothing, and is measured by no apprehension of consequences. He remembered that he must avoid Spitalfields Market, full of men who would stop him; and he knew that in many places where a man would be befriended many would make a virtue of stopping a boy. To the right along Bell Lane he made an agonised burst of speed, and for a while he saw not nor remembered anything; heard no more than dreadful shouts drawing nearer his shoulders, felt only the fear. But he could not last. Quick enough when fresh, he was tiny and ill fed, and now he felt his legs trembling and his wind going. Something seemed to beat on the back of his head, till he wondered madly if it were the shop-boy with a stick. He turned corners, and chose his way by mere instinct, ashen-faced, staring, open-mouthed. How soon would he give in, and drop? A street more—half a street—ten yards? Rolling and tripping, he turned one last corner and almost fell against a vast, fat, unkempt woman whose clothes slid from her shoulders.

"Ere y' are, boy,' said the woman, and flung him by the shoulder through the doorway before which she stood.

He was saved at his extremity, for he could never have reached the street's end. The woman who had done it (probably she had boys of her own on the crook) filled the entrance with her frowsy bulk, and the chase straggled past. Dicky caught the stair-post for a moment's support, and then staggered out at the back of the house. He gasped, he panted, things danced blue before him, but still he clutched his jacket hem and the music box lying within. The back door gave on a cobble-paved court, with other doors, two costers' barrows, and a few dusty fowls. Dicky sat on a step where a door was shut, and rested his head against the frame.

The beating in his head grew slower and lighter, and presently he could breathe with no fear of choking. He rose and moved off, still panting, and feeble in the legs. The court ended in an arched passage, through which he gained the street beyond. Here he had but to turn to the left, and he was in Brick Lane, and thence all was clear to the Old Jago. Regaining his breath and his confidence as he went, he bethought him of the Jago Row retreat, where he might examine his prize at leisure, embowered amid trucks and barrows. Thither he pushed his way, and soon, in the shade of the upturned barrow, he brought out the music box. Bright and shiny, it had taken no damage in the flight, though on his hands he found scratches, and on his shins bruises, got he knew not how. On the top of the box was the picture of a rosy little boy in crimson presenting a scarlet nosegay to a rosy little girl in pink, while a red brick mansion filled the distance and solidified the composition. The brilliant hoop that made the sides (silver, Dicky was convinced) was stamped in patterns, and the little brass handle was an irresistible temptation. Dicky climbed a truck, and looked about him, peeped from beside the loose fence-plank. Then, seeing nobody very near, he muffled the box as well as he could in his jacket, and turned the handle.

This was indeed worth all the trouble. *Gently Does the Trick* was the tune, and Dicky with his head aside and his ear on the bunch of jacket that covered the box, listened; his lips parted, his eyes seeking illimitable space. He played the tune through, and played it again, and then growing reckless, played it with the box unmuffled, till he was startled by a bang on the fence from without. It was but a passing boy with a stick, but Dicky was sufficiently disturbed to abandon his quarters and take his music elsewhere.

What he longed to do was to take it home and play it to Looey, but that was out of the question: he remembered the watch. But there was Jerry Gullen's canary, and him Dicky sought and found. Canary blinked solemnly when the resplendent box was flashed in his eyes, and set his ears back and forward as, muffled again in Dicky's jacket, it tinkled out its tune.

Tommy Rann should not see it, lest he prevail over its beneficent dedication to the Ropers. Truly, as it was, Dicky's resolution was hard to abide by. The thing acquired at such a cost of patience, address, hard flight, and deadly fear was surely his by right—as surely as the clock had been. And such a thing he might never touch again. But he put by the temptation manfully, and came out by Jerry Gullen's front door. He would look no more on the music box, beautiful as it was: he would convey it to the Ropers before temptation came again.

It was not easy to devise likely means. Their door was shut fast, of course. For a little while he favoured the plan of setting the box against the threshold, knocking and running off. But an opportunity might arise of doing the thing in a way to give him some glimpse of the Ropers' delight, an indulgence he felt entitled to. So he waited a little, listened a little, and at last came out into the street, and loafed.

It was near six o'clock, and a smell of bloater hung about Jerry Gullen's door and window; under the raised sash Jerry Gullen, close-cropped and foxy of face, smoked his pipe, sprawled his elbows, and contemplated the world. Dicky, with the music box stowed out of sight, looked as blank of design and as destitute of possession as he could manage; for there were loafers near Mother Gapp's, loafers at the Luck Row corner—at every corner —and loafers by the 'Posties', all laggard of limb and alert of eye. He had just seen a child, going with an empty beer can, thrown down, robbed of his coppers and a poor old top, and kicked away in helpless tears; and the incident was commonplace enough, or many would have lacked pocket-money. Whosoever was too young, too old, or too weak to fight for it must keep what he had well hidden, in the Jago.

Down the street came Billy Leary, big, flushed and limping, and hanging to a smaller man by a fistful of his coat on the shoulder. Dicky knew the small man for a good toy-getter—(which=watch stealer)—and judged he had had a good click, the proceeds whereof Billy Leary was battening upon in beershops. For Billy Leary rarely condescended to anything less honourable than bashing, and had not yet fallen so low as to go about stealing for himself. His missis brought many to the cosh, and his chief necessity—another drink—he merely demanded of the nearest person with the money to buy it, on pain of bashing. Or he walked into the nearest public-house, selected the fullest pot, and spat in it: a ceremony that deprived the purchaser of further interest in the beer, and left it at his own disposal. There were others, both Ranns and Learys, who pursued a similar way of life; but Billy Leary was biggest among them—big men not being common in the Jago—and rarely came to a difficulty: as, however, he did once come, having invaded the pot of a stranger, who turned out to be a Mile End pugilist exploring Shoreditch. It was not well for any Jago who had made a click to have Billy Leary know of it; for then the clicker was apt to be sought out, clung to, and sucked dry; possibly bashed as well, when nothing more was left, if Billy Leary were still but sober enough for the work.

Dicky gazed after the man with interest. It was he whom his father was to fight in a week or so—perhaps in a few days: on the first Sunday, indeed, that Leary should be deemed fit enough. How much of the limp was due to yesterday's disaster and how much to to-day's beer, Dicky could not judge. But there seemed little reason to look for a long delay before the fight. As Dicky turned away a man pushed a large truck round the corner from Edge Lane, and on the footpath beside it walked the parson, calm as ever, with black clothes and tall hat, whole and unsoiled.

The Reverend Henry Sturt had made himself known in the Jago in the course of that afternoon. He had traversed it from end to end, street by street and alley by alley. His self-possession, his readiness, his unbending firmness, abashed and perplexed the Jagos, and his appearance just as the police had left could but convince them that he must have some mysterious and potent connection with the force. He had attempted very little in the way of domiciliary visiting, being content for the time to see his parish, and speak here a word and there another with his parishioners. An encounter with Kiddo Cook did as much as anything toward securing him a proper deference. In his second walk through Old Jago Street, as he neared the Feathers, he was aware of a bunch of grinning faces pressed against the bar window, and as he came abreast, forth stepped Kiddo Cook from the door, impudently affable, smirking and ducking with mock obsequiousness, and offering a quart pot.

'An' 'ow jer find jerself, sir?' he asked, with pantomime cordiality. 'Hof'ly shockin' these 'ere lower classes, ain't they? Er—yus; disgustin', weally. Er—might I—er—prepose—er—a little refreshment? Ellow me.'

The parson, grimly impassive, heard him through, took the pot, and instantly jerking it upward, shot the beer, a single splash, into Kiddo's face. 'There are things I must teach you, I see, my man,' he said, without moving a muscle, except to return the pot.

Kiddo Cook, coughing, drenched and confounded, took the pot instinctively and backed to Mother Gapp's door, while the bunch of faces at the bar window tossed and rolled in a joyous ecstasy: the ghost whereof presently struggled painfully among Kiddo's own dripping features, as he realised the completeness of his defeat, and the expedience of a patient grin. The parson went calmly on.

Before this, indeed when he left the Ropers' room, and just after Dicky had started out, he had looked in at the Perrotts' quarters to speak about the clock. But plainly no clock was there, and Mrs Perrott's flaccid indignation at the suggestion, and her unmistakable ignorance of the affair, decided him to carry the matter no further, at any rate for the present. Moreover, the little hunchback's tale was inconclusive. He had seen no clock in Dicky's possession—had but met him on the stairs with a bulging jacket. The thing might be suspicious, but the new parson knew better than to peril his influence by charging where he could not convict. So he duly commiserated Hannah Perrott's troubles, suggested that the baby seemed unwell and had better be taken to a doctor, and went his way about the Jago.

Now he stopped the truck by Dicky's front door and mounted to the Ropers' room. For he had seen that the Jago was no place for them now, and had himself found them a suitable room away by Dove Lane. And so, emboldened by his company, the Ropers came forth, and with the help of the man who had brought the truck, carried down the pieces of their bedstead, a bundle of bedding, the two chairs, the pink vases, and the strip of old carpet, and piled them on the truck with the few more things that were theirs.

Dicky, with his hand on the music box in the lining of his jacket, sauntered up by the tail of the truck, and, waiting his chance, plunged his gift under the bundle of bedding, and left it there. But the little hunchback's sharp eyes were jealously on him, and 'Look there!' he squealed. ''E put 'is 'and in the truck an' took somethink!'

'Ye lie!' answered Dicky, indignant and hurt, but cautiously backing off; 'I ain't got nothink.' He spread his hands and opened his jacket in proof. 'Think I got yer bloomin' bedstead?'

He had nothing, it was plain. In fact, at the tail of the truck there was nothing he could easily have moved at all, certainly nothing he could have concealed. So the rest of the little removal was hurried, for heads were now at windows, the loafers began to draw about the truck, and trouble might break out at any moment: indeed, the Ropers could never have ventured from their room but for the general uneasy awe of the parson. For nothing was so dangerous in the Jago as to impugn its honesty. To rob another was reasonable and legitimate, and to avoid being robbed, as far as might be, was natural and proper. But to accuse anybody of a theft was unsportsmanlike, a foul outrage, a shameful abuse, a thing unpardonable. You might rob a man, bash a man, even kill a man; but to 'take away his character'—even when he had none—was to draw down the execrations of the whole Jago; while to assail the pure fame of the place—to 'give the street a bad name'—this was to bring the Jago howling and bashing about your ears.

The truck moved off at last, amid murmurings, mutterings, and grunts from the onlookers. The man of the truck pulled, Roper shoved behind, and his wife, with her threadbare decency and her meagre, bruised face, carried the baby, while the hunchbacked boy went by her side. All this under convoy of the Reverend Henry Sturt.

A little distance gave more confidence to a few, and, when the group had reached within a score of yards of Edge Lane, there came a hoot or two, a 'Yah!' and other less spellable sounds, expressive of contempt and defiance. Roper glanced back nervously, but the rest held on their way regardless. Then came a brickbat, which missed the woman by very little and struck the truck wheel. At this the parson stopped and turned on his heel, and Cocko Harnwell, the flinger, drove his hands into his breeches pockets and affected an interest in Mother Gapp's window; till, perceiving the parson's eyes directed sternly upon him, and the parson's stick rising to point at him, he ingloriously turned tail and scuttled into Jago Court.

And so the Ropers left the Jago. Dove Lane was but a stone's-throw ahead when some of the load shifted, and the truck was stopped to set the matter right. The chest was pushed back, and the bedding was lifted to put against it, and so the musical box came to light. Roper picked it up and held it before the vicar's eyes. 'Look at that, sir,' he said. 'You'll witness I know nothing of it, won't you? It ain't mine, an' I never saw it before. It's bin put in for spite to put a theft on us. When they come for it you'll bear me out, sir, won't you? That was the Perrott boy as was put up to do that, I'll be bound. When he was behind the truck.'

But nobody came for Dicky's gift, and in the Jago twilight Dicky vainly struggled to whistle the half-remembered tune, and to persuade himself that he was not sorry that the box was gone.

11

JOSH PERROTT reached home late for tea but in good humour.
He had spent most of the day at the Bag of Nails, dancing attendance on the High Mobsmen. Those of the High Mob were the
flourishing practitioners in burglary, the mag, the mace, and the
broads, with an outer fringe of such dippers—such pickpockets—
as could dress well, welshers, and snidesmen. These, the grandees
of rascality, lived in places far from the Jago, and some drove in
gigs and pony traps. But they found the Bag of Nails a convenient and secluded exchange and house of call, and there they
met, made appointments, designed villainies, and tossed for
sovereigns: deeply reverenced by the admiring Jagos, among
whom no ambition flourished but this—to become also of these
resplendent ones. It was of these that Old Beveridge had spoken
one day to Dicky, in language the child but half understood. The
old man sat on a kerb in view of the Bag of Nails, and smoked a
blackened bit of clay pipe. He hauled Dicky to his side, and,
pointing with his pipe, said: 'See that man with the furs?'

'What?' Dicky replied. 'Mean 'im in the ice-cream coat, smokin'
a cigar? Yus.'

'And the other with the brimmy tall hat, and the red face, and
the umbrella?'

'Yus.'

'What are they?'

''Igh mob. 'Ooks. Toffs.'

'Right. Now, Dicky Perrott, you Jago whelp, look at them—
look hard. Some day, if you're clever—cleverer than anyone in
the Jago now—if you're only scoundrel enough, and brazen
enough, and lucky enough—one of a thousand—maybe you'll be
like them: bursting with high living, drunk when you like, red
and pimply. There it is—that's your aim in life—there's your pattern. Learn to read and write, learn all you can, learn cunning,
spare nobody and stop at nothing, and perhaps—' he waved his
hand towards the Bag of Nails. 'It's the best the world has for
you, for the Jago's got you, and that's the only way out, except
gaol and the gallows. So do your devilmost, or God help you,

Dicky Perrott—though He won't: for the Jago's got you!'

Old Beveridge had eccentric talk and manners, and the Jago regarded him as a trifle 'balmy', though anything but a fool. So that Dicky troubled little to sift the meaning of what he said.

Josh Perrott's mission among the High Mob had been to discover some Mobsman who might be disposed to back him in the fight with Billy Leary. For though a private feud was the first cause of the turn-up, still business must never be neglected, and a feud or anything else that could produce money must be made to produce it, and when a fight of exceptional merit is placed before spectators, it is but fair that they should pay for their diversion.

But few Mobsmen were at the Bag of Nails that day. Sunday was the day of the chief gatherings of the High Mob: Sunday the market-day, so to speak, of the Jago, when such rent as was due weekly was paid (most of the Jago rents were paid daily and nightly) and other accounts were settled or fought out. Moreover, the High Mob were perhaps a trifle shy of the Jago at the time of a faction fight; and one was but just over, and that cut short at a third of the usual span of days. So that Josh waited long and touted vainly, till a patron arrived who knew him of old; who had employed him, indeed, as 'minder'—which means a protector or a bully, as you please to regard it—on a racecourse adventure involving bodily risk. On this occasion Josh had earned his wages with hard knocks given and taken, and his employer had conceived a high and thankful opinion of his capacity. Wherefore he listened now to the tale of the coming fight, and agreed to provide something in the way of stakes, and to put something on for Josh himself: looking for his own profit to the bets he might make at favourable odds with his friends. For Billy Leary was notorious as being near prime ruffian of the Jago, while Josh's reputation was neither so evil nor so wide. And so it was settled, and Josh came pleased to his tea; for assuredly Billy Leary would have no difficulty in finding another notable of the High Mob to cover the stakes.

Dicky was at home, sitting by Looey on the bed; and when he called his father it seemed pretty plain to Josh that the baby was out of sorts. 'She's rum about the eyes,' he said to his wife. 'Blimy if she don't look as though she was goin' to squint.'

Josh was never particularly solicitous as to the children, but he saw that they were fed and clothed—perhaps by mere force of habit of his more reputable days of plastering. He had brought home tripe, rolled in paper, and stuffed into his coat pocket, to make a supper on the strength of the day's stroke of business. When this was boiled, he and Dicky essayed to drive morsels into Looey's mouth, and to wash them down with beer; but to no end but choking rejection. Whereat Josh decided that she must go to the dispensary in the morning. And in the morning he took her, with Dicky at his heels; for not only did his wife still nurse her neck, but in truth she feared to venture abroad.

The dispensary was no charitable institution, but a shop so labelled in Meakin Street, one of half a dozen such kept by a medical man who lived away from them, and bothered himself as little about them as was consistent with banking the takings and signing the death-certificates. A needy young student, whose sole qualification was cheapness, was set to do the business of each place, and the uniform price for advice and medicine was sixpence. But there was a deal of professional character in the blackened and gilt-lettered front windows, and the sixpences came by hundreds. For hospital letters but rarely came Meakin Street way. Such as did were mostly in the hands of tradesmen, who subscribed for the purpose of getting them, and gave them to their best customers, as was proper and business-like. And so the dispensary flourished, and the needy young student grew shifty and callous, and no doubt there were occasional faith-cures. Indeed, cures of simple science were not at all impossible. For there was always a good supply of two drugs in the place—Turkey rhubarb and sulphuric acid: both very useful, both very cheap and both going very far in varied preparation, properly handled. An ounce or two of sulphuric acid, for instance, costing something fractional, dilutes with water into many gallons of physic. Excellent medicines they made too, and balanced each other very well by reason of their opposite effects. But indeed they were not all, for sometimes there were two or three other drugs in hand, interfering, perhaps troublesomely, with the simple division of therapeutics into the two provinces of rhubarb and sulphuric acid.

Business was brisk at the dispensary: several were waiting, and medicine and advice were going at the rate of two minutes for sixpence. Looey's case was not so clear as most of the others: she could not describe its symptoms succinctly, as 'a pain here', or 'a tight feeling there'. She did but lie heavily, staring blankly upward (she did not mind the light now), with the little cast in her eyes, and repeat her odd little wail; and Dicky and his father could tell very little. The young student had a passing thought that he might have known a trifle more of the matter if he had had time to turn up Ross on nerve and brain troubles—were such a proceeding consistent with the dignity of the dispensary; but straightway assigning the case to the rhubarb province, made up a powder, ordered Josh to keep the baby quiet, and pitched his sixpence among the others, well within the two minutes.

And faith in the dispensary was strengthened, for indeed Looey seemed a little better after the powder; and she was fed with spoonfuls of a fluid bought at a chandler's shop, and called milk.

12

'DICKY PERROTT, come 'ere,' said Mr Aaron Weech in a voice of sad rebuke, a few days later. 'Come 'ere, Dicky Perrott.'

He shook his head solemnly as he stooped. Dicky slouched up.

'What was that you found the other day an' didn't bring to me?'

'Nuffin'.' Dicky withdrew a step.

'It's no good you a-tellin' me that, Dicky Perrott, when I know better. You know very well you can't pervent me knowin'.' His little eyes searched Dicky's face, and Dicky sulkily shifted his own gaze. 'You're a wicked, ungrateful young 'ound, an' I've a good mind to tell a p'liceman to find out where you got that clock. Come 'ere now—don't you try runnin' away. Wot! after me a-takin' you in when you was 'ungry, an' givin' you cawfy an' cake, an' good advice like a father, an' a bloater an' all, an' you owin' me thrippence 'a'peny besides, then you goes an'—an' takes yer findin's somewhere else!'

'I never!' protested Dicky stoutly. But Mr Weech's cunning, equal to a shrewd guess that since his last visit Dicky had probably had another 'find', and quick to detect a lie, was slack to perceive a truth.

'Now don't you go an' add on a wicked lie to yer sinful ungratefulness, wotever you do,' he said severely. 'That's wuss, an' I alwis know. Doncher know the little 'ymn?—

> An' 'im as does one fault at fust
> An' lies to 'ide it, makes it two.

It's bad enough to be ungrateful to me as is bin so kind to you, an' it's wuss to break the fust commandment. If the bloater don't inflooence you, the 'oly 'ymn ought. 'Ow would you like me to go an' ask yer father for that thrippence 'a'peny you owe me? That's wot I'll 'ave to do if you don't mind.'

Dicky would not have liked it at all, as his frightened face testified.

'Then find somethink an' pay it at once, an' then I won't. I won't be 'ard on you, if you'll be a good boy. But don't git playin' no more tricks—'cos I'll know all about 'em. Now go an' find somethink quick.'

And Dicky went.

13

TEN DAYS after his first tour of the Old Jago, the Reverend Henry Sturt first preached in the parish church made of a stable, in an alley behind Meakin Street, but a few yards away, though beyond sight and sound of the Jago. There, that Sunday morning was a morning of importance, a time of excitement, for the fight between Billy Leary and Josh Perrott was to come off in Jago Court. The assurance that there was money in the thing was a sovereign liniment for Billy Leary's bruises—for they were but bruises—and he hastened to come by that money, lest it melt by caprice of the backers, or the backers themselves fall at unlucky odds with the police. He made little of Josh Perrott, his hardness and known fighting power notwithstanding. For was there not full a stone and a half between their weights? and had Billy not four or five inches the better in height and a commensurate advantage in reach? And Billy Leary's own hardness and fighting power were well proved enough.

It was past eleven o'clock. The weekly rent—for the week forthcoming—had been extracted, or partly extracted, or scuffled over. Old Poll Rann, who had made money in sixty-five years of stall-farming and iniquity, had made the rounds of the six houses she rented, to turn out the tenants of the night who were disposed to linger. Many had already stripped themselves to their rags at pitch-and-toss in Jago Court; and the game still went busily on in the crowded area and in overflow groups in Old Jago Street; and men found themselves deprived, not merely of the money for that day's food and that night's lodging, but even of the last few pence set by to back a horse for Tuesday's race. A little-regarded fight or two went on here and there as usual, and on kerbs and doorsteps sat women, hideous at all ages, filling the air with the rhetoric of the Jago.

Presently down from Edge Lane and the 'Posties' came the High Mobsmen, swaggering in check suits and billycocks, gold chains and lumpy rings: stared at, envied, and here and there pointed out by name or exploit. 'Him as done the sparks in from Regent Street for nine centuries o' quids'; 'Him as done five stretch for a snide bank bill an' they never found the 'oof'; 'Him as maced the bookies in France an' shot the nark in the boat'; and so forth. And the High Mob being come, the fight was due.

Of course, a fight merely as a fight was no great matter of interest: the thing was too common. But there was money on this; and again, it was no common thing to find Billy Leary defied, still less to find him challenged. Moreover, the thing had a Rann and Leary complexion, and it arose out of the battle of less than a fortnight back. So that Josh Perrott did not lack for partisans, though not a Rann believed he could stand long before Billy Leary. Billy's cause, too, had lost some popularity because it had been reported that Sally Green, in hospital, had talked of 'summonsing' Norah Walsh in the matter of her mangled face: a scandalous device to overreach, a piece of foul practice repugnant to all proper feeling; more especially for such a distinguished Jago as Sally Green—so well able to take care of herself. But all this was nothing as affecting the odds. They ruled at three to one on Billy Leary, with few takers, and went to four to one before the fight began.

Josh Perrott had been strictly sober for a full week. And the family had lived better, for he had brought meat home each day. Now he sat indifferently at the window of his room, and looked out at the crowd in Jago Court till such time as he might be wanted. He had not been out of the room that morning: he was saving his energy for Billy Leary.

As for Dicky, he had scarce slept for excitement. For days he had enjoyed consideration among his fellows on account of this fight. Now he shook and quivered, and nothing relieved his agitation but violent exertion. So he rushed downstairs a hundred times to see if the High Mob were coming, and back to report that they were not. At last he saw their overbearing checks, and tore upstairs, face before knees, with "Ere they are, father! 'Ere they are! They're comin' down the street, father!' and danced frenzied about the room and the landing.

Presently Jerry Gullen and Kiddo Cook came, as seconds, to take Josh out, and then Dicky quieted a little externally, though he was bursting at the chest and throat, and his chin jolted his teeth together uncontrollably. Josh dragged off his spotted coat and waistcoat and flung them on the bed, and then was helped out of his ill-mended blue shirt. He gave a hitch to his trousers-band, tightened his belt, and was ready.

'Ta-ta, ol' gal,' he said to his wife, with a grin; 'back agin soon.'

'With a bob or two for ye,' added Kiddo Cook, grinning like-wise.

Hannah Perrott sat pale and wistful, with the baby on her knees. Through the morning she had sat so, wretched and help-less, sometimes putting her face in her hands, sometimes break-ing out hopelessly: 'Don't, Josh, don't—good Gawd, Josh, I wish you wouldn't!' or 'Josh, Josh, I wish I was dead!' Josh had fought before, it was true, and more than once, but then she had learned of the matter afterward. This preparation and long waiting were another thing. Once she had even exclaimed that she would go with him—though she meant nothing.

Now, as Josh went out at the door, she bent over Looey and hid her face again. 'Good luck, father,' called Dicky, 'go it!' Though the words would hardly pass his throat, and he struggled to believe that he had no fear for his father.

No sooner was the door shut than he rushed to the window, though Josh could not appear in Jago Court for three or four minutes yet. The sash-line was broken, and the window had been propped open with a stick. In his excitement Dicky dis-lodged the stick, and the sash came down on his head, but he scarce felt the blow, and readjusted the stick with trembling hands, regardless of the bruise rising under his hair.

'Aincher goin' to look, mother?' he asked. 'Wontcher 'old up Looey?'

But his mother would not look. As for Looey, she looked at nothing. She had been taken to the dispensary once again, and now lay drowsy and dull, with little more movement than a general shudder and a twitching of the face at long intervals. The little face itself was thinner and older than ever: horribly flea-bitten still, but bloodlessly pale. Mrs Perrott had begun to think Looey was ailing for something; thought it might be measles or whooping-cough coming, and complained that children were a continual worry.

Dicky hung head and shoulders out of the window, clinging to the broken sill and scraping feverishly at the wall with his toes. Jago Court was fuller than ever. The tossing went on, though now with more haste, that most might be made of the remaining time. A scuffle still persisted in one corner. Some stood to gaze at the High Mob, who, to the number of eight or ten, stood in an exalted group over against the back fences of New Jago Street; but the thickest knot was about Cocko Harnwell's doorstep, whereon sat Billy Leary, his head just visible through the press about him, waiting to keep his appointment.

Then a close group appeared at the archway, and pushed into the crowd, which made way at its touch, the disturbed tossers pocketing their coppers, but the others busily persisting, with no more than a glance aside between the spins. Josh Perrott's cropped head and bare shoulders marked the centre of the group, and as it came, another group moved out from Cocko Harnwell's doorstep, with Billy Leary's tall bulk shining pink and hairy in its midst.

"E's in the court, mother,' called Dicky, scraping faster with his toes.

The High Mobsmen moved up toward the middle of the court, and some from the two groups spread and pushed back the crowd. Still half a dozen couples, remote by the walls, tossed and tossed faster than ever, moving this way and that as the crowd pressed.

Now there was an irregular space of bare cobble stones and house refuse, five or six yards across, in the middle of Jago Court, and all round it the shouting crowd was packed tight, those at the back standing on sills and hanging to fences. Every window was a clump of heads, and women yelled savagely or cheerily down and across. The two groups were merged in the press at each side of the space, Billy Leary and Josh Perrott in front of each, with his seconds.

'Naa then, any more 'fore they begin?' bawled a High Mobsman, turning about among his fellows. 'Three to one on the big 'un—three to one! 'Ere I'll give fours—four to one on Leary! Fourer one! Fourer one!'

But they shook their heads; they would wait a little. Leary and Perrott stepped out. The last of the tossers stuffed away his coppers, and sought for a hold on the fence.

'They're a-sparrin', mother!' cried Dicky, pale and staring, elbows and legs a-work, till he was like to pitch out of the window. From his mother there but jerked a whimpering sob, which he did not hear.

The sparring was not long. There was little of subtlety in the milling of the Jago: mostly no more than a rough application of the main hits and guards, with much rushing and ruffianing. What there was of condition in the two men was Josh's: smaller and shorter, he had a certain hard brownness of hide that Leary, in his heavy opulence of flesh, lacked; and there was a horny quality in his face and hands that reminded the company of his boast of invulnerability to anything milder than steel. Also his breadth of chest was great. Nevertheless all odds seemed against him, by reason of Billy Leary's size, reach, and fighting record.

The men rushed together, and Josh was forced back by weight. Leary's great fists, left and right, shot into his face with smacking reports, but left no mark on the leathery skin, and Josh, fighting for the body, drove his knuckles into the other's ribs with a force that jerked a thick grunt from Billy's lips at each blow.

There was a roar of shouts. 'Go it, father! Fa—ther! Fa—ther!' Dicky screamed from the window, till his voice broke in his throat and he coughed himself livid. The men were at holds, and swaying this way and that over the uneven stones. Blood ran copiously from Billy Leary's nose over his mouth and chin, and, as they turned, Dicky saw his father spit away a tooth over Leary's shoulder. They clipped and hauled to and fro, each striving to break the other's foothold. Then Perrott stumbled at a hole, lost his feet, and went down, with Leary on top.

Cheers and yells rent the air, as each man was taken to his own side by his seconds. Dicky let go the sill and turned to his mother, wild of eye, breathless with broken chatter.

'Father 'it 'im on the nose, mother, like that—'is ribs is goin' black where father pasted 'em—'e was out o' breath fust—there' blood all over 'is face, mother—father would 'a' chucked 'im over if 'e 'adn't tumbled in a 'ole—father 'it 'im twice on the jore —'e—O!'

Dicky was back again on the sill, kicking and shouting, for time was called, and the two men rushed again into a tangled knot. But the close strife was short. Josh had but closed to spoil his man's wind, and, leaving his head to take care of itself, stayed till he had driven left and right on the mark, and then got back. Leary came after him, gasping and blowing already, and Josh feinted a lead and avoided, bringing Leary round on his heel and off again in chase. Once more Josh met him, drove at his ribs, and got away out of reach. Leary's wind was going fast, and his partisans howled savagely at Josh—perceiving his tactics—taunting him with running away, daring him to stand and fight. 'I'll take that four to one,' called a High Mobsman to him who had offered the odds in the beginning. 'I'll stand a quid on Perrott!'

'Not with me you won't,' the other answered. 'Evens, if you like.'

'Right. Done at evens. A quid.'

Perrott, stung at length by the shouts from Leary's corner, turned on Billy and met him at full dash. He was himself puffing by this time, though much less than his adversary, and, at the cost of a heavy blow (which he took on his forehead), he visited Billy's ribs once more.

Both men were grunting and gasping now, and the sound of blows was as of the confused beating of carpets. Dicky, who had been afflicted to heartburst by his father's dodging and running, which he mistook for simple flight, now broke into excited speech once more:

'Father's 'it 'im on the jore ag'in—'is eye's a-bungin' up—*Go it, father, bash 'i-i-i-m*! Father's landin' 'im—'e—'

Hannah Perrott crept to the window and looked. She saw the foul Jago mob, swaying and bellowing about the shifting edge of an open patch, in the midst whereof her husband and Billy Leary, bruised, bloody and gasping, fought and battered infuriately; and she crept back to the bed and bent her face on Looey's unclean little frock; till a fit of tense shuddering took the child, and the mother looked up again.

Without, the round ended. For a full minute the men took and gave knock for knock, and then Leary, wincing from another body-blow, swung his right desperately on Perrott's ear, and knocked him over.

Exulting shouts rose from the Leary faction, and the blow struck Dicky's heart still. But Josh was up almost before Kiddo Cook reached him, and Dicky saw a wide grin on his face as he came to his corner. The leathery toughness of the man, and the advantage it gave him, now grew apparent. He had endured to the full as much and as hard punching as had his foe—even more, and harder; once he had fallen on the broken cobble-stones with all Leary's weight on him; and once he had been knocked down on them. But, except for the sweat that ran over his face and

down his back, and for a missing front tooth and the lip it had
cut, he showed little sign of the struggle; while Leary's left eye
was a mere slit in a black wen, his nose was a beaten mass, which
had ensanguined him (and indeed Josh) from crown to waist, and
his chest and flanks were a mottle of bruises.

'Father's awright, mother—I see 'im laughin'! And 'e's smashed
Leary's nose all over 'is face!'

Up again they sprang for the next round, Perrott active and
daring, Leary cautious and a trifle stiff. Josh rushed in and struck
at the tender ribs once more, took two blows callously on his
head, and sent his left at the nose, with a smack as of a flail on
water. With that Leary rushed like a bull, and Josh was driven
and battered back, for the moment without response. But he
ducked, and slipped away, and came again, fresh and vicious.
And now it was seen that Perrott's toughness of hand was lasting.
Leary's knuckles were raw, cut, and flayed, and took little good
by the shock when they met the other's stubborn muzzle; while
Josh still flung in his corneous fists, hard and lasting as a bag of
bullets.

But suddenly, stooping to reach the mark once more, Josh's
foot turned on a projecting stone, and he floundered forward into
Billy's arms. Like a flash his neck was clipped in the big man's
left arm: Josh Perrott was in chancery. Quick and hard Leary
pounded the imprisoned head, while Jerry Gullen and Kiddo
Cook danced distracted and dismayed, and the crowd whooped
and yelled.

Dicky hung delirious over the sill, and shrieked he knew not
what. He saw his father fighting hard at the back and ribs with
both hands, and Leary hammering his face in a way to make
pulp of an ordinary mazzard. Then suddenly Josh Perrott's right
hand shot up from behind, over Leary's shoulder, and gripped
him at the chin. Slowly, with tightened muscles, he forced his
man back over his bent knee, Leary clinging and swaying, but
impotent to struggle. Then, with an extra wrench from Josh, up
came Leary's feet from the ground, higher, higher, till suddenly
Josh flung him heavily over, heels up, and dropped on him with
all his weight.

The Ranns roared again. Josh was up in a moment, sitting on
Kiddo Cook's knee, and taking a drink from a bottle. Billy Leary
lay like a man fallen from a house-top. His seconds turned him

on his back, and dragged him to his corner. There he lay limp and senseless, and there was a cut at the back of his head.

The High Mobsman who held the watch waited for half a minute and then called 'Time!' Josh Perrott stood up, but Billy Leary was knocked out of knowledge, and heard not. He was beaten.

Josh Perrott was involved in a howling, dancing crowd, and was pushed, grinning, this way and that, slapped on the back, and offered drinks. In the outskirts the tossers, inveterate, pulled out their pence and resumed their game.

Dicky spun about, laughing, flushed, and elated, and as soon as the door was distinct to his dazzled sight, he ran off downstairs. His mother, relieved and even pleased, speculated as to what money the thing might bring. She put the baby on the bed, and looked from the window.

Josh, in the crowd, shouted and beckoned her, pointing and tapping his bare shoulder. He wanted his clothes. She gathered together the shirt, the coat, and the waistcoat, and hurried downstairs. Looey could come to no harm lying on the bed for a few minutes. And, indeed, Hannah Perrott felt that she would be a person of distinction in the crowd, and was not sorry to have an excuse for going out.

'Three cheers for the missis!' sang out Kiddo Cook as she came through the press. 'I said 'e'd 'ave a bob or two for you, didn't I?' Josh Perrott, indeed, was rich—a capitalist of five pounds. For a sovereign a side had been put up, and his backer had put on a sovereign for him at three to one. So that now it became him to stand beer to many sympathisers. Also, he felt that the missis should have some part in the celebration, for was it not her injury that he had avenged on Sally Green's brother? So Hannah Perrott, pleased though timorous, was hauled away with the rest to Mother Gapp's.

Here she sat by Josh's side for an hour. Once or twice she thought of Looey, but with native inertness she let the thought slip. Perhaps Dicky would be back, and at any rate it was hard if she must not take half an hour's relaxation once in a way. At last came Dicky, urgent perplexity in his face, looking in at the door. Josh, minded to be generous all round, felt for a penny.

'Mother,' said Dicky, plucking at her arm, 'Pigeony Poll's at 'ome, nussin' Looey; she told me to tell you to come at once.'

Pigeony Poll? What right had she in the room? The ghost of Hannah Perrott's respectability rose in resentment. She supposed she must go. She arose, mystified, and went, with Dicky at her skirts.

Pigeony Poll sat by the window with the baby in her arms, and pale misgiving in her dull face. 'I—I come in, Mrs Perrott, mum,' she said, with a hush in her thick voice, 'I come in 'cos I see you goin' out, an' I thought the baby'd be alone. She—she's 'ad a sort o' fit—all stiff an' blue in the face and grindin' 'er little mouth. She's left auf now—but I—I dunno what to make of 'er. She's so—so—'

Hannah Perrott stared blankly, and lifted the child, whose arm dropped and hung. The wizenage had gone from Looey's face, and the lids were down on the strained eyes; her pale lips lay eased of the old pinching—even parted in a smile. For she looked in the face of the Angel that plays with the dead children.

Hannah Perrott's chin fell. 'Lor',' she said bemusedly, and sat on the bed.

An odd croaking noise broke in jerks from Pigeony Poll as she crept from the room, with her face bowed in the bend of her arm, like a weeping schoolboy. Dicky stared, confounded. . . . Josh came and gazed stupidly, with his mouth open, walking tip-toe. But at a word from Kiddo Cook, who came in his tracks, he snatched the little body and clattered off to the dispensary, to knock up the young student.

The rumour went in the Jago that Josh Perrott was in double luck. For here was insurance money without a doubt. But in truth that was a thing the Perrotts had neglected.

Hannah Perrott felt a listless relief; Josh felt nothing in particular, except that there was no other thing to be done, and that Mother Gapp's would be a cheerful place to finish the day in, and keep up the missis's pecker.

So that eight o'clock that evening at Perrott's witnessed a darkening room wherein an inconsiderable little corpse lay on a bed; while a small ragamuffin spread upon it with outstretched arms, exhausted with sobbing, a soak of muddy tears: 'O Looey, Looey! Can't you 'ear? Won't you never come to me no more?'

And the Reverend Henry Sturt, walking from church through

Luck Row toward his lodgings in Kingsland Road, heard shouts and riot behind the grimy panes of Mother Gapp's, and in the midst the roar of many voices joined in the Jago chant:

> *Six bloomin' long months in a prison,*
> *Six more bloomin' months I must stay,*
> *For meetin' a bloke in our alley,*
> *An' takin' 'is uxter away!*
>
> *Toora-li—toora-li-looral,*
> *Toora-li—toora-li—lay,*
> *A-coshin' a bloke in our alley,*
> *An' takin' 'is uxter away!*

14

ON AN autumn day four years after his first coming to the Jago, the Reverend Henry Sturt left a solicitor's office in Cheapside, and walked eastward, with something more of hope and triumph in him than he had felt since the Jago fell to his charge. For the ground was bought whereon should be built a church and buildings accessory, and he felt, not that he was like to see any great result from his struggle, but that perhaps he might pursue it better armed and with less of grim despair than had been his portion hitherto.

It had taken him four years to gather the money for the site, and some of it he was paying from his own pocket. He was unmarried, and had therefore no reason to save. Still, he must be careful, for the sake of the parish: the church must be built, and some of the money would probably be wanted for that. Moreover, there were other calls. The benefice brought a trifle less than £200 a year, and out of that, so far as it would go, he paid (with some small outside help) £130 for rent of the temporary church and the adjacent rooms; the organist's salary; the rates and the gas-bills; the cost of cleaning, care, and repair; the sums needed for such relief as was impossible to be withheld; and a thousand small things beside. While the Jagos speculated wildly among themselves as to the vast sums he must make by his job. For what toff would come and live in the Jago except for a consideration of solid gain? What other possible motive could there be indeed?

Still, he had an influence among them such as they had never known before. For one thing, they feared in him what they took for a sort of supernatural insight. The mean cunning of the Jago, subtle as it was, and baffling to most strangers, foundered miserably before his relentless intelligence; and crafty rogues—'wide as Broad Street', as their proverb went—at first sulked, faltered and prevaricated transparently, but soon gave up all hope or effort to deceive him. Thus he was respected. Once he had made it plain that he was no common milch-cow in the matter of gratuities: to be bamboozled for shillings, cajoled for coals, and bullied for blankets; then there became apparent in him qualities of charity and lovingkindness, well-judged and governed, that awoke in places a regard that was in a way akin to affection. And the familiar habit of the Jago slowly grew to call him Father Sturt.

Father Sturt was not to be overreached: that was the axiom gloomily accepted by all in the Jago who lived by what they accounted their wits. You could not juggle shillings and clothing (convertible into shillings) out of Father Sturt by the easy fee-faw-fum of repentance and salvation that served with so many. There were many of the Jagos (mightily despised by some of the sturdier ruffians) who sallied forth from time to time into neighbouring regions in pursuit of the profitable sentimentalist; discovering him—black-coated, earnest, green—sometimes a preacher, sometimes a layman, sometimes one having authority on the committee of a charitable institution; dabbling in the East End on his own account, or administering relief for a mission, or disbursing a Mansion House Fund. He was of two chief kinds: the Merely-Soft—the 'man of wool' as the Jago word went—for whom any tale was good enough, delivered with the proper wistful misery: and the Gullible-Cocksure, confident in a blind experience, who was quite as easy to tap, when approached with a becoming circumspection. A rough and ready method, which served well in most cases with both sorts, was a profession of sudden religious awakening. For this, one offered an aspect either of serene happiness or of maniacal exaltation, according to the customer's taste. A better way, but one demanding greater subtlety, was the assumption of the part of Earnest Inquirer, hesitating on the brink of Salvation. For the attitude was capable of indefinite prolongation, and was ever productive of the boots, the coats, and the half-crowns used to coax weak brethren into the fold. But with Father Sturt, such trouble was worse than useless; it was, indeed, but to invite a humiliating snub. Thus, when Fluffy Pike first came to Father Sturt with the intelligence that he had at last found Grace, then Father Sturt asked if he had found it in a certain hamper—a hamper hooked that morning from a railway van—and if it were of a quality likely to inspire an act of restoration to the goods office. Nothing was to be done with a man of this disgustingly practical turn of mind, and the Jagos soon ceased from trying.

Father Sturt had made more of a stable than the make-shift church he had found. He had organised a club in the stable adjoining, and he lived in the rooms over the shut-up shop. In the club he gathered the men of the Jago indiscriminately, with the sole condition of good behaviour on the premises. And there they smoked, jumped, swung on horizontal bars, boxed, played at cards and bagatelle, free from interference save when interference became necessary. For the women there were sewing-meetings and singing. And all governed with an invisible discipline, which, being brought to action, was found to be of iron.

Now there was ground on which might be built a worthier church; and Father Sturt had in mind a church which should have by its side a cleanly lodging-house, a night-shelter, a club, baths and washhouses. And at a stroke he would establish this habitation and wipe out the blackest spot in the Jago. For the new site comprised the whole of Jago Court and the houses that masked it in Old Jago Street.

This was a dream of the future—perhaps of the immediate future, if a certain new millionaire could only be interested in the undertaking—but of the future certainly. The money for the site alone had been hard enough to gather. In the first place the East London Elevation Mission and Pansophical Institute was asking very diligently for funds—and was getting them. It was to that, indeed, that people turned by habit when minded to invest in the amelioration of the East End. Then about this time there had arisen a sudden quacksalver, a Panjandrum of philanthropy, a mummer of the market-place, who undertook, for a fixed sum, to abolish poverty and sin together; and many, pleased with the new gaudery, poured out before him the money that had gone to maintain hospitals and to feed proved charities. So that gifts were scarce and hard to come by—indeed, were apt to be thought unnecessary, for was not misery to be destroyed out of hand? Moreover, Father Sturt wanted not for enemies among the Sentimental-Cocksure. He was callous and cynical in face of the succulent penitence of Fluffy Pike and his kind. He preferred the frank rogue before the calculating snivel-monger. He had a club at which boxing was allowed, and dominoes—flat ungodliness. He shook hands familiarly every day with the lowest characters: his tastes were vulgar and brutal. And the company at his club was really dreadful. These things the Cocksure said, with shaking of heads; and these they took care should be known among such as might give Father Sturt money. Father Sturt!— the name itself was sheer papistry. And many comforted themselves by writing him anonymous letters, displaying hell before his eyes, and dealing him vivid damnation.

So Father Sturt tramped back to the Jago, and to the strain and struggle that ceased not for one moment of his life, though it left never a mark of success behind it. For the Jago was much as ever. Were the lump once leavened by the advent of any denizen a little less base than the rest, were a native once ridiculed and persuaded into a spell of work and clean living, then must Father Sturt hasten to drive him from the Jago ere its influence suck him under for ever; leaving for his own community none but the entirely vicious. And among these he spent his life: preaching little, in the common sense, for that were but idle vanity in this place; but working, alleviating, growing into the Jago life, flinging scorn and ridicule on evil things, grateful for tiny negative successes—for keeping a few from ill-behaviour but for an hour; conscious that wherever he was not, iniquity flourished unreproved; and oppressed by the remembrance that albeit the Jago death-rate ruled full four times that of all London beyond, still the Jago rats bred and bred their kind unhindered, multiplying apace and infecting the world.

In Luck Row he came on Josh Perrott, making for home with something under the skirt of his coat.

'How d'ye do, Josh?' said Father Sturt, clapping a hand on Josh's shoulder, and offering it as Josh turned about.

Josh, with a shifting of the object under his coat, hastened to tap his cap-peak with his forefinger before shaking hands. He grinned broadly, and looked this way and that, with mingled gratification and embarrassment, as was the Jago way in such circumstances. Because one could never tell whether Father Sturt would exchange a mere friendly sentence or two, or, with concealed knowledge, put some disastrous question about a watch, or a purse, or a breastpin, or what not.

'Very well, thanks, Father,' answered Josh, and grinned amiably at the wall beyond the vicar's elbow.

'And what have you been doing just lately?'

'Oo—odd jobs, Father.' Always the same answer, all over the Jago.

'Not quite such odd jobs as usual, I hope, Josh, eh?' Father Sturt smiled, and twitched Josh playfully by the button-hole as one might treat a child. 'I once heard of a very odd job in the Kingsland Road that got a fine young man six months' holiday. Eh, Josh?'

Josh Perrott wriggled and grinned sheepishly; tried to frown, failed, and grinned again. He had only been out a few weeks from that six moon. Presently he said: 'Awright, Father; you do rub it into a bloke, no mistake.'

The grin persisted as he looked first at the wall, then at the pavement, then down the street, but never in the parson's face.

'Ah, there's a deal of good in a blister sometimes, isn't there, Josh? What's this I see—a clock? Not another odd job, eh?'

It was indeed a small nickel-plated American clock which Josh had under his coat, and which he now partly uncovered with positive protests. 'No, s'elp me, Father, it's all straight—all fair trade, Father—jist a swop for somethink else, on me solemn davy. That's wot it is, Father—straight.'

'Well, I'm glad you thought to get it, Josh,' Father Sturt pursued, still twitching the buttonhole. 'You never have been a punctual churchgoer, you know, Josh, and I'm glad you've made arrangements to improve. You'll have no excuse now, you know, and I shall expect you on Sunday morning—promptly. Don't forget: I shall be looking for you.' And Father Sturt shook hands again, and passed on, leaving Josh Perrott still grinning dubiously, and striving to assimilate the invitation to church.

The clock was indeed an exchange, though not altogether an innocent one: the facts being these. Early that morning Josh had found himself scrambling hastily along a turning out of Brick Lane, accompanied by a parcel of nine or ten pounds of tobacco, and extremely conscious of the hasty scrambling of several other people round the corner. Some of these people turned that corner before Josh reached the next, so that his course was observed, and it became politic to get rid of his parcel before a possible heading-off in Meakin Street. There was one place where this might be done, and that was at Weech's. A muddy yard, one of a tangle of such places behind Meakin Street, abutted on Weech's back fence; and it was no uncommon thing for a Jago on the crook, hard pressed, to pitch his plunder over the fence, double out into the crowd and call on Mr Aaron Weech for the purchase

114

money as soon as opportunity served. The manoeuvre was a simple one, facilitated by the plan of the courts; but it was only adopted in extreme cases, because Mr Aaron Weech was at best but a mean paymaster, and with so much of the upper hand in the bargain as these circumstances conferred, was apt to be meaner than ever. But this case seemed to call for the stratagem, and Josh made for the muddy yard, dropped the parcel over the fence, with a loud whistle, and backed off by the side passage in the regular way.

When he called on Mr Aaron Weech a few hours later, that talented tradesman, with liberal gestures, told out shillings singly in his hand, pausing after each as though that were the last. But Josh held his hand persistently open, till Mr Weech, having released the fifth shilling, stopped altogether, scandalised at such rapacity. But still Josh was not satisfied, and as he was not quite so easy a customer to manage as the boys who commonly fenced at the shop, Mr Weech compromised, in the end, by throwing in a cheap clock. It had been in hand for a long time; and Josh was fain to take it, since he could get no more. And thus it was Dicky, coming in at about five o'clock, was astonished to see on the mantelpiece, amid the greasy ruins of many candle ends, the clock that had belonged to the Ropers four years before.

15

As for Dicky, he went to school. That is to say, he turned up now and again, at irregular intervals, at the Board School just over the Jago border in Honey Lane. When anything was given away, he attended as a matter of course; but he went now and again without such inducement—perhaps because he fancied an afternoon's change, perhaps because the weather was cold and the school was warm. He was classed as a half-timer, an arrangement which variegated the register, but otherwise did not matter. Other boys, half-timers or not, attended as little as he. It was long since the managers had realised the futility of attempting compulsion in the Jago.

Dicky was no fool, and he had picked up some sort of reading and writing as he went along. Moreover, he had grown an expert thief, and had taken six strokes of a birch-rod by order of a magistrate. As yet he rarely attempted a pocket, being, for most opportunities, too small; but he was comforted by the reflection that probably he would never get really tall, and thus grow out of pocket-picking when he was fully experienced, as was the fate of some. For no tall man can be a successful pickpocket, because he must bend to his work, and so advertise it to every beholder.

Meantime Dicky practised that petty larceny which is possible in every street in London; and at odd times he would play the scout among the practitioners of the 'fat's a-running' industry. If one crossed Meakin Street by way of Luck Row and kept his way among the courts ahead, he presently reached the main Bethnal Green Road, at the end whereof stood the great goods depot of a railway company. Here carts and vans went to and fro all day, laden with goods from the depot, and certain gangs among the Jagos preyed on these continually. A quick-witted scout stood on the look-out for such vehicles as went with unguarded tailboards. At the approach of one such he sent the shout '*Fat's a-runnin*'!' up Luck Row, and, quick at the signal, a gang scuttled down, by the court or passage which his waved hand might hint at, seized whatever could be snatched from the cart, and melted away into the courts, sometimes leaving a few hands behind to hinder and misdirect pursuit. Taking one capture with another, the thing paid very well; and besides, there were many vans laden with parcels of tobacco, not from the railway depot but from the tobacco factories hard by, a click from which was apt to prove especially lucrative. Dicky was a notable success as scout. The department was a fairly safe one, but it was not always easy to extract from the gang the few coppers that were regarded as sufficient share for service done. Moreover, Mr Weech was not pleased; for by now Dicky was near to being his most remunerative client, and the cart robberies counted nothing, for the fat's a-running boys fenced their swag with a publican at Hoxton. And though Dicky had grown out of his childish belief that Mr Weech could hear a mile away and see through a wall, he had a cautious dread of the weapon he supposed to lie ever to his patron's hand—betrayal to the police. In other respects things were easier. His father took no heed of what he did, and even his mother had so far accepted destiny as to ask if he had a copper or two, when there was a scarcity. Indeed Hannah Perrott filled her place in the Jago better than of old. She would gossip, she drew no very rigid line as to her acquaintance, and Dicky had seen her drunk. Still, for Old Jago Street she was a quiet woman, and she never brawled nor fought. Of fighting, indeed, Josh could do enough for the whole family, once again four in number. For the place of Looey, forgotten, was supplied by Em, aged two.

When Dicky came home and recognised the clock on the mantelpiece, being the more certain because his mother told him it had come from Weech's, the thing irritated him strangely. Through all those four years since he had carried the clock to Mr Weech, he had never got rid of the wretched hunchback. He, too, went to the Board School in Honey Lane (it lay between Dove Lane and the Jago), but he went regularly, worked hard, and was a favourite with the teachers. So far, Dicky was unconcerned. But scarce an ill chance came to him but, sooner or later, he found the hunchback at the back of it. If ever a teacher mysteriously found out that it was Dicky who had drawn his portrait, all nose and teeth, on the blackboard, the tale had come from Bobby Roper. Whenever Dicky, chancing upon school by ill luck on an afternoon when sums were to be done, essayed to copy answers from his neighbour's slate, up shot the hunchback's hand in an instant, the tale was told, and handers were Dicky's portion. Once, dinnerless and hungry, he had stolen a sandwich from a teacher's desk; and, though he had thought himself alone and unseen, the hunchback knew it, and pointed him out, white malice in his thin face and eager hate in his thrust finger. For a fortnight Dicky dared not pass a little fruit shop in Meakin Street, because of an attempt on an orange, betrayed by his misshapen schoolfellow, which brought him a hard chase from the fruiterer and a bad bruise on the spine from a board flung after him. The hunchback's whole energies—even his whole time—seemed to be devoted to watching him. Dicky, on his part, received no injuries meekly. In the beginning he had tried threats and public jeers at his enemy's infirmity. Then, on some especially exasperating occasion, he pounded Bobby Roper savagely about the head and capsized him into a mud-heap. But bodily reprisal, though he erected it into a practice, proved no deterrent. For the little hunchback, though he might cry at the pummelling, retorted with worse revenge of his own sort. And once or twice bystanders, seeing a deformed child thus treated, interfered with clouts on Dicky's ears. The victim, however, designed another retaliation. He would go to some bigger boy with a tale that Dicky had spoken vauntingly of fighting him and beating him hollow, with one hand. This brought the big boy after Dicky at once, with a hiding: except on some rare occasion when the hunchback rated his instrument of vengeance too high, and Dicky was able to beat him in truth. But this was a very uncommon mistake. And after this Dicky did not wait for specific provocation: he 'clumped' Bobby Roper, or rolled him in the gutter, as a matter of principle, whenever he could get hold of him.

That afternoon Dicky had suffered again. Two days earlier, tea and cake had been provided by a benevolent manager for all who attended the school. Consequently the attendance was excellent, and included Dicky. But his attempt to secrete a pocketful of cake, to carry home for Em, was reported by Bobby Roper; and Dicky was hauled forth, deprived of his plunder, and expelled in disgrace. He waited outside and paid off the score fiercely, by the help of a very long and pliant cabbage stalk. But this afternoon Bill Bates, a boy a head taller than himself and two years older, had fallen on him suddenly in Lincoln Street, and, though Dicky fought desperately and kicked with much

118

effect, had dealt him a thrashing that left him bruised, bleeding, dusty, and crying with rage and pain. This was the hunchback's doing, without a doubt. Dicky limped home, but was something comforted by an accident in Shoreditch High Street, whereby a coster's barrow-load of cough-drops was knocked over by a covered van, and the cough-drops were scattered in the mud. For while the carman and the coster flew at each other's name and address, and defamed each other's eyes and mother, Dicky gathered a handful of cough-drops, muddy, it is true, but easy to wipe. And so he made for home more cheerfully disposed: till the sight of the Ropers' old clock brought the hunchback to mind once more, and in bitter anger he resolved to search for him forthwith, and pass on the afternoon's hiding, with interest.

As he emerged into the street, a hand was reached to catch him, which he dodged by instinct. He rushed back upstairs, and emptied his pockets, stowing away in a safe corner the rest of the cough-drops, the broken ruin he called his knife, some buttons and pieces of string, a bit of chalk, three little pieces of slate pencil and two marbles. Then he went down again into the street, confident in his destitution, and watched, forgetting the hunchback in the excitement of the spectacle.

The loafers from the corners had conceived a sudden notion of co-operation, and had joined forces to the array of twenty or thirty. Confident in their numbers, they swept the street, stopping every passenger—man, woman or child—and emptying all pockets. A straggler on the outskirts of the crowd, a hobbledehoy like most of the rest, had snatched at but had lost Dicky, and was now busy, with four or five others, rolling a woman, a struggling heap of old clothes and skinny limbs, in the road. It was Biddy Flynn, too old and worn for anything but honest work, who sold oranges and nuts from a basket, and who had been caught on her way out for an evening's trade in High Street. She was a fortunate capture, being a lone woman with all her possessions about her. Under her skirt, and tied round her waist with string, she kept her money-bag; and it was soon found and dragged away, yielding two and eightpence farthing and a lucky shoe-tip, worn round and bright. She had, moreover, an old brass brooch; but unfortunately her wedding ring, worn to pin-wire, could not be got past the knotted knuckle—though it would have been worth little in any case. So Biddy Flynn, exhausted with plunging and screaming, was left, and her empty basket was flung at her. She staggered away, wailing and rolling her head, with her hand to the wall; and the gang, sharing out, sucked oranges with relish, and turned to fresh exploits. Dicky watched from the Jago Court passage.

Business slackened for a little while, and the loafers were contemplating a raid in force on Mother Gapp's till, when a grown lad ran in pell-mell from Luck Row with a square parcel clipped under his arm—a parcel of aspect well known among the fat's a-running boys—a parcel that meant tobacco. He was collared at once.

'Stow it, Bill!' he cried breathlessly, recognising his captor. 'The bloke's a-comin'!'

But half-a-dozen hands were on his plunder, it was snatched away, and he was flung back on the flags. There was a clatter on the stones of Luck Row, and a light van came rattling into Old Jago Street, the horse galloping, the carman lashing and shouting: 'Stop 'im! Stop thief!'

The sight was so novel that for a moment the gang merely stared and grinned. This man must be a greenhorn—new to the neighbourhood—to venture a load of goods up Luck Row. And it was tobacco, too. He was pale and flustered, and he called wildly, as he looked this way and that: 'A man's stole somethin' auf my van. Where's 'e gawn?'

'No good, guv'nor,' cried one. 'The ball's stopped rollin'. You've lawst 'im.'

'My Gawd!' said the man, in a sweat, 'I'm done. There's two quids' worth a' 'bacca—an' I on'y got the job o' Monday—bin out nine munse!'

'Was it a parcel like this 'ere?' asked another, chuckling, and lifting a second packet over the tailboard.

'Yus—put it down! Gawd—wotcher up to? 'Ere—'elp! 'elp!'

The gang were over the van, guffawing and flinging out the load. The carman yelled aloud, and fought desperately with his whip—Bill Hanks is near blind of an eye now from one cut; but he was the worse for it. For he was knocked off the van in a heap, and, as he lay, they cleared his pockets, and pulled off his boots; those that had caught the sting of the whip kicking him about the head till it but shifted in the slime at the stroke, an inanimate lump.

There was talk of how to deal with the horse and van. To try to sell them was too large a job, and too risky. So, as it was growing dusk, the senseless carman was put on the floor of the van, the tailboard was raised, and one of the gang led the horse away, to lose the whole thing in the busy streets.

Here was a big haul, and many of the crowd busied themselves in getting it out of sight, and scouting out among the fences to arrange sales. Those who remained grew less active, and hung at the corner of Luck Row, little more than an ordinary corner-group of loafers.

Then Dicky remembered the hunchback, and slouched off to Dove Lane. But he could see nothing of Bobby Roper. The Jago and Dove Lane were districts ever at feud, active or smouldering, save for brief intervals of ostentatious reconciliation, serving to render the next attack on Dove Lane the more savage—for invariably the Jagos were aggressors and victors. Dicky was careful in his lurkings, therefore: lest he should be recognised and set upon by more Dove Lane boys than would be convenient. He knew where the Ropers lived, and he went and hung about the door. Once he fancied he could hear a disjointed tinkle, as of a music-box grown infirm, but he was not sure of it. And in the end he contented himself, for the present, with flinging a stone through the Ropers' window, and taking to his heels.

The Jago was black with night, the rats came and went, and the cosh-carriers lurked on landings. On a step, Pigeony Poll, drunk because of a little gin and no food, sang hideously and wept. The loafers had dispersed to spend their afternoon's makings. The group which Dicky had left by Luck Row corner, indeed, had been discouraged early in the evening in consequence of an attempt at 'turning over' old Beveridge, as he unsuspectingly stalked among them, in from his city round. For the old man whipped out his case-knife and drove it into the flesh of Nobber Sugg's arm, at the shoulder—stabbed, too, at another, and ripped his coat. So Nobber Sugg, with blood streaming through his sleeve, went off with two more to tie up the arm; and old Beveridge, grinning and mumbling fiercely, strode about the street, knife in hand, for ten minutes, ere he grew calm enough to go his way. This Tommy Rann told Dicky, sitting in the back yard and smoking a pipe; a pipe charged with tobacco pillaged from a tin-full which his father had bought, at about fourpence a pound, from a loafer. And both boys crawled indoors deadly sick.

16

JOSH PERROTT was at church on Sunday morning, as Father
Sturt had bid him. Not because of the bidding, but because the
vicar overtook him and Kiddo Cook in Meakin Street, and hauled
them in, professing to be much gratified at their punctuality, and
charging them never to fall away from the habit. The two Jagos,
with dubious grins, submitted as they must, and were in a little
while surprised to find others arriving, friends and acquaintances
never suspected of church-going. The fact was, that Father Sturt,
by dint of long effort, had so often brought so many to his stable-
church, as he had now brought Josh and Kiddo, that the terrors
and embarrassments of the place had worn off, and many, finding
nothing more attractive elsewhere, would make occasional attend-
ances of their own motion. Wet Sundays, particularly, inclined
them to church; where there might be a fire, where at least there
was a clean room, with pictures on the wall, where there were
often flowers, where there was always music, and where Father
Sturt made an address of a quarter of an hour, which nobody
ever suspected of being a sermon; an address which one might
doze over or listen to, as one might be disposed; but which most
listened to, more or less, partly because of an uneasy feeling that
Father Sturt would know if they did not, and partly because it
was very easy to understand, was not oppressively minatory, was
spoken with an intimate knowledge of themselves, and was, indeed, something of a refreshing novelty, being the simple talk of
a gentleman.

Josh Perrott and Kiddo Cook were not altogether sorry they
had come. It was a rest. Stable though it had been, they had
never sat in so pleasant a room before. There was nothing to do,
no constant watch to be kept, no police to avoid, and their wits
had a holiday. They forgot things. Their courage never rose so
high as to build the thought; but in truth pipes would have made
them happy.

The address being done, Father Sturt announced the purchase
of the site for the new church, and briefly described his scheme.
He would give tenants good notice, he said, before the houses

were destroyed. Meantime, they must pay rent; though most of the amounts would be reduced.

And after the benediction, Father Sturt, from his window over the closed shop, saw Josh Perrott and Kiddo Cook guffawing and elbowing one another up Luck Row. Each was accusing the other of having tried to sing.

17

THERE was much talk of Father Sturt's announcement. Many held it a shame that so much money, destined for the benefit of the Jago, should be spent in bricks and mortar, instead of being distributed among themselves. They fell to calculating the price of the land and houses, and to working it out laboriously in the denomination of pots and gallons. More: it was felt to be a grave social danger that Jago Court should be extinguished. What would become of the Jago without Jago Court? Where would Sunday morning be spent? Where would the fights come off, and where was so convenient a place for pitch and toss? But mainly they feared the police. Jago Court was an unfailing sanctuary, a city of refuge ever ready, ever secure. There were times when two or three of the police, hot in the chase, would burst into the Jago at the heels of a flying marauder. Then the runaway would make straight for the archway, and, once he was in Jago Court, danger was over. For he had only to run into one of the ever-open doors at right or left, and out into back yards and other houses; or, better, to scramble over the low fence opposite, through the back door before him, and so into New Jago Street. Beyond the archway the police could not venture, except in large companies. A young constable who tried it once, getting ahead of two companions in his ardour, was laid low as he emerged from the passage, by a fire-grate adroitly let drop from an upper window.

The blotting out of such a godsend of a place as this would be a calamity. The Jago would never be the same again. As it was, the Old Jago was a very convenient, comfortable sort of place, they argued. They could not imagine themselves living anywhere else. But assuredly it would be the Jago no longer without Jago Court. And this thing was to be done, too, with money got together for their benefit! The sole explanation the Jago could supply was the one that at last, with arithmetical variations, prevailed. The landlords were to be paid a sum (varying in Jago estimation from a hundred pounds to a hundred thousand) for the houses and the ground, and of this they were secretly to return to Father Sturt a certain share (generally agreed on as half), as his private fee for bringing about so desirable a transaction. Looked at from all points, this appeared to be the most plausible explanation: for no other could reasonably account for Father Sturt's activity. No wonder he could afford to reduce some of the rents! Was he not already receiving princely wages (variously supposed to be something from ten pounds to thirty pounds a week) from the Government, for preaching every Sunday?

Still the rents were to be reduced: that was the immediate consideration, and nothing but an immediate consideration carried weight in the Jago, where a shilling to-day was to be preferred to a constant income beginning in a month's time. The first effect of the announcement was a rush of applications for rooms in the doomed houses, each applicant demanding to be accommodated by the eviction of somebody already established, but now disinterestedly discovered to be a bad tenant. They were all disappointed, but the residents had better luck than they had hoped. For the unexpected happened, and the money for a part of the new buildings was suddenly guaranteed. Wherefore Father Sturt, knowing that many would be hard put to it to find shelter when the houses came down, and guessing that rents would rise with the demand, determined to ask none for the little while the tenements endured. Scarce had he made his decision known ere he regretted it, popular as it was. For he reflected that the money saved would merely melt, and that at the inevitable turning out, not a soul would be the better off for the relief, but, indeed, might find it harder than ever to pay rent after the temporary easement. It would have been better rigidly to exact the rent, and return it in lump to each tenant as he left. The sum would have been an inducement to leave peaceably—a matter in which trouble was to be expected. But then, what did any windfall of shillings bring in the Jago? What but a drunk? This was one of Father Sturt's thousand perplexities, and he could but hope that, perhaps, he had done right after all.

The old buildings were sold, as they stood, to the house-wreckers, and on the house-wreckers devolved the work of getting the lodgers out. For weeks the day was deferred, but it drew very near at last, and a tall hoarding was put up. Next morning it had vanished; but there was a loud crackling where the Jagos boiled their pots; Dicky Perrott and Tommy Rann had a bonfire

125

in Edge Lane; and Jerry Gullen's canary sweated abroad before a heavy load of cheap firewood.

Then Josh Perrott and Billy Leary, his old enemy, were appointed joint guardians of the new hoarding, each to get half a crown on every morning when the fence was found intact. And in the end there came eviction day, and once more the police held the Jago in force, escorting gangs of men with tumbrils.

As for the Perrotts, they could easily find another room, at the high rent always charged for the privilege of residence in the Jago. To have remained in one room four or five years, and to have paid rent with indifferent good regularity, was a feat sufficiently rare to be notorious, and to cause way to be made for them wherever a room was falling vacant, or could be emptied. They went no farther than across the way, to a room wherein a widow had died over her sack-making two days before, and had sat on the floor with her head between her knees for hours, while her children, not understanding, cried that they were hungry. These children were now gone to the workhouse: more fortunate than the many they left behind. And the room was a very fair one, ten feet square or so.

The rest of the tenants thought not at all of new quarters, and did nothing to find them, till they found themselves and their belongings roofless in Old Jago Street. Then with one accord they demanded lodgings of the vicar. Most of them had never inhabited any rooms so long as they had these which they must now leave—having been ejected again and again because of unpaid rent. Nevertheless, they clamoured for redress as they might have clamoured had they never changed dwellings in their lives.

Nobody resisted the police; for there were too many of them. Moreover, Father Sturt was there, and few had hardihood for any but their best behaviour in his presence. Still, there were disputes among the Jagos themselves, that sometimes came very near to fights. Ginger Stagg's missis professed to recognise a long-lost property in a tin kettle brought into the outer air among the belongings of Mrs Walsh. The miscellaneous rags and sticks that were Cocko Harnwell's household goods got mingled in the roadway with those appertaining to the Fishers; and their assortment without a turn of family combat was a task which tried the vicar's influence to the utmost. Mrs Rafferty, too, was suspected of undue pride in a cranky deal washstand, and thereby of a

126

disposition to sneer at the humbler turn-out of the Regans from the next floor: giving occasion for a shrill and animated row.

The weather was dry, fortunately, and the evicted squatted in the roadway, by their heaps, or on them, squabbling and lamenting. Ginger Stagg, having covered certain crockery with the old family mattress, forgetfully sat on it, and came upon Father Sturt with an indignant demand for compensation.

Father Sturt's efforts to stimulate a search for new lodgings met with small success at first. It was felt that, no doubt, there were lodgings to be had, but they would be open to the fatal objection of costing something; and the Jago temperament could neither endure nor understand payment for what had once been given for nothing. Father Sturt, the Jagos argued, had given them free quarters for so long. Then why should he stop now? If they cleared out in order to make room for his new church, in common fairness he should find them similar lodgings on the same terms. So they sat and waited for him to do it.

At length the vicar set to work with them in good earnest, carried away with him a family or two at a time, and inducted them to rooms of his own finding. And hereat others, learning that in these cases rent in advance was exacted, bestirred themselves: reflecting that if rent must be paid they might as well choose their own rooms as take those that Father Sturt might find. Of course the thing was not done without payments from the vicar's pocket. Some were wholly destitute; others could not muster enough to pay that advance of rent which alone could open a Jago tenancy. Distinguishing the genuine impecuniosity from the merely professed, with the insight that was now a sixth sense with him, Father Sturt helped sparingly and in secret; for a precedent of almsgiving was an evil thing in the Jago, confirming the shiftlessness which was already a piece of Jago nature, and setting up long affliction for the almsgiver. Enough of such precedents existed; and the inevitable additions thereto were a work of anxious responsibility and jealous care.

So the bivouac in Old Jago Street melted away. For one thing, there were those among the dispossessed who would not waste time in unproductive inactivity just then; for war had arisen with Dove Lane, and spoils were going. Dove Lane was no very reputable place, but it was not like the Jago. In the phrase of the district, the Dove Laners were pretty thick, but the Jagos were

thick as glue. There were many market-porters among the Dove
Laners, and at this, their prosperous season, they and their friends
resorted to a shop in Meakin Street, kept by an 'ikey' tailor, there
to buy the original out-and-out benjamins, or the celebrated
bang-up kicksies, cut saucy, with artful buttons and a double
fakement down the sides. And hereabouts they were apt to be
set upon by Jagos; overthrown by superior numbers; bashed;
and cleaned out. Or, if the purchases had been made, they were
flimped of their kicksies, benjies or daisies, as the case might be.
So that a fight with Dove Lane might be an affair of some occasional profit; and it became no loyal Jago to idle in the stronghold.

Father Sturt's task was nearly over, when, returning to Old
Jago Street, he saw Dicky Perrott sitting by a still-remaining
heap—a heap small and poor even among those others. The Perrotts had been decorously settled in their new home since early
morning; but here was Dicky, guarding a heap with a baby on it,
and absorbed in the weaving of rush bags.

'That's right, Dicky my boy,' said Father Sturt in the approving
voice that a Jago would do almost anything—except turn honest
—to hear. And Dicky, startled, looked up, flushed and happy,
over his shoulder.

'Rush bags, eh?' the vicar went on, stooping and handing Dicky
another rush from the heap. 'And whose are they?'

The bags, the rushes, the heap, and the baby, belonged to Mrs
Bates, the widow, who was now in search of a new room. Dicky
had often watched the weaving of fishmongers' frails, and, since it
was work in which he had had no opportunity of indulging, it
naturally struck him as a fascinating pastime. So that he was delighted by the chance which he had taken, and Mrs Bates, for
her part, was not sorry to find somebody to mind her property.
Moreover, by hard work and the skill begot of much practice,
she was able to earn a sum of some three farthings an hour at
the rush bags: a profit which her cupidity made her reluctant to
lose, for even half an hour. And thus to have Dicky carry on the
business—and in his enthusiasm he did it very well—was a further consideration.

Father Sturt chatted with Dicky till the boy could scarce plait
for very pride. Would not Dicky like to work regularly every
day, asked Father Sturt, and earn wages? Dicky could see no
graceful answer but the affirmative; and in sober earnest he

128

thought he would. Father Sturt took hold of Dicky's vanity. Was he not capable of something better than other Jago boys? Why should he not earn regular wages, and live comfortably, well fed and clothed, with no fear of the police, and no shame for what he did? *He* might do it, when others could not. They were not clever enough. They called themselves 'clever' and 'wide'; 'but,' said Father Sturt, 'is there one of them that can deceive me?' And Dicky knew there was not one. Most did no work, the vicar's argument went on, because they had neither the pluck to try nor the intelligence to accomplish. Else why did they live the wretched Jago life instead of take the pleasanter time of the decent labourer?

Dicky, already zealous at work as exampled in rush bag-making, listened with wistful pride. Yes, if he could, he would work and take his place over the envious heads of his Jago friends. But how? Nobody would employ a boy living in the Jago. That was notorious. The address was a topsy-turvy testimonial for miles around.

All the same when Mrs Bates at last took away her belongings, Dicky ran off in delighted amaze to tell his mother and Em that he was going to tea at Father Sturt's rooms.

And the wreckers tore down the foul old houses, laying bare the secret dens of a century of infamy; lifting out the wide sashes of the old 'weavers' windows'—the one good feature in the structures; letting light and air at last into the subterraneous basements where men and women had swarmed, and bred, and died, like wolves in their lairs; and emerging from clouds of choking dust, each man a colony of vermin. But there were rooms which the wreckers—no jack-a-dandies neither—flatly refused to enter; and nothing would make them but much coaxing, the promise of extra pay, and the certainty of much immediate beer.

18

MR GRINDER kept a shop in the Bethnal Green Road. It was announced in brilliant lettering as an 'oil, colour and Italian warehouse', and there, in addition to the oil and the colour, and whatever of Italian there might have been, he sold pots, pans, kettles, brooms, shovels, mops, lamps, nails, and treacle. It was a shop ever too tight for its stock, which burst forth at every available opening, and heaped so high on the paving that the window was half buried in a bank of shining tin. Father Sturt was one of the best customers: the oil, candles and utensils needed for church and club all coming from Mr Grinder's. Mr Grinder was losing his shop-boy, who had found a better situation; and Father Sturt determined that, could but the oilman be persuaded, Dicky Perrott should be the new boy. Mr Grinder was persuaded. Chiefly perhaps, because the vicar undertook to make good the loss, should the experiment end in theft; partly because it was policy to oblige a good customer; and partly, indeed, because Mr Grinder was willing to give such a boy a chance in life, for he was no bad fellow, as oil-and-colourmen go, and had been an errand boy himself.

So that there came a Monday morning when Dicky, his clothes as well mended as might be (for Hannah Perrott, no more than another Jago, could disobey Father Sturt), and a cut-down apron of his mother's tied before him, stood by Mr Grinder's bank of pots and kettles, in an eager agony to sell something, and near blind with the pride of the thing. He had been waiting at the shop-door long ere Mr Grinder was out of bed; and now, set to guard the outside stock—a duty not to be neglected in that neighbourhood—he brushed a tin pot here and there with his sleeve, and longed for some Jago friend to pass and view him in his new greatness. The goods he watched over were an unfailing source of interest; and he learned by much repetition the prices of all the saucepans, painted in blue distemper on the tin, and ranging from eightpence-halfpenny, on the big pots in the bottom row, to three-halfpence on the very little ones at the top. And there were long ranks of little paraffin lamps at a penny—the sort that had set fire to a garret in Half Jago Street a month since, and burnt old Mother Leary to a greasy cinder. With a smaller array of a superior quality at fourpence-halfpenny—just like the one that had burst at Jerry Gullen's, and burnt the bed. While over his head swung doormats at one-and-eightpence, with penny mousetraps dangling from their corners.

When he grew more accustomed to his circumstances, he bethought him to collect a little dirt, and rub it down the front of his apron, to give himself a well-worked and business-like appearance; and he greatly impeded women who looked at the saucepans and the mousetraps, ere they entered the shop, by his anxiety to cut them off from Mr Grinder and serve them himself. He remembered the boy at the toy-shop in Bishopsgate Street, years ago, who had chased him through Spitalfields; and he wished that some lurching youngster would snatch a mousetrap, that he might make a chase himself.

At Mr Grinder's every call Dicky was prompt and willing; for every new duty was a fresh delight, and the whole day a prolonged game of real shopkeeping. And at his tea—he was to have tea each day in addition to three and sixpence every Saturday— he took scarce five minutes. There was a trolley—just such a thing as porters used at railway stations, but smaller—which was his own particular implement, his own to pack parcels on for delivery to such few customers as did not carry away their own purchases: and to acquire the dexterous management of this trolley was a pure joy. He bolted his tea to start the sooner on a trolley-journey to a public-house two hundred yards away.

His enthusiasm for work as an amusement cooled in a day or two, but all his pride in it remained. The fight with Dove Lane waxed amain, but Dicky would not be tempted into more than a distant interest in it. In his day-dreams he saw himself a tradesman, with a shop of his own and the name 'R. Perrott', with a gold flourish, over the door. He would employ a boy himself then; and there would be a parlour, with stuff-bottomed chairs and a shade of flowers, and Em grown up and playing on the piano. Truly Father Sturt was right: the hooks were fools, and the straight game was the better.

Bobby Roper, the hunchback, went past the shop once, and saw him. Dicky, minding his new dignity, ignored his enemy, and for the first time for a year and more, allowed him to pass without either taunt or blow. The other, astonished at Dicky's new occupation, came back and back again, staring, from a safe distance, at Dicky and the shop. Dicky, on his part, took no more notice than to assume an ostentatious vigilance: so that the hunchback, baring his teeth in a snigger of malice, at last turned on his heel and rolled off.

Twice Kiddo Cook passed, but made no sign of recognition beyond a wink; and Dicky felt grateful for Kiddo's obvious fear of compromising him. Once old Beveridge came by, striding rapidly, his tatters flying, and the legend 'Hard Up' chalked on his hat, as was his manner in his town rambles. He stopped abruptly at sight of Dicky, stooped, and said: 'Dicky Perrott? Hum—hum—hey?' Then he hurried on, doubtless conceiving just such a fear as Kiddo Cook's. As for Tommy Rann, his affections were alienated by Dicky's outset refusal to secrete treacle in a tin mug for a midnight carouse; and he did not show himself. So matters went for near a week.

But Mr Weech missed Dicky sadly. It was rare for a day to pass without a visit from Dicky, and Dicky had a way of bringing good things. Mr Weech would not have sold Dicky's custom for ten shillings a week. So that when Mr Weech inquired, and found that Dicky was at work in an oil-shop, he was naturally annoyed. Moreover, if Dicky Perrott got into *that* way of life, he would have no fear for himself, and might get talking inconveniently among his new friends about the business affairs of Mr Aaron Weech. And at this reflection that philanthropist grew thoughtful.

19

DICKY had gone on an errand, and Mr Grinder was at the shop door, when there appeared before him a whiskered and smirking figure, with a quick glance each way along the street, and a long and smiling one at the oil-man's necktie.

'Good mornin', Mr Grinder, good mornin', sir.' Mr Weech stroked his left palm with his right fist and nodded pleasantly. 'I'm in business meself, over in Meakin Street—name of Weech: p'raps you know the shop? I—I jist 'opped over to ask'—Grinder led the way into the shop—'to ask (so's to make things quite sure y'know, though no doubt it's all right) to ask if it's correct you're awfferin' brass roastin'-jacks at a shillin' each.'

'Brass roastin'-jacks at a shillin'?' exclaimed Grinder, shocked at the notion. 'Why, no!'

Mr Weech appeared mildly surprised. 'Nor yut seven-poun' jars o' jam an' pickles at sixpence?' he pursued, with his eye on those ranged behind the counter.

'No!'

'Nor doormats at fourpence?'

'Fourpence? Cert'nly not!'

Mr Weech's face fell into a blank perplexity. He pawed his ear with a doubtful air, murmuring absently: 'Well I'm sure 'e *said* fourpence: an' sixpence for pickles, an' bring 'em round after the shop was shut. But there,' he added, more briskly, 'there's no 'arm done, an' no doubt it's a mistake.' He turned as though to leave, but Grinder restrained him.

'But look 'ere,' he said, 'I want to know about this. Wotjer mean? 'Oo was going to bring round pickles after the shop was shut? 'Oo said fourpence for doormats?'

'Oh, I expect it's jest a little mistake, that's all,' answered Weech, making another motion toward the door; 'an' I don't want to git nobody into trouble.'

'Trouble? Nice trouble I'd be in if I sold brass smoke-jacks for a bob! There's somethink 'ere as I ought to know about. Tell me about it straight.'

Weech looked thoughtfully at the oil-man's top waistcoat button for a few seconds, and then said: 'Yus, p'raps I better. I can feel for you, Mr Grinder, 'avin' a feelin' 'art, an' bein' in business meself. Where's your boy?'

'Gawn out.'

'Comin' back soon?'

'Not yut. Come in the back parlour.'

There Mr Weech, with ingenuous reluctance, assured Mr Grinder that Dicky Perrott had importuned him to buy the goods in question at the prices he had mentioned, together with others —readily named now that the oil-man swallowed so freely—and that they were to be delivered and paid for at night when Dicky left work. But perhaps, Mr Weech concluded, parading an obstinate belief in human nature, perhaps the boy, being new to the business, had mistaken the prices, and was merely doing his best to push his master's trade.

'No fear o' that,' said Grinder, shaking his head gloomily. 'Not the least fear o' that. 'E knows the cheapest doormats I got's one an' six—I 'eard him tell customers so outside a dozen times; an' anyone can see the smoke jacks is ticketed five an' nine'—as Mr Weech had seen, when he spoke of them. 'I thought that boy was too eager an' willin' to be quite genavin,' Dicky's master went on. ''E ain't 'ad me yut, that's one comfort: if anythin' 'ud bin gawn I'd 'a' missed it. But out 'e goes as soon as 'e comes back: you can take yer davy o' that!'

'Ah,' replied Mr Weech, 'it's fearful the wickedness there is about, ain't it? It's enough to break yer 'art. Sich a neighb'r'ood too! Wy, if it was known as I'd give you this 'ere little friendly information, bein' in business meself an' knowin' wot it is, my life wouldn't be safe a hower. It wouldn't, Mr Grinder.'

'Wouldn't it?' said Mr Grinder. 'You mean them in the Jago, I s'pose.'

'Yus. They're a awful lot, Mr Grinder—you've no idear. The father o' this 'ere boy as I've warned you aginst, 'e's in with a desprit gang, an' they'd murder me if they thought I'd come an' told you honest, w'en you might 'a' bin robbed, as is my nature to. They would indeed. So o' course you won't say wot I toldjer, nor 'oo give you this 'ere honourable friendly warnin'—not to nobody.'

'That's awright,' answered the simple Grinder, 'I won't let on.

134

But out 'e goes, promp'. I'm obliged to ye, Mr Weech. Er—r wot'll ye take?'

Weech put away the suggestion with a virtuous palm: 'Nothink at all, Mr Grinder, thanks all the same. I never touch nothink; an' I'm glad to—to do any moral job, so to speak, as comes in my way. "Scatter seeds o' kindness" you know, as the—the Psalm says, Mr Grinder. Your boy ain't back, is 'e?'

And after peering cautiously, Mr Weech went his way.

20

DICKY completed his round, and pushed his unladen trolley Grinder-ward with a fuller sense of responsibility than ever. For he carried money. A publican had paid him four and threepence, and he had taken two and tenpence elsewhere. He had left his proud signature, pencilled large and black, on two receipts, and he stopped in a dozen doorways to count the money over again, and make sure that all was right. Between the halts he added four and three to two and ten mentally, and proved his sum correct by subtracting each in turn from seven and a penny. And at last he stood his trolley on end by the bank of saucepans, and entered the shop.

'Walker's is paid, an' Wilkins is paid,' said Dicky, putting down the money. 'Two an' ten an' four an' three's seven an' a penny.'

Mr Grinder looked steadily and sourly at Dicky, and counted. He pitched the odd penny into the till and shook the rest of the coins in his closed hand, still staring moodily in the boy's face. 'It's three an' six a week you come 'ere at,' he said.

'Yus sir,' Dicky replied, since Grinder seemed to expect an answer. The supreme moment when he should take his first wages had been the week's beacon to him, reddening and brightening as Saturday night grew nearer.

'Three an' six a week an' yer tea.'

Dicky wondered.

'So as if I found out anythink about—say brass roastin'-jacks for instance—I could give ye yer three an' six an' start y'auf, unless I did somethin' wuss.'

Dicky was all incomprehension; but something made him feel a little sick.

'But s'posin' I *didn't* find out anythink about—say seven-pun' jars o' pickles—an' s'pose I wasn't disposed to suspect anythink in regard to—say, doormats; then I could either give ye a week's notice or pay y' a week's money an' clear y' out on the spot, without no more trouble.'

Mr Grinder paused, and still looked at Dicky with calm dislike.

Then he added, as though in answer to himself, 'Yus.' . . .

He dropped the money slowly from his right hand to his left. Dicky's mouth was dry, and the drawers and pickle-jars swam before him at each side of Grinder's head. What did it mean?

"Ere y' are,' cried Mr Grinder, with sudden energy, thrusting his hand across the counter. 'Two three-and-sixes is seven shillin's, an' you can git yer tea at 'ome with yer dirty little sister. Git out o' my shop!'

Dicky's hand closed mechanically on the money, and after a second's pause, he found broken speech. 'W—w—wot for, sir?' he asked huskily. 'I ain't done nothink!'

'No, an' you sha'n't do nothink, that's more. Out ye go! If I see ye near the place agin I'll 'ave ye locked up!'

Dicky slunk to the door. He felt the sobs coming, but he turned at the threshold and said with tremulous lips: 'Woncher gimme a chance, sir? S'elp me, I done me best. I—'

Mr Grinder made a short rush from the back of the shop, and Dicky gave up and fled.

It was all over. There could never be a shop with 'R. Perrott' painted over it, now; there would be no parlour with stuff-bottomed chairs and a piano for Em to play. He was cut off from the trolley for ever. Dicky was thirteen, and at that age the children of the Jago were past childish tears; but tears he could not smother, even till he might find a hiding-place: they burst out shamefully in the open street.

He took dark turnings, and hid his head in doorways. It was very bitter. At last, when the sobs grew fewer, he remembered the money gripped in his wet fist. It was a consolation. Seven shillings was a vast sum in Dicky's eyes; until that day he had never handled so much in his life. It would have been handsome recompense, he thought, for any trouble in the world but this. He must take it home, of course; it might avail to buy sympathy of his father and mother. But then, to think he might have had as much every fortnight of his life, a good tea every day, and the proud responsibility, and the trolley! At this his lips came awry again, his eyes sought his sleeve, and he turned to another doorway.

His glance fell on the white apron, now smudged and greased in good earnest. It made him feel worse; so he untied it and stuffed it away under his jacket. He wondered vaguely what had occurred to irritate Mr Grinder, and why he talked of pickles and doormats; but the sorrow of it all afflicted him to the extinction of such minor speculation. And in this misery he dragged his reluctant feet towards the Old Jago.

21

HE HANDED his father the seven shillings, and received a furious belting for losing his situation. He cried quietly, but it was not because of the strap. All he feared now was to meet Father Sturt. He had rather fifty beltings than Father Sturt's reproaches; and, having disgraced himself with Mr Grinder in some mysterious way which it was beyond his capacity to understand, what but reproaches could he expect from the vicar? The whole world was against him. As for himself, he was hopeless: plainly he must have some incomprehensible defect of nature, since he offended, do as he might, and could neither understand nor redeem his fault. He wondered if it had been so with little Neddy Wright, who had found the world too ruthless for him at ten; and had tied a brick to his neck, as he had seen done with needless dogs, and let himself timidly down into the canal at Haggerstone Bridge.

So he shuffled through Jago Row, when a hand came on his shoulder and a hoarse voice said: 'Wot's the matter, Dicky?'

He turned, and saw the mild, coarse face of Pigeony Poll, the jaw whereof was labouring on something tough and sticky. Poll pulled from her pocket a glutinous paper, clinging about a co-hesive lump of broken toffee—the one luxury of her moneyed times. ''Ave a bit,' she said. 'Wot's the matter?'

But Dicky thrust the hand away and fled, for he feared another burst of tears. His eyes were bad enough as it was, and he longed to hide himself in some hole.

He turned into New Jago Street. Hither it was that Jerry Gullen had betaken himself with his family and the Canary, after the great eviction. Dicky slackened his pace, loitered at Jerry's doorway, and presently found himself in the common passage. It was long since he had had a private interview with Jerry Gullen's canary: for, indeed, he was thirteen—he was no longer a child, in fact!—and it was not well that he should indulge in such foolish weakness. Nevertheless he went as far as the back door. There stood the old donkey, mangy and infirm as ever, but apparently no nearer the end. The wood of the fence was bitten in places, but it was not as yet gnawed to the general whiteness and roundness of that in the Canary's old abode. Canary, indeed, was fortunate to-day, for at the sound of Dicky's step he lifted his nose from a small heap of straw, dust, and mouldy hay, swept into a corner. Dicky stepped into the yard, and put his hand on Canary's neck; presently he glanced guiltily at the windows above. Nobody was looking. And in five minutes Dicky, aged as he was, had told Canary his troubles, while new tears wetted the ragged crest and dropped into the dusty straw.

Now his grief lost some of its edge. Ashamed as he was, he had a shapeless, unapprehended notion that Canary was the sole creature alive that could understand and feel with him. And Canary poked his nose under the old jacket and sniffed in sympathy, as the broken lining tickled him. Dicky's intellectuals began to arrange themselves. Plainly Mr Weech's philosophy was right after all. He was of the Jago, and he must prey on the outer world, as all the Jago did; not stray foolishly off the regular track in chase of visions, and fall headlong. Father Sturt was a creature of another mould. Who was he, Dicky Perrott, that he should break away from the Jago habit, and strain after another nature? What could come of it but defeat and bitterness? As old Beveridge had said, the Jago had got him. Why should he fight against the inevitable, and bruise himself? The ways out of the Jago old Beveridge had told him, years ago. Gaol, the gallows, and the High Mob. There was his chance, his aspiration, his goal: the High Mob. To dream of oil-shops or regular wages was foolishness. His bed was made in the Jago, and he must lie on it. His hope in life, if he might have a hope at all, was to be of the High Mob. Spare nobody, stop at nothing, do his devilmost: old Beveridge had said that years ago. The task was before him, and he must not balk at it. As for gaol and the gallows, well! There they were, and he could not help it; ill ways out of the Jago, both, but still—ways out.

He rubbed his face carefully with his sleeve, put away his foolish ambitions, and went forth with a brave heart: to accomplish his destiny, for well or ill—a Jago rat. To do his devilmost. But to avoid Father Sturt.

Out he went into Shoreditch High Street, and there he prowled the evening away; there and in Norton Folgate. But he touched for nothing—nothing at all. He feared lest his week's honesty had damaged his training. Even an apple on a stall he failed at, and had to run. And then he turned into Bethnal Green Road.

But here a thought checked him suddenly. What of Mr Grinder? He had threatened to have Dicky locked up if he came near the shop again. But a child of the Jago knew too much to be frightened by such a threat as that. He went on. He felt interested to see how his late employer was getting along without him, and who was minding the goods outside the shop. Probably there was nobody: and this gave Dicky an idea.

He had forgotten his smudgy apron, folded and tucked away in the lining of his jacket. Now he pulled it out, and fastened it before him once more. He knew Mr Grinder's habits in the shop, and if he could seize a fitting opportunity he might be able, attired in his apron, to pick up or reach down any article that struck his fancy, fearless of interference from passers-by; for he would seem to be still shop-boy.

With that he hastened, for it was near closing time at Grinder's. He took the opposite side of the road, the better to observe unseen in the darkness. But Mr Grinder had already begun to carry things in from the pavement. As Dicky looked he came out with a long pole wherewith he unhooked from above a clattering cluster of pails and watering-pots, and a bunch of doormats. The doormats he let fall on the flags, while he carried in the pots and pails. Dicky knew that these pots and pails were kept at night in a shed behind the house; so he scuttled across the road, opening the blade of his old knife as he ran. He cut the string that held the mats together, selected a thick one, rolled it under his arm, and edged off into the shadow. Then he ran quietly across to the nearest turning.

Presently Mr Grinder came out, hooked his finger in the string among the mats, and pulled up nothing. He stooped, and saw that the string was cut. He looked about him suspiciously, flung the mats over, and counted them. Then he stood erect; stared up the street, down the street, and across the road, with his mouth open; and made short rushes left and right into the gloom. Then he returned to the mats and scratched his head. Finally, he gave another glance about the street, picked up the mats in his arms and carried them in, counting them as he went. And, the mats bestowed, whenever he came forth for a fresh armful of

141

saucepans, he stood and gazed doubtfully, now this way, now that, about the Bethnal Green Road.

Mr Aaron Weech was pushing his last shutter into its place when 'Clean the knives,' said Dicky Perrott, in perfunctory repetition of the old formula.

Mr Weech seemed taken aback. 'Wot, that?' he asked doubtfully, pointing at the doormat. Then, after a sharp look about the almost deserted street, he ran to Jago Row corner, twenty yards away, and looked down there. Nobody was hiding, and he came back. He led the way into the shop, and closed the door. Then, looking keenly in Dicky's face, he suddenly asked: ''Oo toldjer to bring that 'ere?'

'Told me?' Dicky answered sullenly. 'Nobody told me. Don'cher want it?'

''Ow much did 'e tell ye t' ask for it?'

'Tell me? 'Oo?'

'*You* know. 'Ow much didjer say 'e said?'

Dicky was mystified. 'Dunno wotcher mean,' he replied.

Mr Weech suddenly broke into a loud laugh, but kept his keen look on the boy's face, nevertheless. 'Ah, it's a good joke, Dicky, ain't it?' he said, and laughed again. 'But you can't 'ave me, ye know! Mr Grinder's a old friend o' mine, an' I know 'is little larks. Wot did 'e tell ye to do if I wouldn't 'ave that doormat?'

'Tell me?' asked Dicky, plainly more mystified than ever. 'Wy 'e never told me nothink. 'E gimme the sack this afternoon, an' chucked me out.'

'Then wotcher got yer apron on now for?'

'Oh,' said Dicky, looking down at it, 'I jist put it on agin—o' purpose.' And he glanced at the mat.

Mr Weech understood, and grinned—a genuine grin this time. 'That's right, Dicky,' he said, 'never let yer wits go a-ramblin'. A sharp boy like you's a lot too good for a shop-boy, slavin' away from mornin' till night, an' treated ungrateful. Wot did 'e sack ye for?'

'I dunno. Took a fit in 'is 'ead, I s'pose. Wotcher goin' to gimme for this mat? It's a two an' three mat.'

'Want somethink to eat, doncher?' suggested Mr Weech, glancing at a heap of stale cake.

'No I don't,' Dicky answered, with sulky resolution. 'I want money.'

142

'Awright,' said Mr Weech resignedly. 'You ain't 'ad much to eat an' drink 'ere for a long time, though. But I'll do the 'an'some, seein' you're bin treated ungrateful by Grinder. 'Ere's twopence.'

But Dicky held to the mat. 'Twopence ain't enough,' he said. 'I want fourpence.' He meant to spare nobody—not even Mr Weech.

'Wot? Fourpence?' gasped Mr Weech indignantly. 'Wy, you're mad. Take it away.'

Dicky rolled the mat under his arm and turned to the door.

''Ere,' said Mr Weech, seeing him going, 'I'll make it thrippence, seein' you're bin treated so bad. Thrippence—*and* a slice o' cake,' he added, perceiving that Dicky did not hesitate.

'I don't want no cake,' Dicky answered doggedly. 'I want fourpence, an' I won't take no less.'

The good Weech was unwilling that Dicky should find another market after all, so he submitted to the extortion. 'Ah well,' he said, with a sigh, pulling out the extra coppers, 'jist for this once, then. You'll 'ave to make it up next time. Mindjer, it's on'y 'cos I'm sorry for ye bein' treated ungrateful. Don't *you* go an' treat *me* ungrateful, now.'

Dicky pocketed his pence and made for home, while Mr Weech, chuckling gently at his morning prophecy of a doormat for fourpence, carried the plunder to the room reserved for new and unused stock; promising himself, however, a peep at Grinder's shop in the morning, to make quite sure that Dicky had really left.

So ended Dicky's dealings with the house of Grinder. When Father Sturt next saw the oil-man, and inquired of Dicky's progress, he was met with solemn congratulations that no larcenies were to pay for. Mr Grinder's sagacity, it seemed, had enabled him to detect and crush at the outset Dicky's plans for selling stock wholesale on his own account. Out of consideration for the vicar's recommendation he had refrained from handing the boy over to the police, but had paid him a week in advance and dismissed him. Father Sturt insisted on repaying the money, and went his way with a heavy heart. For if this were what came of the promising among his flock, what of the others? For some while he saw nothing of Dicky; and the incident fell back among a crowd of others in his remembrance: for Dicky was but one among thousands, and the disappointment was but one of many hundreds.

Lying awake that night, but with closed eyes, Dicky heard his mother, talking with his father, suggest that perhaps an enemy had earwigged Grinder, and told him a tale that had brought about Dicky's dismissal: somebody, perhaps, who wanted the situation for somebody else. Josh Perrott did no more than grunt at the guess, but it gave a new light to Dicky. Clearly that would account for Grinder's change. But who could the mischief-maker be?

The little clock on the mantelpiece ticked away busily in the silence, and Dicky instantly thought of the hunchback. He it must have been, without a doubt. Who else? Was he not hanging about the shop, staring and sneering, but a day or two back? And was it not he who had pursued him with malice on every occasion, in school and out? Had not Bobby Roper this very trick of lying tales? Where was the gratuitous injury in all these four years that had not been Bobby Roper's work? Dicky trembled with rage as he lay, and he resolved on condign revenge. The war with Dove Lane was over for the time being, but that made it easier for him to catch his enemy.

22

THE FEUD between the Jago and Dove Lane was eternal, just as was that between the Ranns and the Learys; but, like the Rann and Leary feud, it had its paroxysms and its intervals. And in both cases, the close of a paroxysm was signalised by a great show of amity between the factions. Bob Rann and Billy Leary would drink affably from the same pot, and Norah Walsh and Sally Green would call each other 'mum'; while Jagos and Dove-Laners would mingle in bars and lend pinches of tobacco, and call each other 'matey'. A paroxysm in the war had now passed, and reconciliation was due. The Dove-Laners had been heavily thrashed: their benjamins and kicksies had been impounded in Meakin Street, and they had ceased from buying. Dove Lane itself had been swept from end to end by the victorious Jago, and the populations of both were dotted thickly with bandaged heads. This satisfactory state of things achieved, there was little reason left for fighting. Moreover, if fighting persisted too long at a time, the police were apt to turn up in numbers, subjecting the neighbourhood to much inconvenient scrutiny, and very often coming across Jagos—or even Dove-Laners—'wanted' on old accounts. So peace was declared; and, as a visible sign thereof, it was determined that the Dove-Laners should visit the Jago in a body, there to join in a sing-song at Mother Gapp's. Mother Gapp's was chosen, not only because it *was* Mother Gapp's—an important consideration—but also because of the large room behind the bar, called the 'club-room', which had long ago been made of two rooms and a big cupboard, by the cutting away of crazy partitions from the crazy walls.

Scarce was it dark when the Dove-Laners, in a succession of hilarious groups—but withal a trifle suspicious—began to push through Mother Gapp's doors. Their caps pulled down to their ears, their hands in their pockets, their shoulders humped, and their jackets buttoned tight, they lurched through the Jago, grinning with uneasy affability at the greetings that met them, being less practised than the Jagos in the assumption of elaborate cordiality.

In the club-room of the Feathers there were but three or four of the other party, though the bar was packed. The three or four, of whom Josh Perrott was one, were by way of a committee of stewards deputed to bid the Dove-Laners welcome, and to help them to seats. The Jagos were in some sort in the situation of hosts, and it had been decided after debate that it would ill become them to take their places till their guests were seated. The punctilio of the Jago on such occasions was a marvel ever.

So Josh Perrott stood at one side of the club-room door and Billy Leary at the other, shaking hands with all who entered, and strenuously maintaining cheerful grins. Now the Jago smile was a smile by itself, unlike the smiles in other places. It faded suddenly, and left the face—the Jago face—drawn and sad and startling by contrast, as of a man betrayed into mirth in the midst of great sorrow. So that a persistent grin was known for a work of conscious effort.

The Dove-Laners came in still larger numbers than had been expected, and before long it was perceived that there would be little space in the club-room, if any at all, for the Jagos. Already the visitors seemed to fill the place, but they still kept coming, and found places by squeezing. There was some doubt as to what had best be done. Meanwhile the sing-song began, for at least a score were anxious to 'oblige' at once, and every moment fresh volunteers arose. Many Dove-Laners stood up, and so made more room; but more came, and still more, till the club-room could hold not another, and the very walls were like to burst. Under the low ceiling hung a layer of smoke that obscured the face of the man standing on the table at the end to sing; and under the smoke was a close-packed array of heads, hats, and clay pipes, much diversified by white bandages and black eyes.

Such Dove-Laners as came in now were fain to find places in the bar, if they could; and a crowd of Jagos, men and women, hung about the doors of the Feathers. More fortunate than other boys, Dicky, who would go anywhere to hear what purported to be music, had succeeded in worming himself through the bar and almost to the door of the club-room; but he could get no farther, and now he stood compressed, bounded on the face by Cocko Harnwell's coat-tails, and on the back of the head by Fluffy Pike's moleskin waistcoat, with pearlies down the front and the artful dodge over the pockets. Pud Palmer—one of the reception committee—was singing. He accompanied his chorus by a step dance, and all the company stamped in sympathy—

> 'She's a fighter, she's a biter, she's a swearer, she's a tearer,
>   The gonophs down aar alley they calls 'er Rorty Sal;
>   But as I'm a pertikiler sort o' bloke, I calls 'er Rorty SAIRER,
>   I'm goin'—'

Crack!—CRASH!

Dicky clung to Cocko Harnwell's coat-tails lest he were trampled to death; and for a while he was flung about, crushed and bruised, among rushing men, like a swimmer among breakers, while the air was rent with howls and the smash of glass. For the club-room floor had given way.

It had been built but slightly in the beginning, as floor for two small rooms and a cupboard, with little weight to carry. Old and rotten now, and put to the strain of a multitude, stamping in unison, it had failed utterly, and had let down a struggling mob of men five feet on the barrels in the cellar, panic-stricken and jumbled with tables, pots, wooden forms, lighted pipes, and splintered joinery.

From the midst of the stramash, a Dove-Laner bawled aloud that it was a trap, and instantly Jagos and Dove-Laners were at each other's throats, and it was like to go hard with the few Jagos among the ruins. Billy Leary laid about him desperately with a ragged piece of flooring, while Josh Perrott and Pud Palmer battered Dove-Laners with quart pots. Then it was shouted without that the Dove-Laners were exterminating the Jagos within, and a torrent of Jagos burst through the doors, poured through the bar, and over the club-room threshold into the confusion below.

Dicky, bruised, frightened and flung like a rag this way and that, at last made shift to grasp a post, and climb up on the bar counter. Mother Gapp, a dishevelled maniac, was dancing amid pots and broken glass, black in the face, screaming inaudibly. Dicky stumbled along the counter, climbed over the broken end of a partition, and fell into the arms of Kiddo Cook, coming in with the rush. 'Put the boy out!' yelled Kiddo, turning and heaving him over the heads behind him. Somebody caught Dicky by a leg and an arm, his head hit the door post, the world turned a double-somersault about him, and he came down with a crash.

He was on the flags of Old Jago Street, with all his breath driven out of him.

But he was quickly on his feet again. A crowd beat against the front of Mother Gapp's, and reinforcements came running from everywhere, with the familiar rallying-cry, 'Jago! Jago 'old tight!' Dove Lane had abused the Jago hospitality; woe to the Dove-Laners!

There were scuffles here and there, where Dove-Laners, who had never reached the club-room, or who had been crowded out of it, made for escape. Dicky was shaken and sore, but he pulled himself together resolutely. He had seen a few Dove Lane boys about before he had got into the Feathers, and plainly it was his duty to find them and bash them. Moreover, he wondered what had become of his father. He hastened through the dark passage of the house next to Mother Gapp's, into the back yard, and through the broken fence. There was a door in the club-room wall, and through this he thought to see what was going forward.

The cellar—at any rate, at the farther end—was a pit of writhing forms, and the din rose loud as ever. A short figure stood black against the light, and held by the doorpost, looking down at the riot. Dicky knew it. He sprang at Bobby Roper, pulled him by the arm, and struck at him furiously. The hunchback, whimpering, did his best to retaliate and to get away; but Dicky, raging at the remembrance of his fancied injury, struck savagely, and struck again, till Bobby Roper tripped backward over the projecting end of a broken floorboard, and pitched headlong into the cellar. He struck a barrel and rolled over, falling into the space between that and two other barrels. Dicky looked, but the hunchback did not move. Then some of the Dove-Laners flung pots at the lamps hanging against the club-room walls. Soon they were smashed and fell, and there was a darkness; and under cover thereof the aliens essayed flight.

Dicky was a little frightened at what he had done, but he felt that with Bobby Roper anything was justifiable. Some Dove-Laners escaped by the back door—the cellar was low, and there was not five feet between the barrels and the broken joists—and these Dicky avoided by getting back through the fence. In the end, most of the enemy struggled away by one means or another, and when lights were brought at last the Jagos were found pummelling each other savagely in the gloom.

Father Sturt, apprised of something uncommon by the exodus of members from the club, finally locked the doors and came to investigate. He arrived as the Jagos were extricating themselves from the cellar, and it was he who lifted the little hunchback from among the barrels and carried him into the open air; he also who carried him home. No bone was broken, and no joint was disturbed, but there was a serious shock, many contusions, and a cut on the scalp. So said the surgeon whom Father Sturt took with him to Dove Lane. And Bobby Roper lay a fortnight in bed.

More plaster than ever embellished the heads of Dove Lane and the Jago that night; but for the Jagos there was compensation. For down among the barrels lay many a packet of tobacco, many a pair of boots, and many a corner stuffed with mixed property of other sorts: which Mother Gapp had fenced for many a month back. So that it happened to more than one warrior to carry home again something with which he had run between the 'Posties' long before, and had sold to Mother Gapp for what she would give.

The ground floor of the Feathers stood a battered shell. The damage of four years ago was inconsiderable compared to this. With tears and blasphemy Mother Gapp invaded the hoard of her long iniquity to buy a new floor; but it was the larceny—the taking of the tobacco and the boots, and the many other things from among the barrels—that cut her to the soul. A crool—a crool thing was such robbery—sheer robbery, said Mother Gapp.

Josh Perrott got a bad sprain in the cellar and had to be helped home. More, he took with him not a single piece of plunder, such was his painful disablement.

23

For more than a week Josh Perrott could not walk about. And it was a bad week. For some little while his luck had been but poor, and now he found himself laid up with a total reserve fund of fourteenpence. A coat was pawned with old Poll Rann (who kept a leaving shop in a first floor back in Jago Row) for ninepence. Then Josh swore at Dicky for not being still at Grinder's, and told him to turn out and bring home some money. Dicky had risen, almost too sore and stiff to stand, on the morning after the fight at the Feathers, and he was little better now. But he had to go, and he went, though he well knew that a click was out of the question, for his joints almost refused to bend. But he found that the fat's a-running boys were contemplating business, and he scouted for them with such success as to bring home sevenpence in the evening. Then Kiddo Cook, who had left Mother Gapp's with a double armful on the night of the sing-song, found himself rich enough, being a bachelor, to lend Josh eighteenpence. And a shawl of Hannah Perrott's was pawned. That, though, was redeemed the next day, together with the coat. For Dicky brought home a golden sovereign.

It had been an easy click—scarce a click at all, perhaps, strictly speaking. Dicky had tramped into the city, and had found a crowd outside St Paul's—a well-dressed crowd, not being moved on; for something was going forward in the cathedral. He recognised one of the High Mob, a pogue-hunter—that is a pickpocket who deals in purses. Dicky watched this man's movements, by way of education; for he was an eminent practitioner, and worked alone, with no assistant to cover him. Dicky saw him in the thick of the crowd, standing beside and behind one lady after another; but it was only when his elbow bent to slip something into his own pocket that Dicky knew he had 'touched'. Presently he moved to another part of the crowd, where mostly men were standing, and there he stealthily let drop a crumpled newspaper, and straightway left the crowd. He had 'worked' it as much as he judged safe. Dicky wriggled toward the crumpled paper, slipped it under his jacket, and cleared away also. He knew that there was something in the paper besides news: that, in fact, there were purses in it—purses emptied and shed as soon as might be, because nobody can swear to money, but strange purses lead to destruction. Dicky recked little of this danger, but made his best pace to a recess in a back street, there to examine his pogues; for though the uxter was gone from them, they might yet bring a few coppers from Mr Weech, if they were of good quality. They were a fairly sound lot. One had a large clasp that looked like silver, and another was quite new, and Dicky was observing with satisfaction the shop-shininess of the lining, when he perceived a cunning pocket at the back, lying flat against the main integument—and in it was a sovereign! He gulped at the sight. Clearly the pogue-hunter, emptying the pogues in his pocket by sense of touch, had missed the flat pocket. Dicky was not yet able to run with freedom, but he never ceased from trotting till he reached his own staircase in Old Jago Street. And so the eight or nine days passed, and Josh went out into the Jago with no more than a tenderness about his ankle.

Now, he much desired a good click; so he went across High Street Shoreditch, to Kingsland Railway Station and bought a ticket for Canonbury.

Luck was against him, it was plain. He tramped the northern suburbs from three o'clock till dark, but touched for nothing. He spent money, indeed, for he feared to overwork his ankle, and for that reason rested in divers public-houses. He peeped in at the gates of quiet gardens, in the hope of garden-hose left unwatched, or tennis-rackets lying in a handy summer-house. But he saw none. He pried about the doors of private stable-yards, in case of absent grooms and unprotected bunches of harness; but in vain. He inspected quiet areas and kitchen entrances in search of unguarded spoons—even descended into one area, where he had to make an awkward excuse about buying old bottles, in consequence of meeting the cook at the door. He tramped one quiet road after another on the look out for a dead 'un—a house furnished, but untenanted. But there was never a dead 'un, it seemed, in all the northern district. So he grew tired and short-tempered, and cursed himself for that he had not driven off with a baker's horse and cart that had tempted him early in the afternoon.

It grew twilight, and then dark. Josh sat in a public-house, and took a long rest and some bread and cheese. It would never do to go home without touching, and for some time he considered possibilities with regard to a handful of silver money, kept in a glass on a shelf behind the bar. But it was out of reach, and there were too many people in the place for any attempt by climbing on the counter. Josh grew savage and soured. Plastering itself was not such troublesome work; and at least the pay was certain. It was little short of ten o'clock when he left the public-house and turned back toward Canonbury. He would have *something* on the way, he resolved, and he would catch the first train home. He would have to knock somebody over in a dark street, that was all. It was nothing new, but he would rather have made his click another way this time, because his tender ankle might keep him slow, or even give way altogether; and to be caught in a robbery with violence might easily mean something more than mere imprisonment; it might mean a dose of the 'cat': and the cat was a thing the thought or the mention whereof sent shudders through the Old Jago.

But no: nobody worth knocking down came his way. Truly luck was out to-night. There was a spot by the long garden wall of a corner house that would have suited admirably, and as Josh lingered there, and looked about him, his eye fell on a ladder, reared nearly upright against the back wall of that same corner house, and lashed at the roof. It passed by the side of the second floor window, whereof the top sash was a little open. That would do. It was not his usual line of work, but it looked very promising.

He stuck his stick under his waistcoat by way of the collar, and climbed the wall with gingerly care, giving his sound foot all the hard work. The ladder offered no difficulty, but the bottom sash of the window was stiff, and he cracked a pane of glass in pushing at the frame with his stick. The sash lifted, however, in the end, and he climbed into the dark room, being much impeded by the dressing-table. All was quiet in the house, and the ticking of a watch on the dressing-table was distinct in the ear. Josh felt for it and found it, with a chain hanging from the bow.

The house was uncommonly quiet. Could it possibly be a dead 'un after all? Josh felt that he ought to have inspected the front windows before climbing the wall, but the excitement of the long-delayed chance had ruined his discretion. At any rate he would reconnoitre. The door was ajar and the landing was dark.

Down in the drawing-room a gross, pimply man, in shirt-sleeves and socks, sat up on the sofa at the sound of an opened window higher in the house. He took a drink from the glass by his side, and listened. Then he rose and went softly upstairs.

Josh Perrott came out on the landing. It was a long landing, with a staircase at the end, illuminated from somewhere below: so that it was not a case of a dead 'un after all. He tiptoed along to take a look down the stairs, nevertheless. Then he was conscious of a loud breathing, as of an over-gorged cow, and up behind the stair-rails rose a fat head, followed by a fat trunk, between white shirt-sleeves.

Josh sank into the shadow. The man had no light, but discover him he must, sooner or later, for the landing was narrow. Better sooner, and suddenly. As the man's foot was on the topmost stair, Josh sprang at him with a straight left-hander that took him on the broad chin, and sent him downstairs in a heap, with a crash and a roar. Josh darted back to the room he had just left, scrambled through the window, and slid down the ladder, as he had slid down many another when he was a plasterer's boy. He checked himself short of the bottom, sprang at the wall-coping, flung himself over, and ran up the dark by-street, with the sound of muffled roars and screams faint in his ears.

He ran a street or two, taking every corner as he came to it, and then fell into a walk. In his flight he had not spared his ankle, and now it was painful. Moreover, he had left his stick behind him, in the bedroom. But he was in Highbury, and Canonbury Road Station was less than half a mile away. He grinned silently as he went, for there was something in the aspect of the overfed householder, and in the manner of his downfall, that gave the adventure a comic flavour. He took a peep at his spoil as he passed under a street lamp, for all watches and chains are the same in the dark, and the thing might be a mere Waterbury on a steel guard. But no: both were gold, and heavy: a red clock and slang if ever there was one. And so Josh Perrott hobbled and chuckled his way home.

24

BUT INDEED Josh Perrott's luck was worse than he thought. For the gross, pimply man was a High Mobsman—so very high a mobsman that it would have been slander and libel, and a very great expense, to write him down a mobsman at all. He paid a rent of a hundred and twenty pounds a year, and heavy rates, and put half a crown into the plate at a very respectable chapel every Sunday. He was, in fact, the King of High Mobsmen, spoken of among them as the Mogul. He did no vulgar thievery: he never screwed a chat, nor claimed a peter, nor worked the mace. He sat easily at home, and financed (sometimes planned) promising speculations: a large swindle requiring much ground-baiting and preliminary outlay; or a robbery of specie from a mail train; or a bank fraud needing organisation and funds. When the results of such speculations consisted of money he took the lion's share. When they were expressed in terms of imprisonment they fell to active and intelligent subordinates. So that for years the Mogul had lived an affluent and a blameless life, far removed from the necessity of injudicious bodily exercise, and characterised by every indulgence consistent with a proper suburban respectability. He had patronised, snubbed, or encouraged High Mobsmen of more temerarious habit, had profited by their exploits, and had read of their convictions and sentences with placid interest in the morning papers. And after all this, to be robbed in his own house and knocked downstairs by a casual buster was an outrage that afflicted the Mogul with wrath infuriate. Because that was a sort of trouble that had never seemed a possibility, to a person of his eminence: and because the angriest victim of dishonesty is a thief.

However, the burglar had got clean away, that was plain; and he had taken the best watch and chain in the house, with the Mogul's initials on the back. So that respectable sufferer sent for the police, and gave his attention to the alleviation of bumps and the washing away of blood. In his bodily condition a light blow was enough to let a great deal of blood—no doubt with benefit; and Josh Perrott's blows were not light in any case.

So it came to pass that not only were the police on the look-out for a man with a large gold watch with the Mogul's monogram on the back; but also the word was passed as by telegraph through underground channels, till every fence in London was warned that the watch was the Mogul's; and ere noon next day there was not one but would as lief have put a scorpion in his pocket as that same toy and tackle that Josh Perrott was gloating over in his back room in Old Jago Street.

As for Josh, his ankle was bad in the morning, and swelled. He dabbed at it perseveringly with wet rags, and rubbed it vigorously, so that by one o'clock he was able to lace up his boot and go out. He was anxious to fence his plunder without delay, and he made his way to Hoxton. The watch seemed to be something especially good, and he determined to stand out for a price well above the usual figure. For the sway of common thieves commanded no such prices as did that of the High Mob. All of it was bought and sold on the simple system first called into being seventy years back and more by the prince of fences, Ikey Solomons. A breastpin brought a fixed sum, good or bad, and a roll of cloth brought the fixed price of a roll of cloth, regardless of quality. Thus a silver watch fetched six shillings, never more and never less; a gold watch was worth twice as much; an uncommonly good one—a rich man's watch—would bring as much as eighteen shillings, if the thief were judge enough of its quality to venture the demand. And as it commonly took three men to secure a single watch in the open street—one to 'front', one to snatch, and a third to take from the snatcher—the gains of the toy-getting trade were poor, except to the fence. This time Josh resolved to put pressure on the fence, and to do his best to get something as near a sovereign as might be. And as to the chain, so thick and heavy, he would fight his best for the privilege of sale by weight. Thus turning the thing in his mind, he entered the familiar doorway of the old clothes shop.

'Vot is id?' asked the fence, holding out his hand with the customary air of contempt for what was coming, by way of discounting it in advance. This particular fence, by-the-bye, never bought anything himself. He inspected whatever was brought on behalf of an occult friend; and the transaction was completed by a shabby third party in an adjoining court. But he had an amazingly keen regard for his friend's interests.

Josh put the watch into the extended hand. The fence lifted it to his face, turned it over, and started. He looked hard at Josh, and then again at the watch, and handed it hastily back, holding it gingerly by the bow. 'Don' vant *dot*,' he said; 'nod me—nod 'im, I mean. No, no.' He turned away, shaking his hand as though to throw off contamination. 'Take id avay.'

'Wot's the matter?' Josh demanded, astonished. 'Is it 'cos o' the letters on the back? You can easy send it to church, can't ye?'

A watch is 'sent to church' when it is put into another case. But the fence waved away the suggestion. 'Take id avay I tell you,' he said. 'I—'e von't 'ave nodden to do vid id.'

'Wot's the matter with the chain, then?' asked Josh. But the fence walked away to the back of the shop, wagging his hands desperately, like a wet man seeking a towel, and repeating only: 'Nodden to do vid id—take id avay—nodden to do vid id.'

Josh stuffed his prize back into his pocket, and regained the street. He was confounded. What was wrong with Cohen? Did he suspect a police trick to entrap him? Josh snorted with indignation at the thought. He was no nark! But perhaps the police were showing a pressing interest in Cohen's business concerns just now, and he had suspended fencing for a while. The guess was a lame one, but he could think of none better at the moment, as he pushed his way to the Jago. He would try Mother Gapp.

Mother Gapp would not even take the watch in her hands; her eyes were good enough at that distance. 'Lor', Josh Perrott,' she said, 'wot 'a' ye bin up to now? Want to git me lagged now, do ye? Ain't satisfied with breakin' up the 'ouse an' ruinin' a pore widder that way, ain't ye? You git out, go on. I 'ad 'nough o' you!'

It was very extraordinary. Was there a general reclamation of fences? But there were men at work at the Feathers, putting down boards and restoring partitions; and two of them had been 'gone over' ruinously on their way to work, and now they came and went with four policemen. Possibly Mother Gapp feared the observation of carpenters. Be it as it might, there was nothing for it now but Weech's.

Mr Weech was charmed. 'Dear me, it's a wonderful fine watch, Mr Perrott—a wonderful fine watch. An' a beautiful chain.' But he was looking narrowly at the big monogram as he said it. 'It's reely a wonderful article. 'Ow they do git 'em up, to be sure!

Cost a lot o' money too, I'll be bound. Might you be thinkin' o' sellin' it?'

'Yus o' course,' replied Josh. 'That's wot I brought it for.'

'Ah, it's a lovely watch, Mr Perrott—a lov-erly watch; an' the chain matches it. But you mustn't be too 'ard on me. Shall we say four pound for the little lot?'

It was more than double Josh's wildest hopes, but he wanted all he could get. 'Five,' he said doggedly.

Weech gazed at him with tender rebuke. 'Five pound's a awful lot o' money, Mr Perrott,' he said. 'You're too 'ard on me, reely. I 'ardly know 'ow I can scrape it up. But it's a beautiful little lot, an' I won't 'aggle. But I ain't got all that money in the 'ouse now. I never keep so much money in the 'ouse—sich a neighb'r'ood, Mr Perrot! Bring it round to-morrer mornin' at eleven.'

'Awright, I'll come. Five quid, mind.'

'Ah yus,' answered Mr Weech, with a reproving smile. 'It's reely more than I ought!'

Josh was jubilant, and forgot his sore ankle. He had never handled such a sum as five pounds since his fight with Billy Leary, years ago; when, indeed, he had stooped to folly in the shape of lavish treating, and so had not enjoyed the handling of the full amount.

Mr Weech, also, was pleased. For it was a great stroke of business to oblige so distinguished a person as the Mogul. There was no telling what advantages it might not lead to in the way of trade.

That night the Perrotts had a hot supper, brought from Walker's cookshop in paper. And at eleven the next morning Josh, twenty yards from Mr Weech's door, with the watch and chain in his pocket, was tapped on the arm by a constable in plain clothes, while another came up on the other side. 'Mornin', Perrott,' said the first constable cheerily. 'We've got a little business with you at the station.'

'Me? Wot for?'

'Oh well, come along; p'raps it ain't anything—unless there's a gold watch an' chain on you, from Highbury. It's just a turnin' over.'

'Awright,' replied Josh resignedly. 'It's a fair cop. I'll go quiet.'

'That's right, Perrott; it ain't no good playin' the fool, you know.' They were moving along; and as they came by Weech's shop, a whiskered face, with a patch of shining scalp over it, peeped from behind a curtain that hung at the rear of the bloaters and plumcake in the window. As he saw it, Josh ducked suddenly, wrenching his arm free, and dashed over the threshold. Mr Weech, whiskers and apron flying, galloped through the door at the back, and the constables sprang upon Josh instantly and dragged him into the street. 'Wotcher mean?' cried the one who knew him, indignantly, and with a significant glance at the other. 'Call that goin' quiet?'

Josh's face was white and staring with rage. 'Awright,' he grunted through his shut teeth, after a pause. 'I'll go quiet now. I ain't got nothin' agin *you*.'

25

Dicky's morning theft that day had been but a small one—he had run off with a new two-foot rule that a cabinet-maker had carelessly left on an unfinished office table at his shop door in Curtain Road. It was not much, but it might fetch some sort of a dinner at Weech's, which would be better than going home, and, perhaps, finding nothing. So about noon, all ignorant of his father's misfortune, he came by way of Holywell Lane and Bethnal Green Road to Meakin Street.

Mr Weech looked at him rather oddly, Dicky fancied, when he came in, but he took the two-foot rule with alacrity, and brought Dicky a rasher of bacon, and a slice of cake afterward. This seemed very generous. More: Mr Weech's manner was uncommonly amiable, and when the meal was over, of his own motion, he handed over a supplementary penny. Dicky was surprised; but he had no objection, and he thought little more about it.

As soon as he appeared in Luck Row, he was told that his father had been 'smugged'. Indeed the tidings had filled the Jago within ten minutes. Josh Perrott was walking quietly along Meakin Street—so went the news—when up comes Snuffy and another split, and smugs him. Josh had a go for Weech's door, to cut his lucky out at the back, but was caught. That was a smart notion of Josh's, the Jago opinion ran, to get through Weech's and out into the courts behind. But it was no go.

Hannah Perrott sat in her room, inert and lamenting. Dicky could not rouse her, and at last he went off by himself to reconnoitre about Commercial Street Police Station, and pick up what information he might; while a gossip or two came and took Mrs Perrott for consolation to Mother Gapp's. Little Em, unwashed, tangled and weeping, could well take care of herself and the room, being more than two years old.

Josh Perrott would be brought up to-morrow, Dicky ascertained, at the North London Police Court. So the next morning found Dicky trudging moodily along the two miles of flags to Stoke Newington Road; while his mother and three sympathising friends, who foresaw an opportunity for numerous tiny drops with interesting circumstances to flavour them, took a penny cast on the way in a tramcar.

Dicky, with some doubt as to the disposition of the door-keeping policeman toward ragged boys, waited for the four women, and contrived to pass in unobserved among them. Several Jagos were in the court, interested not only in Josh's adventure, but in one of Cocko Harnwell's, who had indulged, the night before, in an animated little scramble with three policemen in Dalston; and they waited with sympathetic interest while the luck was settled of a long string of drunk-and-disorderlies.

At last Josh was brought in, and lurched composedly into the dock, in the manner of one who knew the routine. The police gave evidence of arrest, in consequence of information received, and of finding the watch and chain in Josh's trousers pocket. The prosecutor, with his head conspicuously bedight with sticking-plaster, puffed and grunted up into the witness-box, kissed the book, and was a 'retired commission agent'. He positively identified the watch and chain, and he not less positively identified Josh Perrott, whom he had picked out from a score of men in the police-yard. This would have been a feat indeed for a man who had never seen Josh, and had only once encountered his fist in the dark, had it not been for the dutiful though private aid of Mr Weech: who, in giving his information, had described Josh and his one suit of clothes with great fidelity, especially indicating a scar on the right cheek-bone which would mark him among a thousand. The retired commission agent was quite sure of the prisoner. He had met him on the stairs, where there was plenty of light from a lamp, and the prisoner had attacked him savagely, beating him about the head and flinging him downstairs. The policeman called by the prosecutor's servant deposed to finding the prosecutor bruised and bleeding. There was a ladder against the back of the house; a bedroom window had been opened; there were muddy marks on the sill; and he had found the stick—produced—lying in the bedroom.

Josh leaned easily on the rail before him while evidence was being given, and said 'No, yer worship,' whenever he was asked if he desired to question a witness. He knew better than to run the risk of incriminating himself by challenging the prosecutor's well-coloured evidence; and, as it was a certain case of committal for trial, it would have been useless in any event. He made the same reply when he was asked if he had anything to say before being committed; and straightway was 'fullied'. He lurched serenely out of the dock, waving his cap at his friends in the court, and that was all. The Jagos waited till Cocko Harnwell got his three months and then retired to neighbouring public-houses; but Dicky remembered his little sister, and hurried home.

The month's session at the Old Bailey had just begun, so that Josh had no long stay at Holloway. Among the Jagos it was held to be a most creditable circumstance that Josh was to take his trial with full honours at the Old Bailey, and not at mere County Sessions at Clerkenwell, like a simple lob-crawler or peter-claimer. For Josh's was a case of burglary with serious violence, such as was fitting for the Old Bailey, and not even a High Mobsman could come to trial with greater glory. 'As like as not it's laggin' dues, after 'is other convictions,' said Bill Rann. And Jerry Gullen thought so too.

Dicky went, with his mother and Em, to see Josh at Newgate. They stood with other visitors, very noisy, before a double iron railing covered with wire-netting, at the farther side whereof stood Josh and other prisoners, while a screaming hubbub of question and answer filled the air. Josh had little to say. He lounged against the farther railing with his hands in his pockets, asked what Cocko Harnwell had got, and sent a message to Bill Rann; while his wife did little more than look dolefully through the wires, and pipe: 'Oh, Josh, wotever shall I do?' at intervals, with no particular emotion; while Em pressed her smudgy little face against the wires, and stared mightily; and while Dicky felt that if he had been younger he would have cried. When time was up, Josh waved his hand and slouched off, and his family turned out with the rest: little Em carrying into later years a memory of father as a man who lived in a cage.

In such a case as this, the Jago would have been for ever disgraced if Josh Perrott's pals had neglected to get up a 'break' or subscription to pay for his defence. Things were never very flourishing in the Jago. But this was the sort of break a Jago could not shirk, lest it were remembered against him when his own turn came. So enough was collected to brief an exceedingly junior counsel, who did his useless best. But the facts were too strong, even for the most inexperienced advocate; the evidence of the prosecutor was nowhere to be shaken, and the jury found a verdict of guilty without leaving the box—indeed, with scarce the formality of collecting their heads together over the rails. Then Josh's past was most unpleasantly raked up before him. He had been convicted of larceny, of assaulting the police, and of robbery with violence. There were two sentences of six months' imprisonment recorded against him, one of three months, and two of a month. Besides fines. The Recorder considered it a very serious offence. Not deterred by the punishments he had already received, the prisoner had proceeded to a worse crime—burglary; and with violence. It was plain that lenience was wasted in such a case, and simple imprisonment was not enough. There must be an exemplary sentence. The prisoner must be kept in penal servitude for five years.

Lagging dues it was, as Bill Rann had anticipated. That Josh Perrott agreed with him was suggested by the fact that from the very beginning he had described himself as a painter; because a painter in prison is apt to be employed at times in painting—a lighter and a more desirable task than falls to the lot of his fellows in other trades.

In a room by the court Josh saw his wife, Dicky, and Bill Rann (Josh's brother-in-law for the occasion) before his ride to Holloway, his one stopping place on the way to Chelmsford Gaol. Little Em had been left sprawling in the Jago gutters. This time Hannah Perrott wept in good earnest, and Dicky, notwithstanding his thirteen years, blinked very hard at the wall before him. The arrangement of Josh's affairs was neither a long nor a difficult labour. 'S'pose you'll 'ave to do wot you can with rush bags, an' sacks, an' match-boxes, an' wot not,' he said to his wife, and she assented. Josh nodded: 'An' if you 'ave to go in the 'ouse'—he meant the workhouse—'well, it can't be 'elped. You won't be no wuss auf 'n me.'

'Oh, *she'll* be awright,' said Bill Rann, jerking his thumb cheerfully toward the missis. 'Wot about you? Think they'll make it Parkhurst?'

Josh shook his head moodily. Parkhurst being the prison reserved for convicts of less robust habit, he had little hope of enjoying its easier conditions. Presently he said: 'I bin put away this time—fair put away.'

'Wot?' answered Bill, 'narkin' dues is it?'

Josh nodded.

"'Oo done it then? 'Oo narked?'

Josh shook his head. 'Never mind,' he said, 'I don't want 'im druv out o' the Jago 'fore I come out. I'd be sorry to miss 'im. *I* know 'im—that's enough.'

And then time was up. Josh suffered the missis to kiss him, and shook hands with Bill Rann. 'Good luck to all you Jagos,' he said. Dicky shook hands too, and said 'Good-bye, father!' in a voice of such laboured cheerfulness that a grin burst for a moment amid Josh's moody features as he was marched away, and so departed for the place—in Jago idiom—where the dogs don't bite.

26

It was Father Sturt's practice to visit every family in his parish in regular order. But small as the parish was—insignificant, indeed, in mere area—its population exceeded eight thousand: so that the round was one of many months, for visiting was but one among innumerable duties. But Josh Perrott's lagging secured his family a special call. Not that the circumstances were in any way novel or at all uncommon; nor even that the vicar had any hope of being able to help. He was but the one man who could swim in a howling sea of human wreckage. In the Jago, wives like Hannah Perrott, temporarily widowed by the absence of husbands 'in the country', were to be counted in scores, and most were in worse case than she, in the matter of dependent children. Father Sturt's house-list revealed the fact that in Old Jago Street alone, near seventy of the males were at that moment on ticket-of-leave.

In the Perrott case, indeed, the sufferers were fortunate, as things went. Mrs Perrott had but herself and the child of two to keep, for Dicky could do something, whether good or bad, for himself. The vicar might try to get regular work for Dicky, but it would be a vain toil, for he must tell an employer what he knew of Dicky's past and of that other situation. He could but give the woman the best counsel at his command, and do what he might to quicken any latent spark of energy. So he did his best, and that was all. The struggle lay with Hannah Perrott.

She had been left before, and more than once; but then the periods had been shorter, and, as a matter of fact, things had fallen out so well that scarce more than a meal here and there had had to be missed, though, when they came, the meals were apt to be but of crusts. And now there was more trouble ahead; for though she began her lonely time with but one small child on hand, she knew that ere long there would be two.

Of course, she had worked before; not only when Josh had been 'in' but at other times, to add to the family resources. She was a clumsy needlewoman: else she might hope to earn some ninepence or a shilling a day at making shirts, by keeping well to the needle for sixteen hours out of the twenty-four; and from the whole sum there would be no deductions, except for needles and cotton, and what the frugal employer might choose to subtract for work to which he could devise an objection. But, as it was, she must do her best to get some sack-making. They paid one and sevenpence a hundred for sacks, and, with speed and long hours, she could make a hundred in four days. Rush bag-making would bring even more, which would be desirable, considering the three-and-sixpence a week for rent: which, with the payments for other rooms, made the rent of the crazy den in Old Jago Street about equal, space for space, to that of a house in Onslow Square. Then there was a more lucrative employment still, but one to be looked for at intervals only: one not to be counted on at all, in fact, for it was a prize, and many sought after it. This was the making of match-boxes. For making one hundred and forty-four outside cases with paper label and sandpaper, and the same number of trays to slide into them—a gross of complete boxes, or two hundred and eighty-eight pieces in all—one got twopence farthing; indeed, for a special size one even got a farthing a gross more; and all the wood and the labels and the sandpaper were provided free: so that the fortunate operator lost nothing out of the twopence farthing but the cost of the paste, and the string for tying up the boxes into regularly numbered batches, and the time employed in fetching the work and taking it back again. And if seven gross were to be got, and could be done in a day—and it was really not very difficult for the skilful hand who kept at work long enough —the day's income was one and threepence three-farthings, less expenses: still better that, than the shirts. But the work was hard to get. As the public-spirited manufacturers complained: people would buy Swedish matches, whereas if people would Support Home Industries and buy no matches but theirs, they would be able to order many a twopence-farthingsworth of boxes more.

There might be collateral sources of income, but these were doubtful and irregular. Probably Dicky would bring in a few coppers now and again. Then judicious attendance at churches, chapels, and prayer-meetings beyond the Jago borders was re-warded by coal-tickets, boots, and the like. It was necessary to know just where and when to go and what to say, else the sole result might be loss of time. There was a church in Bethnal Green, for instance, which it would be foolish to enter before the end of the

Litany, for then you were in good time to get your half-quarter hundredweight of coals; but at other places they might object to so late an appearance. Above all, one must know the ropes. There were several women in the Jago who made almost a living in this way alone. They were experts; they knew every fund, every meeting-house, all the comings and goings of the gullible; insomuch that they would take black umbrage at any unexpected difficulty in getting what they demanded. 'Wy,' one would say, 'I 'ad to pitch sich a bleed'n' 'oly tale I earned it twice over.' But these were the proficient, and proficiency in the trade was an outcome of long experience working on a foundation of natural gifts; and Hannah Perrott could never hope to be among them.

Turning these things in her mind, she addressed herself to the struggle. She managed to get some sacks, but for a week or two she could make nothing like twenty-five a day, though Dicky helped. Her fingers got raw; but she managed to complete a hundred within the first week. They might have been better done, as the employer said when he saw them. But she got her full one and sevenpence. She pawned her boots for fourpence, and wore two old odd ones of Josh's; and she got twopence on a petticoat. Dicky also helped a little; and at the end of a fortnight there came a godsend in the shape of material for matchboxes. Mrs Perrott was slow with them at first; but Dicky was quick, and even little Em began to learn to spread paste.

27

DICKY grew slighter and lanker, dark about the eyes, and weaker. He was growing longitudinally, and that made his lateral wasting the quicker and the more apparent. A furtive, frighted look hung ever in his face, a fugitive air about his whole person. His mother's long face was longer than ever, and blacker under the eyes than Dicky's own, and her weak open mouth hung at the corners as that of a woman faint with weeping. Little Em's knees and elbows were knobs in the midst of limbs of unnatural length. Rarely could a meal be seen ahead; and when it came, it made Dicky doubtful whether or not hunger were really caused by eating. But his chief distress was to see that little Em cried not like a child, but silently, as she strove to thread needles or to smear matchbox labels. And when good fortune brought matchboxes, there was an undue loss on the twopence farthing in the matter of paste. The stuff was a foul mess, sour and faint, and it was kept in a broken tea-cup, near which Dicky had detected his sister sucking her fingers; for in truth little Em stole the paste.

On and off, by one way and another, Mrs Perrott made enough to keep the rent paid with indifferent regularity, and sometimes there was a copper or so left over. She did fairly well, too, at the churches and prayer-meetings; people saw her condition, and now and again would give her something beyond the common dole; so that she learned the trick of looking more miserable than usual at such places.

The roof provided, Dicky felt that his was the task to find food. Alone, he might have rubbed along clear of starvation, but there were his mother and his sister. Lack of victuals shook his nerve and made him timid. Moreover, his terror grew greater than ever at the prospect of being caught in a theft. He lay awake at night and sweated to think of it. Who would bring in things from the outer world for mother and Em then? And the danger was worse than ever. He had felt the police-court birch, and it was bad, very bad. But he would take it every day and take it almost without a tear, rather than the chance of a reformatory. Magistrates were unwilling to send boys to reformatories while both father and mother were at hand to control them, for that were relieving the parents of their natural responsibility; but in a case like Dicky's, a 'schooling' was a very likely thing. So that Dicky, as he prowled, was torn between implacable need and the fear of being cut off from all chance of supplying it.

It was his rule never to come home without bringing something, were it no more than a mildewed crust. It was a resolve impossible to keep at times, but at those times it was two in the morning ere he would drag himself, pallid and faint, into the dark room where the others might be—probably were—lying awake and unfed. Rather than face such a home-coming he had sometimes ventured on a more difficult feat than stealing in the outer world: he had stolen in the Jago. Sam Cash, for instance, had lost a bloater.

Dicky never ate at Weech's now. Rarely, indeed, would he take payment in kind, unless it were for something of smaller value than the average of his poor pilferings; and then he carried the food home. But cheaper things could be bought elsewhere, so that more usually he insisted on money payments: to the grief of Mr Weech, who set forth the odiousness of ingratitude at length; though his homilies had no sort of effect on Dicky's morals.

Father Sturt saw that Hannah Perrott gained no ground in her struggle, and urged her to apply for outdoor parish relief, promising to second her request with the guardians. But with an odd throwback of the respectability of her boiler-making ancestry, she disliked the notion of help from the parish, and preferred to remain as she was; for there at least her ingrained inertness seemed to side with some phantom of self-respect. To her present position she had subsided by almost imperceptible degrees, and she was scarce conscious of a change. But to parish relief there was a distinct and palpable step: a step that, on the whole, it seemed easier not to take. But it was with eagerness that she took a Maternity Society's letter, wherewith the vicar had provided himself on her behalf. For her time was drawing near.

28

Josh perrott well understood the advantage of good prison-behaviour, and after six months in his Chelmsford cell he had earned the right to a visit from friends. But none came. He had scarcely expected that anybody would, and asked for the order merely on the general principle that a man should take all he can get, useful or not. For there would have been a five-shilling fare to pay for each visitor from London, and Hannah Perrott could as easily have paid five pounds. And indeed she had other things to think of.

Kiddo Cook had been less observed of late in the Jago. In simple fact he was at work. He found that a steady week of porterage at Spitalfields Market would bring him sixteen shillings and perhaps a little more; and he had taken Father Sturt's encouragement to try another week, and a week after that. Father Sturt, too, had cunningly stimulated Kiddo's ambitions: still he cherished aspirations to a fruit and vegetable stall, with a proper tarpaulin cover for bad weather; though he cherished them in secret, confident that they were of his own independent conception. Perhaps the Perrotts saw as much of Kiddo as did anybody at this time. For Kiddo, seeing how it went with them (though indeed it went as badly with others too) built up laboriously a solemn and most circumstantial Lie. There was a friend of his, a perfect gentleman, who used a beer-shop by Spitalfields Market, and who had just started an extensive and complicated business in the general provision line. He sold all sorts of fruit and vegetables fresh, and all sorts of meat, carrots, cabbages, saveloys, fried fish and pease-pudding cooked. His motto was: 'Everything of the best.' But he had the misfortune to be quite unable himself to judge whether his goods were really of the best or not, in consequence of an injury to his palate, arising from a blow on the mouth with a quart pot, inflicted in the heat of discussion by a wealthy acquaintance. So that he, being a perfect gentleman, had requested Kiddo Cook, out of the friendship he bore him, to drop in occasionally and test his samples. 'Take a good big whack, you know,' said he, 'and get the advice of a friend or two, if *you* ain't sure.' So Kiddo would take frequent and handsome whacks accordingly, to the perfect gentleman's delight; and, not quite knowing what to do with all the whacks, or being desirous of an independent opinion on them (there was some confusion between these two motives) he would bring Mrs Perrott samples, from time to time, and hope it wouldn't inconvenience her. It never did.

It was late in the dusk of a rainy day that Kiddo Cook stumped into Old Jago Street with an apple in his pocket for Em. It was not much, but money was a little short, and at any rate the child would be pleased. As he climbed the stairs he grew conscious of sounds of anguish, muffled by the Perrotts' door. There might have been sobs, and there seemed to be groans; certainly little Em was crying, though but faintly, and something—perhaps boot-heels—scraped on the boards. Kiddo hesitated a little, and then knocked softly. The knock was unnoticed, so in the end he pushed the door open.

The day had been a bad one with the Perrotts. Dicky had gone out early, and had not returned. His mother had tramped unfed to the sackmakers, but there was no work to be got. She tried the rush bag people, with a like result. Nor was any matchbox material being given out. An unregarded turnip had rolled from a shop into the gutter, and she had seized it stealthily. It was not in nature to take it home whole, and once a corner was cleared, she dragged herself Jago-ward, gnawing the root furtively as she went. And so she joined Em at home late in the afternoon.

Kiddo pushed the door open and went in. At his second step he stood staring, and his chin dropped.

'Good Gawd!' said Kiddo Cook.

He cleared the stairs in three jumps. He stood but an instant on the flags before the house, with a quick glance each way, and then dashed off through the mud.

Pigeony Poll was erratic in residence, but just now she had a room by the roof of a house in Jago Row, and up the stairs of this house Kiddo ran, calling her by name.

'Go over to Perrotts', quick!' he shouted from the landing below as Poll appeared at her door. 'Run, for Gawd's sake, or the woman 'll croak! I'm auf to Father's.' And he rushed away to the vicar's lodgings.

Father Sturt emerged at a run, and made for a surgeon's in

Shoreditch High Street. And when the surgeon reached Hannah Perrott he found her stretched on her ragged bed, tended, with anxious clumsiness, by Pigeony Poll; while Little Em, tearful and abashed, sat in a corner and nibbled a bit of turnip.

Hannah Perrott had anticipated the operation of the Maternity Society letter, and another child of the Jago had come unconsenting into its black inheritance.

Father Sturt met the surgeon as he came away in the later evening, and asked if all were well. The surgeon shrugged his shoulders. 'People would call it so,' he said. 'The boy's alive, and so is the mother. But you and I may say the truth. You know the Jago far better than I. Is there a child in all this place that wouldn't be better dead—still better unborn? But does a day pass without bringing you just such a parishioner? Here lies the Jago, a nest of rats, breeding, breeding, as only rats can; and we say it is well. On high moral grounds we uphold the right of rats to multiply their thousands. Sometimes we catch a rat. And we keep it a little while, nourish it carefully, and put it back into the nest to propagate its kind.'

Father Sturt walked a little way in silence. Then he said: 'You are right, of course. But who'll listen, if you shout it from the housetops? I might try to proclaim it myself, if I had time and energy to waste. But I have none—I must work, and so must you. The burden grows day by day, as you say. The thing's hopeless, perhaps, but that is not for me to discuss. I have my duty.'

The surgeon was a young man, but Shoreditch had helped him over the most of his enthusiasms. 'That's right,' he said, 'quite right. People are so very genteel, aren't they?' He laughed, as at a droll remembrance. 'But, hang it all, men like ourselves needn't talk as though the world was built of hardbake. It's a mighty relief to speak truth with a man who knows—a man not rotted through with sentiment. Think how few men we trust with the power to give a fellow creature a year in gaol, and how carefully we pick them! Even damnation is out of fashion, I believe, among theologians. But any noxious wretch may damn human souls to the Jago, one after another, year in year out, and we respect his right: his sacred right.'

At the 'Posties' the two men separated. The rain, which had abated for a space, came up on a driving wind, and whipped Dicky Perrott home to meet his new brother.

29

THINGS grew a little easier with the Perrotts. Father Sturt saw that there was food while the mother was renewing her strength, and he had a bag of linen sent. More, he carried his point as to parish relief by main force. It was two shillings and three quartern loaves a week. Unfortunately the loaves were imprinted with the parish mark, or they might have been sold at the chandler's, in order that the whole measure of relief might be passed on to the landlord (a very respectable man, with a chandler's shop of his own) for rent. As it was, the bread perforce was eaten, and the landlord had the two shillings, as well as eighteenpence which had to be got in some other way. Of course, Hannah Perrott might have 'taken in lodgers' in the room, as others did, but she doubted her ability to bully the rent out of them, or to turn them out if they did not pay. Whatever was pawnable had gone already, of course, except the little nickel-plated clock. That might have produced as much as sixpence, but she had a whim to keep it. She regarded it as a memorial of Josh, for it was his sole contribution to the family appointments.

Dicky, with a cast-off jacket from the vicar's store, took to hanging about Liverpool Street Station in quest of bags to carry. Sometimes he got bags, and coppers for carrying them: sometimes he got kicks from porters. An hour or two of disappointment in this pursuit would send him off on the prowl to 'find' new stock for Mr Weech. He went farther afield now: to the market-places in Mile End and Stepney, and to the river-side, where there were many chances—guarded jealously, however, by the pirate boys of the neighbourhood, who would tolerate no interlopers at the wharves. In the very early morning, too, he practised the sandbag fake in the Jago. For there were those among the Jagos who kept (two even bred) linnets and such birds, and prepared them for julking, or singing matches at the Bag of Nails. It was the habit of the bird-fanciers to hang their little wooden cages on nails out of the window, and there they hung through the night: for it had been noted, as a surprising peculiarity in linnets, that a bird would droop and go off song after a dozen or so of nights in a Jago room, in company with eight, ten, or a dozen human sleepers, notwithstanding the thoughtful shutting of windows. So that any early riser, provided with a little bag packed with a handful or so of sand, could become an opulent bird-owner in half an hour. Let but the sand-bag be pitched with proper skill at the bottom of a cage, and that cage would leave the nail, and come tumbling and fluttering down into the ready hands of the early riser. The sand-bag brought down the cage and fell quietly on the flags, which was why it was preferred before a stone. The sand-bag faker was moved by no particular love of linnets. His spoil was got rid of as soon as the bird-shops opened in Club Row. And his craft was one of danger.

Thus the months went with Dicky, and the years. There were changes in the Jago. The baby was but three months old when Father Sturt's new church was opened, and the club set going in new buildings; and it was at that time that Josh Perrott was re-moved to Portland. Even the gradual removal of the Old Jago itself was begun. For the County Council bought a row of houses at the end of Jago Row, by Honey Lane, with a design to build big barrack-dwellings on the site. The scenes of the Jago Court eviction were repeated, with less governed antics. For the County Council knew not Jago ways; and when deputations came forth weeping and protesting the impossibility of finding new lodgings, and beseeching a respite, they were given six weeks more, and went back delighted into free quarters. At the end of the six weeks a larger deputation protested a little louder, wept a great deal more, and poached another month; for it would seem an un-popular thing to turn the people into the street. Thus in the end, when the unpopular thing had to be done, it was with sevenfold trouble, loud cursing of the County Council in the public street, and many fights. But this one spot of the Jago cleared, the County Council began to creep along Jago Row and into Half Jago Street; and after long delay the crude yellow brick of the barrack dwellings rose above the oft-stolen hoardings, and grew, storey by storey. Dicky was fourteen, fifteen, sixteen. If Josh Perrott had only earned his marks, he would soon be out now.

30

J<small>OSH</small> <small>PERROTT</small> earned his marks, and in less than four years from his conviction he came away from Portland. It was a mere matter of hours ere his arrival in London, when Dicky, hands in pockets, strolled along Old Jago Street, and by the 'Posties' to High Street.

Dicky was almost at his seventeenth birthday. He had grown his utmost, and stood five feet two. He wore a cap with a cloth peak and ear-laps tied at the top with strings, slap-up kicksies, cut saucy, and a bob-tail coat of the out-and-out description: though all these glories were torn and shabby, and had been bought second-hand. He was safe from any risk of the reformatory now, being well over the age; and he had had the luck never to have been taken by the police since his father's lagging—though there were escapes too narrow to be thought about with comfort. It was a matter for wonderment, and he spoke of it with pride. Here he was, a man of long experience, and near seventeen years old, yet he had never been in prison. Few, very few of such an age could say that.

Sometimes he saw his old enemy, the hunchback, who worked at a shoemaker's, but he saw him with unconcern. He cared nothing for tale-bearing now. The memory of old injuries had dulled, and, after all, this was a merely inconsiderable hunchback, whom it were beneath his dignity to regard with anything but tolerant indifference. Bob Roper steered clear at such encounters, and showed his teeth like a cat, and looked back malevolently. It didn't matter.

Dicky was not married, either in the simple Jago fashion or in church. There was little difference, as a matter of fact, so far as facility went. There was a church in Bethnal Green where you might be married for sevenpence if you were fourteen years old, and no questions asked—or at any rate they were questions answers whereunto were easy to invent. You just came in, drunk if possible, with a batch of some scores, and rowdied about the church with your hat on, and the curate worked off the crowd at one go, calling the names one after another. You sang, or you shouted, or you drank out of a bottle, or you flung a prayer-book at a friend, as the fancy took you; and the whole thing was not a bad joke for the money, though after all sevenpence is half a gallon, and not to be wasted. But Dicky had had enough to do to look after his mother and Em and little Josh—as Hannah Perrott had called the baby. Dicky, indeed, had a family already. More: the Jago girls affected him with an odd feeling of repulsion. Not of themselves, perhaps, though they were squalid drabs long ere they were ripe for the sevenpenny church: but by comparison with the clean, remote shop-girls who were visible through the broad windows in the outer streets.

Dicky intended the day to be a holiday. He was not going 'out', as the word went, for ill-luck had a way of coming on notable days like this, and he might easily chance to 'fall' before his father got home. He was almost too big now for carrying bags at Liverpool Street, because small boys looked cheaper than large ones—not that there was anything especially large about Dicky, beyond his height of five feet two; and at the moment he could think of nothing else that might turn a copper. He stood irresolute on the High Street footway, and as he stood, Kiddo Cook hove in sight, dragging a barrow-load of carrots and cabbages. Kiddo had not yet compassed the stall with the rain-proof awning. But it was almost in sight, for the barrow could scarce hold all that he could sell; and there was a joke abroad that he was to be married in Father Sturt's church: some facetiously suggesting that Mother Gapp would prove a good investment commercially, while others maintained the greater eligibility of old Poll Rann.

"Tcheer, Dicky!' said Kiddo, pulling up and wiping his cap-lining with a red cotton handkerchief. 'Ol' man out to-day, ain't 'e?'

'Yus,' Dicky answered. ''Spect 'im up to-night.'

Kiddo nodded, and wiped his face. "Spose the mob'll git up a break for 'im,' he said; 'but 'e'll 'ave a bit o' gilt from stir as well, won't 'e? So 'e'll be awright.' And Kiddo stuffed his handkerchief into his trousers pocket, pulled his cap tight, and bent to his barrow-handles.

Dicky turned idly to the left, and slouched to the corner of Meakin Street. There he loafed for a little while, and then went as aimlessly up the turning. Meakin Street was much as ever. There were still the chandlers' shops, where tea and sugar were sold by the farthingsworth, and the barber's where hair was fashionably cut for three halfpence: though Jago hair was commonly cut in another place and received little more attention. There was still Walker's cook-shop, foggy with steam, its windows all a-trickle, and there was the Original Slap-up Tog Emporium, with its kicksies and its benjamins cut saucy as ever, and its double fakements still artful. At the 'dispensary' there was another young student, but his advice and medicine were sixpence, just as his remote predecessor's had been for little Looey, long forgotten. And farther down on the opposite side, Mr Aaron Weech's coffee-shop, with its Sunday-school festival bills, maintained its general Band-of-Hope air, and displayed its shrivelled bloaters, its doubtful cake, and its pallid scones in an odour of respectability and stale pickles. Dicky glanced in as he came by the door, and met the anxious eye of Mr Weech, whom he had not seen for a fortnight. For Dicky was no boy now, but knew enough to sell at Cohen's or elsewhere whenever possible, and to care not a rap for Mr Weech.

As that tradesman saw Dicky, he burst into an eager smile, and came forward. 'Good mornin'—er—' with a quick glance—'Mr Perrott! Good mornin'! You're quite a stranger, reely!'

Mister Perrott! Mr Weech was very polite, Dicky stopped, and grunted a cautious salutation.

'Do come in, Mr Perrott. Wy, is the good noos right wot I 'ear, about yer father a-comin' 'ome from—from the country?'

Dicky confirmed the news.

'Well, I *am* glad t' 'ear that now.' Mr Weech grinned exceedingly, though there was something lacking in his delight. 'But there, wot'll you 'ave, Mr Perrott? Say anythink in the 'ole shop and welcome! It's sich an 'appy occasion, Mr Perrott, I couldn't think o' chargin' you a 'a'peny. 'Ave a rasher, now, do. There's one on at this very moment. Sairer! ain't that rasher done yut?'

Dicky did not understand this liberality, but he had long since adopted the policy of taking all he could get. So he sat at a table, and Mr Weech sat opposite.

'Jist like ole times, ain't it?' said Mr Weech. 'An' that reminds me I owe you a shillin'. It's that pair o' noo boots you chucked over the back fence a fortnight ago. W'en I come to look at 'em, they was better'n wot I thought, an' so I says to meself, "This won't do," says I. "On'y ninepence for a pair o' boots like them ain't fair," I says, "an' I'd rayther be at a lawss on 'em than not be fair. Fair's fair, as the apostle David says in the Proverbs, an' them boots is worth very near *one*-an'-nine. So I'll give Mr Perrott another shillin'," I says, "the very next time I see 'im." An' there it is.'

He put the shilling on the table, and Dicky pocketed it, nothing loth. The thing might be hard to understand, but that concerned him not. There was the shilling. Likewise, there was the bacon, and the coffee that went with it, and Dicky went at them with a will, recking nothing of why they were there, and nothing of any matter which might make the giver anxious in the prospect of an early meeting with Josh.

'Ah,' Mr Weech went on, 'it'll be quite a pleasure to see yer father agin, that it will. Wot a blessed release! "Free from the lor O 'appy condition," as the 'ymn says. I 'ope 'e'll be well an' 'arty. An' if—*if* there should be anythink in the way of a friendly lead or a subscription or wot not, I 'ope—remember this, Mr Perrott, won'tcher?—I 'ope you'll let me 'ave a chance to put down something good. Not as I can reely afford it, ye know, Mr Perrott— trade's very pore, an' it's sich a neighb'r'ood!—but I'll do it for yer father—yus, if it's me last copper. Ye won't forgit that, will ye? An' if 'e'd like any little relish w'en 'e comes 'ome—sich as a 'addick or a bit o' 'am—wy, I'll wrop it up an' send it.'

This was all very handsome, and Dicky wished some notion of the sort had occurred to Mr Weech on a few of the dinnerless days of the past four years. But he went away wondering if it might not be well to regard Mr Weech with caution for a while. For there must be a reason for all this generosity.

31

It was in Mother Gapp's that Josh Perrott and his family met. Hannah had started out with an idea of meeting him at Waterloo Station; but, finding herself an object of distinction and congratulation among the women she met, she had lingered by the way, accepting many little drops, to prove herself not unduly proud, and so had failed of her intent. Josh, on his part, had not been abstinent. He had successfully run the gauntlet of Prisoners' Aid Societies and the like, professing to have 'a job waiting for him' in Shoreditch, and his way across London had been freely punctuated at public-houses; for his prison gratuity was a very pleasant and useful little sum. And now, when at last they met, he was not especially gracious. He wanted to know, not only why he had found nobody at home, but also why Hannah had never been to see him at Portland. As to the second question, the obvious and sufficient answer was that the return fare to Portland would have been some twenty-five shillings: a sum that Hannah had never seen together since Josh left her. As to the first, she protested, with muddled vehemence, that she had gone to meet him, and had missed him by some mistake as to arrival platforms. So that at length, urged thereto by the rest of the hour's customers at the Feathers, Josh kissed her sulkily and ordered her a drink. Em was distrustful at first, but drank her allowance of gin with much relish, tipping the glass again and again to catch the last drop; and little Josh, now for the first time introduced to Josh the elder, took a dislike to his father's not particularly sober glare and grin, and roared aloud upon his knee, assailing him, between the roars, with every curse familiar in the Jago, amid the genial merriment of the company. Dicky came in quietly, and stood at his father's elbow with the pride natural to a dutiful son on such an occasion. And at closing-time they all helped each other home.

In the morning Josh rose late. He looked all the better for his lagging, browner than ever in the face, smarter and stouter. In a corner he perceived a little heap of made match-boxes, and, hard by, the material for more. It was Em's work of yesterday morning. 'Support 'ome industeries,' said Josh musingly. 'Yus. Two-pence-farden a gross.' And he kicked the heap to splinters.

He strolled out into the street, to survey the Jago. In the bulk it was little changed, though the County Council had made a difference in the north-east corner, and was creeping farther and farther still. The dispossessed Jagos had gone to infect the neighbourhoods across the border, and to crowd the people a little closer. They did not return to live in the new barrack-buildings; which was a strange thing, for the County Council was charging very little more than double the rents which the landlords of the Old Jago had charged. And so another Jago, teeming and villainous as the one displaced, was slowly growing, in the form of a ring, round about the great yellow houses. But the new church and its attendant buildings most took Josh's notice. They were little more than begun when last he walked Old Jago Street in daylight, and now they stood, large and healthy, amid the dens about them, a wonder and a pride. As he looked, Jerry Gullen and Bill Rann passed.

'Wayo, brother-in-law!' sang out Bill Rann, who remembered the Old Bailey fiction of four years back, and thought it a capital joke.

'Nice sort o' thing, ain't it?' said Jerry Gullen with indignant sarcasm, jerking his thumb toward the new church. 'The street's clean ruined. Wot's the good o' livin' 'ere now? Wy, a man mustn't even do a click, blimey!'

'An' doncher?' asked Josh with a grin. Hereat another grin broke wide on Jerry Gullen's face, and he went his way with a wink and a whistle.

'And so you're back again, Josh Perrott!' said old Beveridge, seedier than ever, with the 'Hard Up' fresh chalked on the changeless hat. 'Back again! Pity you couldn't stay there, isn't it? Pity we can't all stay there.'

Josh looked after the gaunt old figure with much doubt and a vague indignation: for such a view was foreign to his understanding. And as he looked Father Sturt came out of the church, and laid his hand on Josh's shoulder.

'What!' exclaimed the vicar, 'home again without coming to see me! But there, you must have been coming. I hope you haven't been knocking long? Come in now, at any rate. You're looking wonderfully well. What a capital thing a holiday is, isn't it—a

179

good long one?' Taking Josh by the arm he hauled him, grinning, sheepish, and almost blushing, toward the club door. And at that moment Sam Cash came hurrying round Luck Row corner, with his finger through a string, and on that string a bunch of grouse.

'Dear me,' said Father Sturt, turning back, but without releasing Josh's arm. 'Here's our dear friend, Sam Cash, taking home something for his lunch. Come, Sam, with such a fine lot of birds as that, I'm sure you'll be proud to tell us where they came from. Eh?'

For a moment Sam Cash was a trifle puzzled, even offended. Then there fell over his face the mask of utter inexpression which the vicar had learned to know. Said Sam Cash, stolidly: 'I bin 'avin' a little shootin' with a friend.'

'Dear, dear, what a charming friend! And where are his moors? Nowhere about the Bethnal Green Road, I suppose, by the goods depot? Come now, I'm sure Josh Perrott would like to know. You didn't get any shooting in your little holiday, did you, Josh?' Josh grinned, delighted, but Sam shuffled uneasily, with a hopeless sidelong glance as in search of a hole wherein to hide. 'Ah, you see,' Father Sturt said, 'he doesn't want his friend's hospitality to be abused. Let me see—two, four, six—why there must be nine or ten brace, and all at one shot, too! Sam always makes his bag at one shot, you know, Josh, whatever the game is. Yes, wonderful shooting. And did you shoot the label at the same time, Sam? Come, I *should* like to look at that label!'

But the wretched Sam was off at a bolt, faster than a police pursuit would have sent him, while Josh guffawed joyously. To be 'rotted' by Father Sturt was the true Jago terror, but to the Jagos looking on it was pure delight. Theft was a piece of the Jago nature; but at least Father Sturt could wither the pride of it by such ridicule as the Jago could understand.

'There—he's very bashful for a sportsman, isn't he, Josh?' the vicar proceeded. 'But you must come and see the club at once. You shall be a member.'

Josh spent near an hour in the new buildings. Father Sturt showed him the club, the night shelter, the church, and his own little rooms. He asked, too, much about Josh's intention for the future. Of course, Josh was 'going to look for a job'. Father Sturt knew he would say that. Every Jago had been going to look for a job ever since the vicar first came to the place. But he professed to take Josh's word seriously, and offered to try to get him taken on as a plasterer at some of the new County Council buildings. He flattered Josh by reminding him of his command of a regular trade. Josh was a man with opportunities, and he should be above the pitiable expedients of the poor untradesmanlike about him. Indeed, he should leave the Jago altogether, with his family, and start afresh in a new place, a reputable mechanic.

To these things Josh Perrott listened with fidgety deference, answering only 'Yus, Father,' when it seemed to be necessary. In the end he promised to 'think it over,' which meant nothing, as the parson well knew. And in the mood in which Josh came away he would gladly have risked another lagging to serve Father Sturt's convenience; but he would rather have suffered one than take Father Sturt's advice.

He made the day a holiday. He had been told that he was in for a little excitement, for it was held that fitting time had arrived for another scrap with Dove Lane; but the affair was not yet moving. Snob Spicer had broken a window with a Dove-Laner's head, it was true, but nothing had come of it, and etiquette demanded that the next card should be played by Dove Lane. For the present, the Jago was content to take thought for Josh's 'friendly lead'. Such a thing was everybody's right on return from a lagging, and this one was fixed for a night next week.

All that day Mr Weech looked out anxiously, but Josh Perrott never passed his way.

32

BILL RANN called for Josh early the next morning, and they strolled down Old Jago Street in close communion.

'Are you on for a job?' asked Bill. ''Cos I got one cut an' dried —a topper, an' safe as 'ouses.'

'Wot sort o' job's this?'

'Wy a bust—unless we can screw it.'

This meant a breaking-in, with a possibility of a quieter entrance by means of keys. It was unpleasantly suggestive of Josh's last exploit, but he answered: 'Awright. Depends, o' course.'

'O, it's a good un.' Bill Rann grinned for no obvious reason, and slapped his leg to express rapturous amusement. 'It's a good un—you can take yer davy o' that. I bin a thinkin' about it for a fortnight, but it wants two. Damme, it's nobby!' And Bill Rann grinned again, and made two taps of a step-dance. 'Wotjer think,' he pursued, suddenly serious, 'wotjer think o' screwin' a fence?'

It was a novel notion, but in Josh's mind, at first flush, it seemed unsportsmanlike. 'Wot fence?' asked Josh.

Bill Rann's grin burst wide again. He bent low, with outstretched chin, and stuck his elbows out as he answered: 'Wy, ole Weech!'

Josh bared his teeth—but with no smile—looking sharply in the other's upturned face. Bill Rann, bent nearly double, and with hands in pockets, flapped his arms in the manner of wings, chuckled aloud, and, jerking his feet back and forth, went elaborately through the first movement of the gallows-flap. 'Eh? eh?' said he. ''Ow's that strike ye, ole cock?'

Josh answered not, but his parted lips stretched wide, and his tongue-tip passed quickly over them while he thought.

'It'll be a fair cop for 'im,' Bill pursued eagerly. ''E's treated us all pretty mean, one time or other. Wy, I bet 'e *owes* us fifty quid atween us, wot with all the times 'e's squeeged us for a bit. It'll on'y be goin' to bring away our own stuff!'

'G-r-r-r!' Josh growled, glaring fiercely; 'it was 'im as put me away for my laggin'! Bleed'n' swine!'

Bill Rann stopped, surprised. 'Wot—'im?' he exclaimed. 'Ole Weech narked ye? 'Owjer know that?'

Josh told the tale of his negotiations in the matter of the Mogul's watch, and described Weech's terror at sight of his dash at the shop-door. 'I'm on,' said Josh in conclusion. 'It's one way o' payin' 'im, an' it'll bring a bit in. On'y 'e better not show 'isself w'ile I'm abaat! 'E wouldn't git auf with a punch on the chin, like the bloke at 'Ighbury!' Josh Perrott ended with a tigerish snarl and a white spot at the curl of each of his nostrils.

'Blimey!' said Bill Rann; 'an' so it was 'im, was it? I often wondered 'oo you meant. Well, flimpin' 'im's the best way. Won't 'e sing a bleed'n' 'ymn w'en 'e finds 'is stuff weeded!' Bill flung back his head and laughed again. 'But there—let's lay it out.' And the two men fell to the discussion of methods.

Weech's back fence was to be his undoing. It was the obvious plan. The front shutters were impracticable in such a place as Meakin Street; but the alleys in the rear were a perfect approach. Bill Rann had surveyed the spot attentively, and, after expert consideration, he had selected the wash-house window as the point of entrance. Old boxes and packing-wood littered the yard, and it would be easy to mount a selected box, shift the catch of the little window, and wriggle in, feet first, without noise. True, the door between the wash-house and the other rooms might be fastened, but it could be worked at under cover; and Bill Rann had a belief that there must be a good deal of 'stuff' in the wash-house itself. There would be nobody in the house but Weech, because the wretched old woman, who swept the floors and cooked bloaters, was sent away at night; so that every room must be unoccupied but one.

As for tools, Josh had none, but Bill Rann undertook to provide them; and in the matter of time it was considered that that same night would be as good as any. It would be better than most, in fact, for it was Wednesday, and Bill Rann had observed that Mr Weech went to the bank in High Street, Shoreditch, pretty regularly on Thursday mornings.

This day also Mr Weech kept a careful watch for Josh Perrott, but saw him not.

33

HANNAH PERROTT did her best to keep Josh from going out that night. She did not explain her objections, because she did not know precisely what they were, though they were in some sort prompted by his manner; and it was solely because of her constitutional inability to urge them with any persistence that she escaped forcible retort. For Josh was in a savage and self-centred mood.

'Wy, wot's up?' asked Bill Rann, when they met, looking doubtfully in his pal's face. 'You ain't bin boozin', 'ave ye?'

Josh repelled the question with a snarl. 'No I ain't,' he said. 'Got the tools?' There was a thickness in his voice, with a wildness in his eye, that might well explain his partner's doubt.

'Yus. Come under the light. I couldn't git no twirls, an' we sha'n't want 'em. 'Ere's a screwdriver, an' two gimlets, an' a knife for the winder-ketch, an' a little james, an' a neddy—'

'A neddy!' Josh cut in, scornfully pointing his thumb at the instrument, which some call life-preserver. 'A neddy for Weech! G-r-r-r! I might take a neddy to a *man*!'

'That's awright,' Bill replied. 'But it 'ud frighten 'im pretty well, wouldn't it? Look 'ere. S'pose we can't find the oof. Wy shouldn't we wake up Mr Weech very quiet an' respeckful, an' ask 'im t' 'elp us? 'E's all alone, an' I'm sure 'e'll be glad to 'blige, w'en 'e sees this ere neddy, without waitin' for a tap. Wy, blimey, I b'lieve 'e'd be afraid to sing out any'ow, for fear o' bringin' in the coppers to find all the stuff 'e's bought on the crook! It's all done, once we're inside!'

It was near midnight, and Bill Rann had observed Weech putting up his shutters at eleven. So the two Jagos walked slowly along Meakin Street, on the side opposite Weech's, with sharp eyes for the windows.

All was quiet; there was no visible light—none from the skylight over the shop door, none from the window above, none from the garret window above that. They passed on, crossed the road, strolled back, and listened at the door; there was no sound from within. The clock in a distant steeple struck twelve, and was joined at the fourth stroke by the loud bell of St Leonard's close by; and ere the last mild note had sounded from the farthest clock in the awakened chorus, Josh Perrott and Bill Rann had taken the next turning, and were pushing their way to the alleys behind Weech's.

Foul rat-runs, these alleys, not to be traversed by a stranger. Josh and Bill plunged into one narrow archway after another, each of which might have been the private passage of a house, and came at last, stealthy and unseen, into the muddy yard.

Weech's back fence was before them, and black house-backs crowded them round. There were but one or two lights in the windows, and those windows were shut and curtained. The rear of Weech's house was black and silent as the front. They peered over the fence. The yard was pitch-dark, but faint angular tokens here and there told of heaped boxes and lumber. 'We won't tip 'im the whistle this time,' whispered Bill Rann, with a smothered chuckle. 'Over!'

He bent his knee, and Josh straddled from it over the rickety fence with quiet care, and lowered himself gingerly on the other side. 'Clear 'ere,' he whispered. 'Come on.' Since Bill's display of the tools Josh had scarce spoken a word. Bill wondered at his taciturnity, but respected it as a business-like quality in the circumstances.

It was but a matter of four or five yards to the wash-house window, but they bent and felt their way. Josh took up an old lemonade-case as he went, and planted it on the ground below the window, stretching his hand for the knife as he did so. And now he took command and foremost place.

It was an old shoemaker's knife, with too long a handle; for there was a skew-joint in the sash, and the knife would not bend. Presently Bill Rann, below, could see that Josh was cutting away the putty from the pane, and in five minutes the pane itself was put into his hand. He stooped, and laid it noiselessly on the soft ground.

Josh turned the catch and lifted the sash. There was some noise, but not much, as he pushed the frame up evenly, with a thumb at each side. They waited; but it was quite still, and Josh, sitting on the sill, manoeuvred his legs, one at a time, through the narrow opening. Then, turning over, he let himself down, and beckoned Bill Rann to follow.

Bill Rann had a small tin box, with an inch of candle on the inside of one end, so that when the wick was lit the contrivance made a simple but an effective lantern, the light whereof shone in front alone, and could be extinguished at a puff. Now a match was struck, and a quick view taken of the wash-house.

There was not much about; only cracked and greasy plates, jars, tins, pots and pans, and in a corner a miscellaneous heap, plainly cheap pilferings, covered with a bit of old carpet. The air was offensive with the characteristic smell of Weech's—the smell of stale pickles.

'There ain't nothin' to waste time over 'ere,' said Josh aloud. 'Come on!'

'Shut up, you damn fool!' exclaimed Bill Rann, in a whisper. 'D'jer want to wake 'im?'

'Umph! Why not?' was the reply, still aloud. Bill began to feel that his pal was really drunk. But, silent once more, Josh applied himself to the door of the inner room. It was crank and old, worn and battered at the edges. Josh forced the wedge end of the jemmy through the jamb, splintering the perished wood of the frame, and, with a push, forced the striking-box of the lock off its screws. There was still a bolt at the top; that at the bottom had lost its catch—but this gave as little trouble as the lock. Bill Rann strained the door open from below, the jemmy entered readily, and in a few seconds the top bolt was in like case with the bottom.

They entered the room behind the shop, and it was innocent and disappointing. A low table, four horse-hair covered chairs, a mirror, three coloured wall-texts, two china figures and a cheap walnut sideboard—that was all. The slow step of a policeman without stopped, with a push at the shop-door, to test its fastenings, and then went on; and stronger than ever was the smell of stale pickles.

To try the shop would be mere waste of time. Weech's pocket was the till, and there could be no other prize. A door at the side of the room, latched simply, gave on the stairs. 'Take auf yer boots,' Bill whispered, unlacing his own, and slinging them across his shoulder by the tied laces.

But Josh would not, and he said so, with an oath. Bill could not understand him. *Could* it be drink? Bill wished him a mile away. 'Awright,' he whispered, 'you set down 'ere w'ile I slip upstairs an' take a peep. I bet the stuff's in the garret. Best on'y one goes, quiet.'

Josh sat, and Bill, taking the lantern, crept up the stairs noiselessly, save for one creak. He gained the stair-head, listened a moment, tip-toed along the small landing, and was half way up the steep and narrow garret stairs, when he heard a sound, and stopped. Somebody was on the lower flight.

There was a heavy tread, with the kick of a boot against stair or skirting-board; and then came noisy steps along the landing. Josh was coming up in his boots! Bill Rann was at his wits' end. He backed down the garret stairs, and met Josh at the foot. 'Are ye balmy?' he hissed fiercely, catching Josh by the collar and pulling him into the turn of the stairs. 'D'ye want another five stretch?'

A loud creak and a soft thump sounded from behind the door at the other end of the landing; and then a match was struck. 'Keep back on the stairs,' Bill whispered. ''E's 'eard you.' Josh sat on a stair, perfectly still, with his legs drawn up out of sight from the door. Bill blew out his light. He would not venture open intimidation of Weech now, with Josh half muzzy, lest some burst of lunacy brought in the police.

A soft treading of bare feet, the squeak of a door handle, a light on the landing, and Aaron Weech stood at his open door in his shirt, candle in hand, his hair rumpled, his head aside, his mouth a little open, his unconscious gaze upward; listening intently. He took a slight step forward. And then Bill Rann's heart turned over and over.

For Josh Perrott sprang from the stair, and, his shoulders humped and his face thrust out, walked deliberately across the landing. Weech turned his head quickly; his chin fell on his chest as by jawbreak; there were but dots amid the white of his eyes; his head lay slowly back, as the candle tilted and shot its grease on the floor. The door swung wider as his shoulder struck it, and he screamed, like a rabbit that sees a stoat. Then, with a wrench, he turned, letting drop the candle, and ran shrieking to the window, flung it open, and yelled into the black street. ''Elp! 'Elp! P'lice! *Murder! Murder! Murder! Murder!*'

'Run, Josh—run, ye blasted fool!' roared Bill Rann, bounding across the landing, and snatching at his arm.

'Go on—go on! I'm comin'!' Josh answered without turning his head. And Bill took the bottom flight at a jump. The candle flared as it lay on the floor, and spread a greasy pool about it.

'*Murder! Murder! Mu-r-r—*'

Josh had the man by the shoulder, swung him back from the window, gripped his throat, and dragged him across the carpet as he might drag a cat, while Weech's arms waved uselessly, and his feet feebly sought a hold on the floor.

'Now!' cried Josh Perrott, glaring on the writhen face below his own, and raising his case-knife in the manner of a cleaver, 'sing a hymn! Sing the hymn as 'll do ye most good! You'll cheat me when ye can, an' when ye can't you'll put me five year in stir, eh? Sing a hymn, ye snivellin' nark!'

From the street there came the noise of many hurrying feet and of a scattered shouting. Josh Perrott made an offer of slashing the slaty face, checked his arm, and went on.

'You'll put down somethin' 'an'some at my break, will ye? An' you'll starve my wife an' kids all to bones an' teeth four year! Sing a hymn, ye cur!'

He made another feint at slashing. Men were beating thunderously at the shop door, and there were shrill whistles.

'Won't sing yer hymn? There ain't much time! My boy was goin' straight, an' earnin' wages: someone got 'im chucked. A man 'as time to think things out, in stir! Sing, ye son of a cow! Sing! Sing!'

Twice the knife hacked the livid face. But the third hack was below the chin; and the face fell back.

The bubbling Thing dropped in a heap, and put out the flaring candle. Without, the shouts gathered to a roar, and the door shook under heavy blows. 'Open—open the door!' cried a deep voice.

He looked from the open window. There was a scrambling crowd, and more people were running in. Windows gaped, and thrust out noisy heads. The flash of a bull's-eye dazzled him, and he staggered back. 'Perrott! Perrott!' came a shout. He had but glanced out, but he was recognised.

He threw down his knife, and made for the landing, slipping on the wet floor and stumbling against the Heap. There were shouts from behind the house now; they were few, but they were close. He dashed up the narrow stairs, floundered through the back garret, over bags and boxes and heaps of mingled commodities, and threw up the sash. Men were stumbling invisibly in the dark yard below. He got upon the sill, swung round by the dormer-frame, and went, hands and knees, along the roof. Yells and loud whistles rose clamant in the air, and his own name was shouted to and fro. Then the blows on the shop-door ceased with a splintering crash, and there was a trampling of feet on floorboards.

The roofs were irregular in shape and height, and his progress was slow. He aimed at reaching the roof of Father Sturt's old club building, still empty. He had had this in mind from the moment he climbed from the garret-window; for in the work of setting the drains in order an iron ventilating pipe had been carried up from the stable-yard to well above the roof. It was a stout pipe, close by the wall, to which it was clamped with iron attachments. Four years had passed since he had seen it, and he trusted to luck to find it still standing, for it seemed his only chance. Down below people scampered and shouted. Crowds had sprung out of the dark night as by magic; and the police— they must have been lying in wait in scores. It seemed a mere matter of seconds since he had scaled the back fence; and now people were tearing about the house behind him, and shouting out of windows to those below. He hoped that the iron pipe might not be gone.

Good—it was there. He peered from the parapet down into the stable-yard, and the place seemed empty. He gripped the pipe with hands and knees, and descended.

The alley had no back way: he must take his chance in Meakin Street. He peeped. At the street end there was a dark obstruction, set with spots of light: a row of police. That way was shut; he must try the Jago—Luck Row was almost opposite, and no Jago would betray him. The hunters were already on the roofs. Men shouted up to them from the street, and kept pace with them, coming nearer. He took a breath and dashed across, knocking a man over at the corner.

Up Luck Row, into Old Jago Street he ran, past his own home, and across to a black doorway, just as Father Sturt, roused by the persistent din, opened his window. The passage was empty, and for an instant he paused, breathless. But there were howls without, and the pelting of many feet. The man knocked over at the corner had given the alarm, and the hunt was up.

Into the back yard and over the fence; through another passage into New Jago Street; with a notion to gain the courts by Honey Lane and so away. But he was thinking of the Jago as it had been—he had forgotten the demolishment. As he neared Jago Row the place of it lay suddenly before him—an open waste of eighty yards square, skirted by the straight streets and the yellow barracks, with the Board School standing dark among them. And along the straight streets more men were rushing, and more police. They were new-comers: why not venture over? He rubbed his cheek, for something like a film of gum clung to it. Then he remembered, and peered closely at his hands. Blood, sticking and drying and peeling; blood on hands and face, blood on clothes, without a doubt. To go abroad thus were to court arrest, were he known or not. It must be got off; but how? To go home was to give himself up. The police were there long since—they swarmed the Jago through. Some half dismantled houses stood at hand, and he made for the nearest.

There were cellars under these houses, reached from the back yards. Many a Jago had been born, had lived, and had died in such a place. A cellar would hide him for an hour, while he groped himself clean as he might. Broken brickwork littered the space that had been the back yard. Feeling in the dark for the steps, which stood in a little pit, his foot turned on a stone, and he pitched headlong.

The cellar itself was littered with rubbish, and he lay among it a little while, breathless and bruised. When he tried to rise, he found his ankle useless. It was the old sprain, got at Mother Gapp's before his lagging, and ever ready to assert itself. He sat among the brickbats to pull off the boot—that was foul and sticky too—and he rubbed the ankle. He had been a fool to think of the cellar: why not any corner among the walls above? He had given way to the mere panic instinct to burrow, to hide himself in a hole, and he had chosen one wherefrom there was no second way of escape—none at all but by the steps he had fallen in at. Far better to have struck out boldly across the streets by Columbia Market to the canal: who could have seen the smears in the darkness? And in the canal he might have washed the lot away, secure from observation, under a bridge. The thing might be possible, even now, if he could stand the pain. But no, the foot was useless when he tried it. He was trapped like a rat. He rubbed and kneaded the ankle diligently, and managed to draw the boot on. But stand on both legs he could not. He might have crawled up the steps on hands and knees, but what was the use of that? So he sat, and waited.

Knots of men went hurrying by, and he caught snatches of their talk. There had been a murder—a man was murdered in his bed—it was a woman—a man had murdered his wife—there were two murders—three—the tale went every way, but it was always Murder, Murder, Murder. Everybody was saying Murder: till in the passing footsteps, in the vague shouts in the distance, and presently in the mere black about him he heard the word still—Murder, Murder, Murder. He fell to contrasting the whispered fancy with the real screams in that bedroom. He wondered what Bill Rann thought of it all, and what had become of the james and the gimlets. He pictured the crowd in Old Jago Street, pushing into his room, talking about him, telling the news. He wondered if Hannah had been asleep when they came, and what she said when they told her. And more people hurried past the ruined house, all talking Murder, Murder, still Murder.

The foot was horribly painful. Was it swelling? Yes, he thought it was; he rubbed it again. What would Dicky do? If only Dicky knew where he was! That might help. There was a new burst of shouts in the distance. What was that? Perhaps they had caught Bill Rann; but that was unlikely. They knew nothing of Bill—they had seen but one man. Perhaps they were carrying away the Heap on a shutter: that would be no nice job, especially down the steep stairs. There had been very little in the wash-house, and nothing in the next room; the garrets were pretty full of odd things, but no doubt the money was in the bedroom. The smell of stale pickles was very strong.

So his thoughts chased one another—eager, trivial, crowded—till his head ached with their splitting haste. To take heed for the future, to plan escape, to design expedients—these were merely impossible, sitting there inactive in the dark. He thought of the pipe he had slid down, what it cost, why they put it there, who the man was that he ran against at Luck Row, whether or not he hurt him, what the police would do with the bloaters and cake and bacon at the shop, and—again—of the smell of stale pickles.

Father Sturt was up and dressed, standing guard on the landing outside the Perrotts' door. The stairs were full of Jagos—mostly women—constantly joined by new-comers, all anxious to batter the door and belabour the hidden family with noisy sympathy and sedulous inquiries: all, that is, except the oldest Mrs Walsh in the Jago, who, possessed by an unshakable conviction that Josh's wife must have 'druv 'im to it', had come in a shawl and a petticoat to give Hannah a piece of her mind. But all were driven back and sent grumbling away by Father Sturt.

Every passage from the Jago was held by the police, and a search from house to house was begun. With clear consciences the Jagos all could deny any knowledge of Josh Perrott's whereabouts; but a clear conscience was little valued in those parts, and one after another affirmed point blank that the man seen at the window was not Perrott at all, but a stranger who lived a long way off. This, of course, less by way of favouring the fugitive than of baffling the police: the Jago's first duty. But the police knew the worth of such talk, and the search went on.

Thus it came to pass that in the grey of the morning a party in New Jago Street, after telling each other that the ruins must be carefully examined, climbed among the rubbish, and were startled by a voice from underground.

'Awright,' cried Josh Perrott in the cellar. 'I'm done; it's a cop. Come an' 'elp me out o' this 'ole.'

34

THE Lion and Unicorn had been fresh gilt since he was there before, but the white-headed old gaoler in the dock was much the same. And the big sword—what did they have a big sword for, stuck there, over the red cushions, and what was the use of a sword six foot long? But perhaps it wasn't six foot after all—it looked longer than it was; and no doubt it was only for show, and probably a dummy with no blade. There was a well-dressed black man sitting down below among the lawyers. What did he want? Why did they let him in? A nice thing—to be made a show of, for niggers! And Josh Perrott loosened his neckcloth with an indignant tug of the forefinger, and went off into another train of thought. He had a throbbing, wavering headache, the outcome of thinking so hard about so many things. They were small things, and had nothing to do with his own business; but there were so many of them, and they all had to be got through at such a pace, and one thing led to another.

Ever since they had taken him he had been oppressed by this plague of galloping thought, with few intervals of rest, when he could consider immediate concerns. But of these he made little trouble. The thing was done. Very well then, he would take his gruel like a man. He had done many a worse thing, he said, that had been thought less of.

The evidence was a nuisance. What was the good of it all? Over and over and over again. At the inquest, at the police court, and now here. Repeated, laboriously taken down, and repeated again. And now it was worse than ever, for the judge insisted on making a note of everything, and wrote it down slowly, a word at a time. The witnesses were like barrel-organs, producing the same old tune mechanically, without changing a note. There was the policeman who was in Meakin Street at twelve-thirty on the morning of the fourth of the month, when he heard cries of Murder, and proceeded to the coffee-shop. There was the other policeman who also 'proceeded' there, and recognised the prisoner, whom he knew, at the first-floor window. And there was the sergeant who had found him in the cellar, and the doctor who had made an examination, and the knife, and the boots, and all of it. It was Murder, Murder, Murder still. Why? Wasn't it plain enough? He felt some interest in what was coming—in the sentence, and the black cap, and so on—never having seen a murder trial before. But all this repetition oppressed him vaguely amid the innumerable things he had to think of, one thing leading to another.

Hannah and Dicky were there, sitting together behind the glass partition that rose at the side of the dock. Hannah's face was down in her hands, and Dicky's face was thin and white, and he sat with his neck stretched, his lips apart, his head aside to catch the smallest word. His eyes, too, were red with strained, unwinking attention. Josh felt vaguely that they might keep a bolder face, as he did himself. His sprained foot was still far from well, but he stood up, putting his weight on the other. He might have been allowed to sit if he had asked, but that would look like weakness.

There was another judge this time, an older one, with spectacles. He had come solemnly in, after lunch, with a bunch of flowers in his hand, and Josh thought he made an odd figure in his long red gown. Why did he sit at the end of the bench, instead of in the middle, under the long sword? Perhaps the old gentleman, who sat there for a little while and then went away, was the Lord Mayor. That would account for it. There was another room behind the bedroom at Weech's, which he had never thought about. Perhaps the money was there, after all. Could they have missed any hiding-place in the shop parlour? No: there was the round table, with the four chairs about it, and the little sideboard; besides the texts on the wall, and two china figures on the mantelpiece—that was all. There was a copper in the wash-house, but there was nothing in it. The garret was a very good place to keep things in; but there was a strong smell of stale pickles. He could smell it now—he had smelt it ever since.

The judge stopped a witness to speak of a draught from a window. Josh Perrott watched the shutting of the window—they did it with a cord. He had not noticed a draught himself. But pigeons were flying outside the panes and resting on the chimney-stacks. Pud Palmer tried to keep pigeons in Jago Row, but one morning the trap was found empty. A poulterer gave fourpence each for them. They were ticketed at eighteenpence a pair in the

shop, and that was fivepence profit apiece for the poulterer. Tenpence a pair profit on eleven pairs was nearly ten shillings—ten
shillings all but tenpence. They wouldn't have given any more in
Club Row. A man had a four-legged linnet in Club Row, but
there was a show in Bethnal Green Road with a two-headed
sheep. It was outside there that Ginger Stagg was pinched for
lob-crawling. And so on, and so on, till his head buzzed again.

His counsel was saying something. How long had he been talking? What was the good of it? He had told him that he had no
defence. The lawyer was enlarging on the dead man's iniquities,
talking of provocation, and the heat of passion, and the like. He
was aiming desperately at a recommendation to mercy. That was
mere foolery.

But presently the judge began to sum up. They were coming to
something at last. But it was merely the thrice-told evidence once
more. The judge blinked at his notes, and went at it again; the
policeman with his whistle, and the other with his lantern, and
the doctor, and the sergeant, and the rest. It was shorter this
time, though. Josh Perrott turned and looked at the clock behind
him, with the faces over it, peering from the gallery. But when
he turned to face the judge again, he had forgotten the time, and
crowded trivialities were racing through the narrow gates of his
brain once more.

There was a cry for silence, and then a fresh voice spoke.
'Gentlemen of the jury, have you agreed upon your verdict?'

'We have.' The foreman was an agitated, colourless man, and
he spoke in a low tone.

'Do you find the prisoner at the bar guilty, or not guilty?'

'Guilty.'

Yes, that was right; this was the real business. His head was
clear and ready now.

'And is that the verdict of you all?'

'Yes.'

Was that Hannah sobbing?

A pale parson in his black gown came walking along by the
bench, and stood like a tall ghost at the judge's side, his eyes
raised and his hands clasped. The judge took a black thing from
the seat beside him, and arranged it on his head. It was a sort of
soft mortarboard, Josh noted curiously, with a large silk tassel
hanging over one side, giving the judge, with his wig and his

spectacles and his red gown, a horribly jaunty look. No brain could be clearer than Josh Perrott's now.

'Prisoner at the bar, have you anything to say why sentence of death should not be passed on you according to law?'

'No sir—I done it. On'y 'e was a worse man than me!'

The Clerk of Arraigns sank into his place, and the judge spoke.

'Joshua Perrott, you have been convicted, on evidence that can leave no doubt whatever of your guilt in the mind of any rational person, of the horrible crime of wilful murder. The circumstances of your awful offence there is no need to recapitulate, but they were of the most brutal and shocking character. You deliberately, and with preparation, broke into the house of the man whose death you have shortly to answer for in a higher court than this: whether you broke in with a design of robbery as well as of revenge by murder I know not, nor is it my duty to consider: but you there, with every circumstance of callous ferocity, sent the wretched man to that last account which you must shortly render for yourself. Of the ill-spent life of that miserable man, your victim, it is not for me to speak, nor for you to think. And I do most earnestly beseech you to use the short time yet remaining to you on this earth in true repentance, and in making your peace with Almighty God. It is my duty to pronounce sentence of that punishment which not I, but the law of this country, imposes for the crime which you have committed. The sentence of the Court is: that you be taken to the place whence you came, and thence to a place of execution: and that you be there Hanged by the Neck till you be Dead: and may the Lord have Mercy on your Soul!'

'Amen!' It was from the tall black figure.

Well, well, that was over. The gaoler touched his arm. Right. But first he took a quick glance through the glass partition. Hannah was falling over, or something—a mere rusty swaying bundle—and Dicky was holding her up with both arms. Dicky's face was damp and grey, and twitching lines were in his cheeks. Josh took a step toward the partition, but they hurried him away.

35

ALL THIS hard thinking would be over in half an hour or so. What was to come now didn't matter; no more than a mere punch in the eye. The worst was over on Saturday, and he had got through that all right. Hannah was very bad, and so was Dicky. Em cried in a bewildered sort of way, because the others did. Little Josh, conceiving that his father was somehow causing all the tears, kicked and swore at him. He tried to get Hannah to smile at this, but it was no go; and they had to carry her out at last. Dicky was well-plucked though, bad as he was. He felt him shake and choke when he kissed him, but he walked out straight and steady, with the two children. Well, it was over. . . .

He hoped they would get up a break in the Jago for Hannah and the youngsters. His own break had never come off—they owed him one. The last break he was at was at Mother Gapp's, before the Dove-Laners fell through the floor. It must have cost Mother Gapp a deal of money to put in the new floor; but then she had made a lot in her time, what with one thing and another. There was the fencing, and the houses she had bought in Honey Lane, and the two fourpenny doss-houses in Hoxton that they said were hers, and—well, nobody could say what else. Some said she came of the gipsies that used to live at the Mount years ago. The Mount was a pretty thick place now, but not so thick as the Jago: the Jagos were thick as glue and wide as Broad Street. Bob the Bender fell in Broad Street, toy-getting, and got a stretch and a half. . . .

Yes, yes, of course, they always tolled a bell. But it was rather confusing with things to think about.

Ah, they had come at last. Come, there was nothing more to think about now; nothing but to take it game. Hold tight—Jago hold tight. . . . 'No thank you, sir—nothing to say, special. On'y much obliged to ye, thank ye kindly, for the grub an'—an' bein' kind an' wot not. Thanks all of ye, come to that. Specially you, sir.' It was the tall black figure again. . . .

What, this was the chap, was it? Seedy-looking. Sort of undertaker's man to look at. All right—straps. Not cords to tie, then.

Waist; wrists; elbows; more straps dangling below—do them presently. This was how they did it, then. . . . This way?

'I am the resurrection and the life, saith the Lord: he that believeth in Me, though he were dead, yet shall he live: and whosoever liveth and believeth in Me shall never die.'

A very big gate, this, all iron, painted white. Round to the right. Not very far, they told him. It was dark in the passage, but the door led into the yard, where it was light and open, and sparrows were twittering. Another door: in a shed.

This was the place. All white, everywhere—frame too; not black after all. Up the steps. . . . Hold tight: not much longer. Stand there? Very well.

'Man that is born of a woman hath but a short time to live, and is full of misery. He cometh up, and is cut down, like a flower: he fleeth as it were a shadow, and never continueth in one stay.

'In the midst of life. . . .'

36

IT WAS but a little crowd that stood at the Old Bailey corner while the bell tolled, to watch for the black flag. This was not a popular murder. Josh Perrott was not a man who had been bred to better things; he did not snivel and rant in the dock; and he had not butchered his wife nor his child, nor anybody with a claim on his gratitude or affection; so that nobody sympathised with him, nor got up a petition for pardon, nor wrote tearful letters to the newspapers. And the crowd that watched for the black flag was a small one, and half of it came from the Jago.

While it was watching, and while the bell was tolling, a knot of people stood at the Perrotts' front doorway, in Old Jago Street. Father Sturt went across as soon as the sleepers of the night had been seen away from the shelter, and spoke to Kiddo Cook, who stood at the stair-foot to drive off intruders.

'They say she's been settin' up all night, Father,' Kiddo reported, in a hushed voice. 'An' Poll's jest looked in at the winder from Walsh's, and says she can see 'em all kneelin' round a chair with that little clock o' theirs on it. It's—it's more'n 'alf an hour yut.'

'I shall come here myself presently, and relieve you. Can you wait? You mustn't neglect trade, you know.'

'I'll wait all day, Father, if ye like. Nobody sha'n't disturb 'em.'

When Father Sturt returned from his errand, 'Have you heard anything?' he asked.

'No, Father,' answered Kiddo Cook. 'They ain't moved.'

There were two faint notes from a distant steeple, and then the bell of St Leonard's beat out the inexorable hour.

37

KIDDO COOK prospered. The stall was a present fact, and the awning was not far off; indeed, he was vigilantly in search of a second-hand one, not too much worn. But with all his affluence he was not often drunk. Nothing could be better than his pitch—right out in the High Street, in the busiest part, and hard by the London and County branch bank. They called it Kiddo's Bank in the Jago, and made jokes about alleged deposits of his. If you bought a penn'orth of greens from Kiddo, said facetious Jagos, he didn't condescend to take the money himself; he gave you a slip of paper, and you paid at the bank. And Kiddo had indulged in a stroke of magnificence that no other Jago would have thought of. He had taken *two* rooms, in the new County Council dwellings. The secret was that Father Sturt had agreed to marry Kiddo Cook and Pigeony Poll. There would be plenty for both to do, what with the stall and the regular round with the barrow.

The wedding-day came when Hannah Perrott had been one week a widow. For a few days Father Sturt had left her alone, and had guarded her privacy. Then, seeing that she gave no sign, he went with what quiet comfort he might, and bespoke her attention to her concerns. He invented some charring work in his rooms for her. She did it very badly, and if he left her long alone, she would be found on the floor, with her face in a chair-seat, crying weakly. But the work was something for her to do and to think about, and by dint of bustling it and magnifying its importance, Father Sturt brought her to some degree of mindfulness and calm.

Dicky walked that morning in a sort of numb, embittered fury. What should he do now? His devilmost. Spare nobody and stop at nothing. Old Beveridge was right that morning years ago. The Jago had got him, and it held him fast. Now he went doubly sealed of the outcasts: a Jago with a hanged father. Father Sturt talked of work, but who would give *him* work? And why do it, in any case? What came of it before? No, he was a Jago and the world's enemy; Father Sturt was the only good man in it; as for the rest, he would spoil them when he could. There was something for to-morrow night, if only he could get calmed down enough by then. A builder's yard in Kingsland with an office in a loft, and money in a common desk. Tommy Rann had found it, and they must do it together; if only he could get this odd numbness off him, and have his head clear. So much crying, perhaps, and so much trying not to, till his head was like to burst. Deepeyed and pale, he dragged round into Edge Lane, and so into New Jago Street.

Jerry Gullen's canary was harnessed to the barrow, and Jerry himself was piling the barrow with rags and bottles. Dicky stood and looked; he thought he would rub Canary's head, but then he changed his mind, and did not move. Jerry Gullen glanced at him furtively once or twice, and then said: 'Good ole moke for wear, ain't 'e?'

'Yus,' Dicky answered moodily, his talk half random. ''E'll peg out soon now.'

''Im? Not 'im. Wy, I bet 'e'll live longer'n you will. 'E ain't goin' to die.'

'I think 'e'd like to,' said Dicky, and slouched on.

Yes, Canary would be better off, dead. So would others. It would be a comfortable thing for himself if he could die quietly then and there. But it would never do for mother and the children to be left helpless. How good for them all to go off easily together, and wake in some pleasant place, say a place like Father Sturt's sitting-room, and perhaps find—but there, what foolishness!

What was this unendurable stupor that clung about him like a net? He knew everything clearly enough, but it was all in an atmosphere of dull heedlessness. There would be some relief in doing something violent—in smashing something to little pieces with a hammer.

He came to the ruined houses. There was a tumult of yells, and a crowd of thirty or forty lads went streaming across the open waste, waving sticks.

'Come on! come on, Jago! 'Ere they are!'

A fight! Ah, what more welcome! And Dove Lane, too—Dove Lane, that had taken to bawling the taunt, 'Jago cut-throats', since....

He was in the thick of the raid. 'Come on, Jago! Jago! 'Ere they are!' Past the Board School and through Honey Lane they went, and into Dove Lane territory. A small crowd of Dove-Laners broke and fled. Straight ahead the Jagos went, till they were suddenly taken in flank at a turning by a full Dove Lane mob. The Jagos were broken by the rush, but they fought stoutly, and the street was filled with a surge of combat.

'Jago! Jago hold tight!'

Thin, wasted and shaken, Dicky fought like a tiger. He had no stick till he floored a Dove-Laner and took his from him, but then he bludgeoned apace, callous to every blow, till he fought through the thick, and burst out at the edge of the fray. He pulled his cap tight, and swung back, almost knocking over, but disregarding, a leather-aproned, furtive hunchback, who turned and came at his heels.

'Jago! Jago hold tight!' yelled Dicky Perrott. 'Come on, Father Sturt's boys!'

He was down. Just a punch under the arm from behind. As he rolled, face under, he caught a single glimpse of the hunchback, running. But what was this—all this?

A shout went up. 'Stabbed! Chived! They chived Dicky Perrott!'

The fight melted. Somebody turned Dicky on his back, and he moaned, and lay gasping. He lifted his dabbled hands, and looked at them, wondering. They tried to lift him, but the blood poured so fast that they put him down. Somebody had gone for a surgeon.

'Take me 'ome,' said Dicky faintly, with an odd gurgle in his voice. 'Not 'awspital.'

The surgeon came running, with policemen at his heels. He ripped away the clothes from about the wound, and shook his head. It was the lung. Water was brought, and cloths, and an old door. They put Dicky on the door, and carried him toward the surgery; and two lads who stayed by him were sent to bring his friends.

The bride and bridegroom, meeting the news on the way home, set off at a run, and Father Sturt followed.

'Good Gawd, Dicky,' cried Poll, tearing her way to the shutter as it stopped at the surgery door, 'wot's this?'

Dicky's eye fell on the flowered bonnet that graced the wedding, and his lip lifted with the shade of a smile. 'Luck, Pidge!'

He was laid out in the surgery. A crowd stood about the door, while Father Sturt went in. The vicar lifted his eyebrows questioningly, and the surgeon shook his head. It was a matter of minutes.

Father Sturt bent over and took Dicky's hand. 'My poor Dicky,' he said, 'who did this?'

'Dunno, Fa'er.'

The lie—the staunch Jago lie. Thou shalt not nark.

'Fetch mother an' the kids. Fa'er!'

'Yes, my boy?'

'Tell Mist' Beveridge there's 'nother way out—better.'

GLOSSARY OF SLANG AND
CRIMINAL TERMS

Balmy: barmy, stupid
Bang-up: very fine
Barney: lark, spree, quarrel
Benjamin: coat
Benjy: waistcoat
Break: collection made for someone recently out of prison
Boat, in the: sentenced to penal servitude
Broads: playing cards
Buster: burglar
Chancery, in: in an awkward situation
Chat, to screw a: to break into a house
Chiv(e): (v) to cut, stab (n) knife
Claim: to steal
Click: robbery, theft
Clock, red: gold watch
Cop: to steal
Croak: to die
Daisies: boots (rhyming slang—daisy roots)
Davy: affidavit
Dipper: pick-pocket
Fag: pick-pocket
Fall: to be arrested
Fence: receiver of stolen goods
Flimp: to rob
Friendly lead: subscription by whip-round usually held in a pub
Fully: to commit a person for trial
Gilt: money
Gonoph: thief esp. skilled pick-pocket
Go out: to follow the profession of thieving
Hook: pick-pocket
Ikey: Jew esp. receiver of stolen goods
James (jemmy): iron crow-bar
Kicksies: trousers
Lag: to sentence to penal servitude

Lagging dues: liable to be sentenced to penal servitude
Lob-crawling: till-robbing
Lucky, to cut one's: to make a getaway
Mace: (n) swindler (v) *To work the Mace*: to swindle by obtaining goods on false pretences
Mag, on the: engaged in swindling esp. as confidence trickster
Magsman: swell confidence trickster
Mazzard: head, face
Milling: boxing
Moke: donkey
Nark: (v) to inform (n) informer
Narking dues: arrested because of information provided by a nark
Neddy: loaded bludgeon or stick
Nick: to steal
Nobby: smart, stylish
Oof: money
Pecker, to keep one's pecker up: to remain cheerful
Peter: bag, box, trunk
Pogue: purse
Prop: tie-pin, brooch
Quid: pound
Quod: (v) to serve time (n) prison
Rorty: dashing, lively
Rum: odd
Screw: to break into
Slang: watch chain
Smug: to arrest
Sneak: to steal, pilfer
Snide: counterfeit
Snidesman: coiner of counterfeit
Sparks: diamonds
Split: (v) to inform (n) 1. informer, 2. detective
Stall-farming: prob. helping pick-pockets
Stir: prison
Stramash: rough-and-tumble
Stretch: one year esp. prison sentence
Swag: stolen goods
Toke: bread
Topper: something of outstanding quality

Toy: watch
Toy getter: watch stealer
Toy and tackle: watch and chain
Turn over: to search/rob someone
Twirl: skeleton key
Uxter: money
Weed: to take, steal
Welsh: to inform
Welsher: informer
Yannups: money

BIBLIOGRAPHICAL NOTE

FOR DETAILS of Morrison's early life see: *Who's Who* (1897); R. F. Sharp, *Dictionary of English Authors* (1904); Kunitz and Haycraft, *Twentieth Century Authors* (New York 1942). Articles by Morrison in *Palace Journal*: 'Whitechapel', III, 24 April 1889; 'On Blackwell Pier', III, 8 May 1889; 'Christmas Eve in the Streets', V, 25 December 1889. Other relevant articles: 'A Street', *Macmillan's*, LXIV, October 1891; 'What is a Realist?', *New Review*, XVI, March 1897; 'A Workman's Budget', *Cornhill*, LXXXIII, April 1901; 'Hooliganism', *Pall Mall Magazine*, XXIII, 1901. Letter to the *Spectator*, LXXIV, 16 March 1895. Interviews with Morrison; *Bookman* (London), VII, January 1895; *Daily News*, 12 December 1896; see also: C.R., 'The Methods of Mr Morrison', *Academy*, L, 12 December 1896; for Morrison and Henley: K. Williamson, *W. E. Henley* (1930). Quotation from Pett Ridge, see Arnold Bennett's *Journals*, I (1932).

For Jay and the Old Nichol see Jay's three books of memoirs and an interview 'To Check the Survival of the Fittest', *London*, 12 March 1896. Letters in defence of Morrison: *Fortnightly Review*, LXVII, January 1897; *St. James's Gazette*, 8 December 1896. See also H. Walker, *East London* (1896). For L.C.C. statistics see *The Housing Question in London 1855–1900* (1900) which also contains the full text of the Prince of Wales' speech on the Boundary Street Scheme.

Most of the major and many of the minor periodicals reviewed *A Child of the Jago*. Of special relevance are: H. G. Wells, 'A Slum Novel', *Saturday Review*, LXXXII, 28 November 1896; Anon., 'How Realistic Fiction is Written', *St. James's Gazette*, XXXIII, 2 December 1896; Harold Boulton, 'A Novel of the Lowest Life', *British Review*, I, 9 January 1897; H. D. Traill, 'The New Realism', *Fortnightly Review*, LXVII, January 1897. Also an interesting early article on Morrison by Robert Blatchford, 'On Realism', *My Favourite Books* (1900).

Later Studies of Morrison; V. S. Pritchett, 'An East End Novelist', *New Statesman*, XXVII, 22 January 1944, reprinted in *The Living Novel* (1946); Jocelyn Bell, 'A Study of A.M.', *Essays and*

Studies (1952); T. Harper Smith, 'A Child of the Jago', *East London Papers*, II, i (1959); Vincent Brome, 'Four Realist Novelists' (Writers and their Work 1965); P. J. Keating, 'Who Knows Arthur Morrison?', *East London Papers*, x, i, 1967.